Ashes

MEN OF HIDDEN CREEK

HJ WELCH

ASHES

Remi couldn't bear to see Kris so broken and defeated. He could tell Kris was trying to hold it together, but Kris kept scratching at the kitchen table and looking away from Remi as he blinked back angry tears.

The one time Kris had stuck his neck out and believed in himself, he'd been shot down in flames. It made Remi so frustrated. Why couldn't other people see what Kris had? He was full of passion and drive. He shone so bright it made everyone else in the room fade into the shadows.

Maybe it was just Remi who saw Kris like that?

He couldn't help it, though, not anymore. Kris was no longer Leon's kid brother to Remi. He was a friend.

More than a friend.

Before he could stop himself, Remi reached over the kitchen table where they were sitting and grasped Kris's hand, rubbing the back of his knuckles with his thumb. Kris's skin was so soft.

Kris turned his silvery-blue eyes toward Remi in surprise. Remi couldn't blame him. He'd never allowed himself to do anything like this before with another guy. But with Kris, the pull was too strong to ignore.

"Don't give up," Remi urged, squeezing Kris's hand. "Don't let them win."

Kris scoffed and slipped his hand free, tugging Remi's heart right along with it. "Thanks," he said, shaking his head and biting his glossy lip. "But, really – what was I thinking? I'm just a silly bartender." He gave Remi a tight smile that didn't meet his eyes and mimed flicking back his short blond-and-purple hair. "I'm just here to look pretty. No one wants to hear what I think."

Remi frowned and seized Kris's hand again, cradling it between his two larger, calloused ones. "*I* want to hear what you think," he said firmly. "You're so much more than just a pretty face."

Kris blinked at Remi, looking from his face to where their palms were pressed together. This time, he didn't pull his hand away.

"You think I'm pretty?" he asked in a small voice.

Remi was shaking inside. He'd spent so long living a shadow of his own life, not reaching out to find true joy in anything. Since he'd let Kris into his world, he'd felt like Dorothy arriving into Oz, seeing everything in Technicolor for the first time.

Remi could run into a burning building without pause. But faced with the prospect of opening up about his feelings for Kris, he was terrified. He'd been trained not to let his fear get the better of him, however. He couldn't back down now.

"Uh, yeah," Remi said. He did his best to keep his voice steady and not flinch his gaze away from Kris's. "I do, actually."

Their gazes locked while Remi's heart slammed in his chest. Kris's eyes were wide as he took a couple of short, shallow breaths. Was he preparing to run away? Had Remi ruined everything? Was-

"I think you're pretty, too," Kris uttered in a rush.

Relief rushed through Remi like cool water over his skin. Did that mean Kris felt the same way? "Yeah?" he asked.

For a second they just looked at each other, like neither of them knew quite what to do. Their hands were still joined, the connection electric between them.

"Remi, I..." Kris said.

This was it. The moment Remi had been building up to for the past couple of weeks. Goddamn it, it was time to stop being afraid.

"I'm an idiot," Remi blurted out with a nervous laugh. He lifted up Kris's hand between his own and held it to his chest. "Oh my god. You've been here the whole time. Like, literally forever." He laughed louder in relief. "Kris. You're not stupid or silly or any of that crap you were saying. You're amazing. You're one in a million and...I, uh, fuck."

He bit his lip and cast his eyes around, determined to do this right. He closed his eyes and took a breath. There was too much at stake if he messed this up.

"I like you, I think."

There was a pause. "You like me?" Kris asked, his voice a nervous squeak.

Remi peeked between one cracked eyelid and grimaced. "Like...*like* you, like you. Yeah, I think so. But, if that's not cool, just forget I said anything. You're a guest here and I would never want to make you feel, uh-"

"I like you, too," Kris interrupted. But then he gave Remi a wary look. "It doesn't bother you that I'm a man?"

Remi took a deep, steadying breath. When he released it, he gave Kris the most confident smile he could muster. "No," he said clearly. "It doesn't bother me. I'm…I'm fully aware of that fact."

Kris rubbed his fingers against Remi's hand. Then he stood up from the kitchen table but didn't let go of Remi's hand. He walked around, his lip between his teeth again as he brought his other hand up over Remi's. He held them against his stomach. Remi could feel the hardness of his abs on the back of his thumb through the cotton vest. For a petit guy, he was surprisingly firm and muscular.

Very different to most of the ladies Remi had been with in the past. But this was what he had yearned for so many times and never allowed himself to indulge in. A new kind of touch.

Their legs were touching where Kris was standing just between Remi's knees. Despite the Texan summer heat outside, Remi was still in jeans. But Kris's shorts hardly covered his booty and Remi saw him shiver as the denim rubbed against his lean thighs.

"Have you done this before?" Kris asked. Remi didn't need to check if he meant being intimate with another guy.

Remi looked up at him. "No," he said softly. "I wanted to, someday. But there wasn't anyone…there wasn't anyone before you."

Kris's breathing hitched. "Me?"

"Yeah," said Remi. He could hear the naked hope in his voice. "You're pretty awesome, Kris. Like, seriously. I just didn't really see what that meant."

"Oh, uh," said Kris, flustered. He was so adorable Remi's heart ached. "So," Kris uttered. "What *does* it mean?"

Remi grinned but then swallowed nervously. "That I'd like to kiss you. A lot. It's pretty all-consuming right now, actually. So, um, if that's something you'd like-"

In the blink of an eye, Kris swung one leg, then another over Remi's legs so he was straddling his lap. Remi gasped as the hardening bump in Kris's shorts rubbed up against Remi's matching bulge. Kris moved his hands to the back of Remi's neck.

Remi squeaked.

Kris looked as terrified as Remi felt, studying Remi's face with his gorgeous silver-blue eyes. Then he took a deep breath in. "Will you kiss me?" he whispered.

Elation flew through Remi as he seized Kris's lower back and behind his neck, their mouths crashing together. Remi groaned as Kris pressed his lithe body against Remi's bigger form. Remi hugged him close as their tongues and lips battled. Where their skin touched, it felt like Remi was on fire.

"Oh my god," Kris gasped as Remi moved his mouth to taste Kris's neck, sucking and kissing and biting. "Holy fuck, yes."

They were nothing alike. Not in temperament or to look at. And yet Remi couldn't feel more complete with Kris nestled in his embrace.

Remi knew they would feel even more perfect with no clothes on.

He forced himself to pull his lips away from Kris's creamy skin. "Can I take you to bed?" Remi managed to rasp.

Kris's eyes widened. Then he bit his lower lip and giggled, rolling his hips against Remi's lap, rubbing their cocks together. Remi couldn't help but gasp in shock. *Fuck,* that felt good. Kris giggled again.

"Yes," Kris hissed. "God, *yes.*"

Remi stood, wrapping his arms around Kris, keeping him safe. Kris crossed his ankles around Remi's bulky waist and held onto the back of Remi's neck. He looked down at him, his chest visibly rising and falling as he panted. There was little hiding the erection poking against the muscles of Remi's stomach now.

Kris's expression turned a little serious as he looked down at Remi through his blond eyelashes. "Are you sure?" he asked with sincerity.

Much like rushing into a burning building, Remi didn't hesitate. He gave Kris what he hoped was a smoldering look and leaned up to kiss him softly. Unlike before, this kiss was sweet, seductive. Filled with promise.

"You might have to teach me a couple of things," Remi admitted. He was excited by the prospect.

Kris grinned down at him, their lips still touching. "Oh," he said as Remi began to walk them out of the kitchen. "I'd be happy to."

1

———

KRIS

*N*ights like this at Bottom's Up were all starting to blend into one for Kris Novak. He sighed and looked out over Hidden Creek's one and only gay bar and tried to maintain his usual perky, flirty demeanor.

Fridays were generally the busiest day of the week, even more so than Saturdays. Guys, and some girls, would get off work and come to blow off steam to start their weekends. There were a number of faces Kris had never seen before tonight, as well. He thought he'd caught one of the guys say something about a wedding. There were definitely people from nearby towns as well, probably looking for a change of scenery.

Tourists. Kris absolutely didn't mind out-of-towners. In fact, he yearned for new people and different experiences. But it was a fine line between welcoming newcomers and putting up with those who just came to gawp and laugh at the suburban gay scene. Whether it was gay guys from Houston or straight visitors just passing through, Kris would rather not be the butt of anyone's joke.

He had to say the crowd tonight were generally behaving them-selves and having a great time shaking their asses to Britney and Shakira. Which was a good thing, as Kris was close to feeling the pressure behind the bar as he ran around like a tornado fixing drinks and dishing out winks and smiles.

"You're a pretty one, aren't you," a big guy commented as he handed over a ten.

Kris flicked his eyes over the dude. Muscular, tattooed, sparkling smile. Just how he liked them. He wasn't seriously flirting, though, just having a bit of fun. Kris had gotten good at reading these things. So he kissed the air, plucked the ten from the dude's thick fingers and spun around to skip to the cash register.

Within seconds he was already serving the next customer, and the next. It was coming up to eleven and the bar was in full party-mode.

So, of course, that was when his one and only colleague had to leave.

"I'm so sorry," Ben said as he wrapped up his last couple of orders. He threw Kris a genuinely apologetic look. "I've been here since opening twelve hours ago. I'll be sick if I have to stay any longer."

Kris scoffed and looked up at his friend. Kris looked up at most other men, but he'd decided to get over his petit stature long ago. 'Great things come in small packages,' his mom had always told him.

"Go, shoo," Kris said, flicking a dishcloth at the other guy's ass. "She's got this under control," he said, referring to himself. He mimed flicking his short hair over his shoulder and winked at the guys nearest them waiting to be served. "You think she can't handle this lot? They're just a bunch of kitty-cats." One of the guys blushed. Kris wondered if he might be able to get a phone number there.

"Thanks, darling," Ben said. He hugged Kris and kissed his cheek. "Good luck."

Kris didn't say it, but he would probably need it. Not for the first time, his manager, PJ, had fucked up the staff scheduling, leaving Kris by himself out front until close. So not only did he have to man the fort all alone, he had to do so while struggling with the new point of sales system PJ had implemented. Kris swore the man was obsessed with updating unnecessarily every six months.

Not that Kris had been working at the bar much longer than six months. He'd only turned twenty-one just before Christmas and therefore become old enough to serve alcohol. It had seemed like a fun idea to meet more guys, not just from Hidden Creek. But working under PJ was the opposite of fun in reality.

Kris did like most of the customers, however. He stood up straighter as someone he didn't recognize managed to snag one of the bar stools and sit down. Kris knew pretty much all of the regulars by sight, if not by name, by now. He'd tried it on with most of the guys, usually to no avail. They all thought he was adorable, like a puppy. A novelty twink. Not a man with real, burning needs.

He didn't know this small girl, though, as she glanced nervously about. Or...did he? Her short pixie haircut had thrown him, but as she played with a beer coaster, Kris thought he might remember her being a sophomore when he was a senior at Hidden Creek High. She'd had brown wavy hair past her shoulders then. Now it was short and dyed black.

If Kris was right, that meant she was eighteen and absolutely too young to be in a bar, drinking alcohol at least. But he hated being a party pooper. He also hated making women feel like they weren't wanted. Yes, technically this was a *gay* bar. But that didn't mean all manner of queer people and allies weren't welcome, too.

He bounced over and batted his false lashes at the girl. "Hey, there," he said in a friendly manner. "You're too cute. Do you mind if I see your ID?"

The girl blanched, her skin looking even paler against her dark hair in the swirling disco lights of the shadowy bar. "Sure," she shouted over the thumping music. She fished out a wallet from her jeans pocket and swallowed as she handed over her driving license.

It read Harrison Brown.

Kris caught himself before he frowned. He knew before he looked at it that the ID would be fake. He hadn't anticipated it would be in a male name. The gender was classified as male on the ID as well. Kris quickly added the name to the short hair and the tight T-shirt over a flat chest and came to the obvious conclusion.

This wasn't a girl.

He only took a second to consider his options. Then he smiled back up at Harrison and gave him back his license. Harrison looked surprised that Kris was fooled by the ID.

Kris leaned in toward the younger guy. The music was probably loud enough to drown out his words. But he didn't want any of the other dudes hanging around to hear anything or even read his lips, just in case.

"I'm happy for you to stay," he said with a wink. "But soft drinks only, yeah?" Harrison looked frightened for a second. But Kris nodded at him. "It's cool," he promised.

Harrison relaxed a fraction and smiled. "Thank you," he said with sincere gratitude. "I – can I have a cranberry juice? Please?"

Kris winked again. "Excellent choice," he said. No one would be able to see there wasn't any vodka in that.

He sympathized with the young kid. It wasn't that long ago Kris has also been desperate just to find a queer space where he didn't feel so exposed. Somewhere he could just be himself. It was one of the reasons he'd been so eager to take this job, after all.

"Hey!"

A slightly hostile voice cut through the music as Kris poured Harrison his cranberry juice. Kris glanced over at a gym bunny type of guy with several identical buddies. All blond with glowing skin and big muscles, but not in the rugged way that Kris preferred. These were like perfect, hairless Ken dolls. The one who'd spoken raised a sculpted eyebrow at Kris.

"If you ladies are done flirting, we'd like some beers," he drawled with a smirk.

Anger flashed through Kris, but he remained smiling. Customer service was the main aspect of his job, after all. He wouldn't let this dick rile him. "Just a minute, handsome," he said, even though it made him feel a bit sick. He placed the juice in front of Harrison. "Do you want to pay now or start a tab?" he asked, purposefully stalling so Ken Doll had to wait a little longer.

"Uh, tab, please," Harrison said. Kris remembered when starting a tab had felt like a grown-up thing to do, too.

Kris rung up the juice, then finally turned to the Ken doll guys and worked very hard not to feel nervous. The crowd was starting to dwindle as it approached twelve o'clock, pairing off and leaving for the night. But there were still enough patrons that these guys wouldn't cause a scene. At least, that was what Kris hoped.

Ken Doll flicked his eyes up and down Kris's small frame with an unimpressed but also predatory gaze. Like a cat that would eat a particularly puny mouse if he had to. Rather than shrink away, Kris preened. He always wore next to nothing at work, so he only had on a pair of short denim shorts, a white mesh tank and his army boots. But with the makeup he had on, purple-tipped hair and leather choker, he didn't feel quite so naked. Despite what guys like that might think, those 'fem' things felt like protection to him.

He batted his false eyelashes and leaned on the bar, shimmying his chest. "What can I get you fellas?"

"Beer," Ken Doll said with a slight curl of his lip. "Five. In bottles. No pink fucking umbrellas or any sparkly shit like that."

His buddies laughed, but Kris didn't show any signs that they bothered him. He just twirled around to grab the plastic bottles and pop the lids off them one by one, pinging the caps away in a cathartic rhythm.

In truth, guys like this made him feel like he was back in high school, dealing with pea-brained jocks. But since he'd come out in junior year, he'd vowed never to get ruffled by them again. At least on the outside.

The guys seemed disappointed not to get a reaction, so they paid silently and slunk off to the upstairs of the bar. Kris breathed a sigh of relief.

The place wasn't huge, but big enough to have a second level and space by the right of the counter for a pool table, air hockey and foosball. The dance floor had a set of curtains at the end on the wall to give the illusion of a stage. Not that PJ bothered to book any live acts, but the patrons liked taking photos in front of them.

Now the crowd was thinning slightly, Kris felt like he could breathe. He still had to serve customers as fast as he could, but now at least he could manage and not be totally overwhelmed.

Nothing pissed off drunk people like having to wait for more booze. Or so he'd observed.

Without asking him to, Kris replenished Harrison's cranberry juice when the first glass ran low, then another later on. He was clearly more at ease now, although he didn't talk to other people or make any real eye contact with anyone aside from Kris. He was content to play on his phone and look about every now and again. As if he couldn't quite believe his own daring for being there.

That was, until fifteen minutes before closing. The doors flung open and a trio of unfortunately familiar girls Kris's own age came stumbling through. They were in heels and short skirts, covered in glitter and clearly toasted. Kris gave them three seconds before they tottered to the bar screeching 'Yas qween!' and 'Werk it, gurl!'

Mandy, Trixie and Lola. All girls Kris also knew from school. The cheer squad, specifically. Kris had made many friends during his time as a Hidden Creek Honeybee cheerleader. These were not any of them.

They were exactly the kind of people who treated Bottom's Up like an exhibit at the zoo. A place to come and giggle at all the crazy queers and grope the guys with six-packs whether they wanted it or not. Luckily, they had only been bothering Kris the past few weeks while they had been back from college. It didn't mean he was any happier to see them now.

He wasn't the only one to presumably recognize the girls.

Before Kris could say anything, Harrison bolted from his seat and practically sprinted for the door.

Without paying for his cranberry juices.

Kris sighed. That was unfortunate. Not least of all because that was the moment PJ had decided to grace him with his presence.

"Hey," he cried as he strode down the length of the bar, scowling. "Did that girl just bolt without paying?"

Kris rolled his eyes and rang up the three juices on the register as Mandy and her friends grabbed the empty bar stool and snagged another two as well to fall onto. The bar was certainly emptying now as people headed home for the night, usually in pairs. Kris's heart gave a little pang. It wasn't that he *needed* a boyfriend. It would just be nice to go home with the same guy more than once. To have something that was more than just sex.

"That *boy* had an emergency," Kris said as he sorted out the bill. And it *was* an emergency. He wasn't sure how long Harrison had been experimenting with presenting as his true gender, but Kris was sure Harrison wouldn't want Mandy and company blabbing to anyone about him being here. Who knew what his family or work situation was?

"His drinks are coming out of your check," PJ grumbled as he started punching at one of the other tills to presumably start the cash pickup. He would remove most of the money to put into the safe, leaving Kris with fifty dollars in change to serve the last few patrons. Namely, Mandy and company.

PJ was several inches taller than Kris with brunet hair and a goatee. Rectangular glasses were the only really distinctive part of his appearance. The guy was painfully bland, looks-wise. Personality-wise, he seemed to be permanently grumpy. Like he got a parking ticket every single goddamned morning.

Kris found him tiresome. PJ always sucked the energy from the room. But Kris did his best to be friendly. "It was only a couple of dollars on juice," he assured PJ with a smile. "I'm happy to cover for the guy until he comes back another day."

"How old was he, anyway?" PJ asked as he pulled up whatever

report he was looking for on the new POS system. "He looked like a fetus."

"Twenty-one," Kris said automatically. Then he turned to his giggling former classmates before PJ could pry any more. "What can I get you ladies?"

"Oh my god, Kris," Mandy cackled, flicking back her strawberry-blonde hair. "You get gayer every time we see you!"

"You bet, baby," Kris said with a wink, refusing to take it as an insult.

"You might as well be a woman if you're gonna wear that much glitter," Lola snorted, almost toppling off her stool. "Does anyone here actually fuck you, Kris? I thought gay guys wanted *guys,* you know?"

Trixie's giggling became almost hysterical. *"I'd fuck him,"* she told the other two in a loud whisper behind her hand.

Kris sighed and plastered on his best I'm-done-with-this-bullshit smile. "What can I get you gorgeous ladies?" he asked again. "Three porn star martinis?"

The girls squealed. "You remembered!" Mandy cried, as if he was a puppy who had learned a new trick.

He was glad, however, that they liked cocktails rather than wine or beer. It meant he could spend some time making the three concoctions and grab a few seconds peace and quiet.

Or so he thought. PJ came up to him as he was shaking together the first drink, brandishing his phone. "We got another one," PJ muttered.

Kris's heart sank. As much as he didn't really get along with PJ, he did feel sorry for him in this situation. The bar had been getting increasingly frequent threats on their social media from anonymous or dummy accounts. Real homophobic shit, but vague enough the police didn't really have anything to go on. Still, it was a punch in the gut to read yet another message saying how the LGBT community was a 'bunch of fucking perverts' and how they were all going to 'die of AIDS and roast in hell.'

PJ wasn't even queer. He'd just opened a gay bar because there was a gap in the Hidden Creek market. He was pretty ambivalent on the whole prejudice and hate speech side of things. He just resented having his business threatened.

"Shit, sorry," Kris mumbled back. He didn't want customers to know they had any issues. There hadn't been any *direct* threats of an attack or anything, after all.

PJ shrugged and put his phone away. "Just so you're aware," he said, already walking away with the cash pickup to put in the safe. "I'll be out back until close, then I'm heading home. See you later."

Any sympathy for his manager vanished. Kris gritted his teeth and focused on making the three cocktails. He was perfectly capable of getting through the rest of his shift alone. He just shouldn't have to.

The bar emptied quite quickly after that, he was pleased to note. Mandy and her friends were the last to leave when he shut the music off. Thankfully, he saw them ordering a cab rather attempting to drive anywhere.

"Bye, qween!" they shrieked as they left, clinging onto each other for support. Kris hoped they made it home safely, even if they were obnoxious. He wondered where Harrison had gotten to and hoped even more that he was safe. Hidden Creek was a nice town with low crime rates, but still. He needed to be extra careful.

The cleaners would come around in the morning, so it was up to Kris to just lock the tills, wipe down the bar, shut all the lights off and make sure the building was secure for the night. Luckily, he didn't have to go far at all to make his way home. But he still dragged his feet as he punched his code into the door's security pad and made his way into the bar's back hallway. He trudged up the stairs to his apartment on the third floor.

The one and only apartment had once been an office or something when the bar had been a warehouse. Kris wasn't entirely sure. He just knew that PJ let him rent it for a really decent rate. Another reason he couldn't quite bring himself to hate the guy.

Kris sighed loudly once he'd closed and locked the door, leaning back against it and rolling his neck until it clicked. What the hell was he doing with his life, really? Sure, he had his own place and a half-decent wage. But spending night after night watching other people having fun was only making him feel lonelier.

"Oh, hon, get a grip," he said aloud. "You have friends."

This was true. Only, he wanted someone who was *more* than just a friend. For all his flirtiness and bravado, he longed to be like those guys that always came in together. Like his new buddies, Hunter and Chase, or Gabe and Ryan. As much as Kris liked no-strings sex and fun hookups, he wished he didn't have to come home to an empty apartment.

"I'm so rude, aren't I, Tay Tay?" he scoffed. He walked over to the three-foot-wide fish tank by his bed and tapped the glass gently to get his fancy goldfish's attention. "I'm not alone." Taylor Swift swished her double-finned tail and swam to say hello. She wasn't quite a puppy or a kitten, but she was Kris's and he couldn't help but love her cute personality traits.

Like what a little fatso she was. He laughed as he shook a number of pellets into the water for her and watched her zip around, chomping them all up.

"Good girl," he said fondly.

By the time he stripped and took his makeup off, he couldn't be bothered to eat. He just fell into the bed in the middle of the room. The space was basically one room with a bathroom the size of a closet attached and a hotplate on top of a small fridge. But it was all Kris's and it was quiet.

Because the ceilings were so high in the bar, the view from his window was more like being on the fourth floor. He did enjoy looking out over the town during the day when it was busy or at night when it twinkled. It made him feel more connected to the town below.

He sighed and plugged his phone in to charge before snuggling under his bedsheets. His life was fine, for heaven's sake. He knew he was only twenty-one and had all the time in the world. He should be less impatient for more. Tomorrow was another day. He didn't know what it would bring.

Or who.

As sleep claimed him, he allowed himself to fantasize about a strong pair of arms holding him tight. Maybe one day not so far off that would be more than just a dream.

2

———

REMI

*A*s much as Remi Washington loved his job, there were other places he would rather be on a Friday night than stuck up a tree, in the dark, trying to sweet-talk a kitten down who couldn't seem to care less she was perched several feet above a swimming pool.

"Oh, Smoky, be careful!" the old dear, Mrs. Albany, called below, ringing her hands. Remi gritted his teeth and clung to the flimsy branch, reaching another couple of inches closer to the gray kitten. "Thank you so much, sweetheart," the elderly lady cried up to Remi. "I just don't know how she got herself up there."

Remi knew exactly how. She was a sassy little thing who, judging from the way she was smugly licking her paws, would spend her life getting humans to run around after her because she was too adorable. He sighed. He loved cats, but this one wasn't helping him out at all.

"Here, kitty kitty kitty," he cooed, lying on his stomach to reach as far as he could with one hand, clutching the wood with the other. "Come to Uncle Remi."

"Hey, Remi," one of his fellow firefighters, Channing, called up from by the pool. "You having trouble getting a little pussy?"

Remi rolled his eyes at his crew all standing around watching, and now laughing, at him. "Remind me again why Alondra isn't doing this?" he asked with a raised eyebrow they probably couldn't see in the ambient lighting around the yard.

Alondra, the only female member of the third watch, pointed to her foot inside the big chunky regulation boot they all had to wear. "Sprained ankle from kickboxing," she said with over-the-top remorse.

"Yeah, right," Remi grumbled. "You did that weeks ago."

He knew his coworkers were punishing him for eating the last donut at the station earlier without asking. Alondra was tiny and nimble. Remi was over six foot and spent half of his free time lifting weights down the gym.

The tree creaked underneath him.

"You wanna hurry it up, buddy?" Greg hollered with a cackle. Holby smacked his arm and pointed to the distraught-looking owner of both the house and the kitten. Greg cleared his throat and nodded at Mrs. Albany before looking at Remi again. "I mean, do you need any help?"

"We could get the ladder in?" Captain Bishop suggested, his deep voice rumbling from closer to the truck where old Travis was probably already napping.

"No," Remi grunted. "Y'all will only tear up Mrs. Albany's nice lawn. I got this."

"I'll go warm up the ladder," Remi heard Greg mumble before he trotted back off to the truck.

Remi shook his head. "I can do this," he said more to himself than anyone else. But when he reached for Smoky the kitten again, she hopped further down the branch, swishing her tail and meowing shrilly. "Goddamn it." He sighed.

"Oh, do be careful," Mrs. Albany cried.

Remi forced himself to smile down at her. "I promise I will, ma'am."

But at that moment the branch gave a terrible crack. Smoky froze, snapping her head to look at Remi. Then she dashed down the branch, deftly avoiding his grasp, running over his back and scaling the tree to the lawn where Mrs. Albany reached down to snatch her into her arms.

"Oh!" she cried. "You did it!"

The branch cracked again. Remi only had a second to grab onto it with both hands, as if that might somehow stop the inevitable, before the whole thing gave way and he dropped with a lurch, plummeting into the swimming pool.

When he reemerged, his coworkers were doubled up with laughter. Greg came jogging back from the truck, his hands in his hair. "Aww, I always miss the good stuff!" he bemoaned.

Remi gasped for air and spluttered out chlorinated water. "Mother fucker!" he cried.

Mrs. Albany covered Smoky's ears with a shocked expression on her elderly face. Smoky, the little bastard, looked damned pleased with herself.

The team made Remi strip off before allowing him or his drenched suit and gear back into the truck. At least Holby threw him a blanket for him to drape over his shoulders. It wasn't that he was ashamed of his body. He was extremely in shape. But it made it easier to take all his buddies' ribbing while not just sitting in his underwear.

Back at the station, most of the crew set about organizing some late supper. But all Remi wanted to do was take a shower and get all the chlorine off his skin.

After a call, they quite often piled into the bathroom together, except for Alondra who had naturally managed to secure her own shower cubicle in the women's room. After a more strenuous job, they all generally needed a freshen up. But seeing as the rest of the team had stood around watching Remi get bested by a kitten, the upside was he now had the entire bathroom to himself.

He washed the suds from his hair and body in about a minute. When a call could come through at any time, he didn't want to be running back through the station with soap in his eyes.

But he was enjoying the solitude. It was rare he got a moment to himself during his twenty-four-hour shift unless he tried to grab a nap, but then Travis was usually in the breakroom snoring. Remi closed his eyes and rolled his shoulders, relaxing. The only sound was the water running down his body.

It occurred to him that it had been a while since he'd had some fun in the shower.

He wiped the water from his eyes and looked around. He was still alone and he had left the rest of the team in the kitchen and around the TV. It was unlikely any of them would get the mad urge to take a shower in the next five minutes.

He grinned, feeling mischievous, and wrapped his fingers around his cock.

Ordinarily, the idea of doing this anywhere vaguely public would make him too nervous. But he'd found some new porn last week that he couldn't stop replaying in his head. He didn't see any harm in knocking a quick one out.

It wasn't like he hadn't watched two dudes fucking before. He'd given most porn a try in his twenty-six years. But there had been something so fun and playful about the guys he'd discovered last week. And it had brought Remi's mind back to a place it had been hovering over for a few years now.

What would it be like to try having sex with another guy, just once?

He didn't have anybody in mind as he began to stroke his shaft. He'd seen a few guys around the gym from time to time. Slim fit guys that had lit something inside him that he was normally too afraid to acknowledge in the cold light of day.

But with his eyes closed under the running water, he wondered what it might be like to hold a body like that for a change? What would it feel like to have a guy suck his cock? Would it be any different? Would he know what he was doing any better?

Remi had watched enough porn of guys jacking off to know he found the sight fucking erotic. He tried telling himself that every guy found all kinds of porn hot. It didn't mean they wanted to do it for real. But as his rhythm increased, he found himself visualizing some cute guy sucking him off, touching his own cock as he did.

Wow, fuck, yeah. That was doing the trick. Remi bit his lip harder and rubbed the head of his cock with his thumb before squeezing the shaft hard. He was close, but he wanted to build up his orgasm a bit more. He wasn't sure he'd ever have the guts to do this anytime again soon, so he wanted to make the most of it.

Which is of course why the alarm chose to sound at that moment.

"Fuck!" he cried, slamming the water off and grabbing a towel, his dick immediately softening with the shock. He barely gave himself a once-over with the towel before shoving his feet through his dry pants, forgoing underwear to give him that extra couple of seconds.

"Engine five," the composed voice from dispatch announced over the PA system as Remi ran from the bathroom, pulling his polo over his head. *"Ladder three. Building fire. Corner of Jefferson and Row Street."*

Shit. An actual fire. *Another* one? For months, Hidden Creek had gone without a blaze. Then after some shady business involving the CIA in April, they'd had three separate callouts for explosions. Now this?

He was a big guy, but he could fucking run when he needed. So he sprinted through the empty common room where everyone had abandoned their toast and bags of chips. Then he skidded to a halt in front of the engine at the same time as the rest of his half a dozen crew, stepping into his suit.

"What have we got?" he asked as he and the rest of them jumped into the engine, lacing up his boots. Channing was behind the wheel. Within seconds they were peeling away from the house, the siren blaring and the lights flashing against the night. No matter how many times he did this, even after almost seven years, his heart rate still sped up every time.

It didn't help that it had kind of already been elevated.

His almost orgasm was a million miles from his mind, though, as they sped through the town, heading past Victory Boulevard. He and the rest of the crew looked at Captain Bishop as the seconds ticked by. Every single one counted in an emergency situation.

"Three-story building appears to be on fire," the captain said, looking between the guys and Alondra. "Call came from the only tenant. Says he lives above a bar. He's stuck on the top floor."

Remi's blood ran cold and he leaned across to look down the street. He could just make out the orange glow of the fire in the distance against the night sky. "Fuck," he said. He hadn't recognized the address from the street names, but he knew where he was now.

He resisted the urge to ask Channing to drive faster. They would get there as soon as they possibly could. That didn't stop Remi's heart from racing.

"What?" Holby asked, always the first to pick up when someone wasn't doing so good.

"The bar," Remi said, turning back to Captain Bishop. "It's the gay bar on the intersection, right? Bottom's Up?"

That got a snigger from old Travis, but Remi was too preoccupied to shoot him a glare.

"I believe so," said the captain. He narrowed his eyes at Remi. "What is it, son?"

Remi turned back to look out the front window. The sirens from both the engine and the truck were howling in his ears. As they reached the intersection, he could see the whole first floor of the bar was already up in flames. It was hard to tell in the dark, but it looked like the smoke might already be turning black.

Fuck, fuck, fuck. They couldn't be too late. They couldn't.

"I know who lives there," Remi said through dry lips.

And they were going to damn well get him out.

3

———————

KRIS

Kris's first thought was that he must be seriously dehydrated from work because he was coughing as he woke up. He was dreaming he couldn't breathe or swallow properly, when he realized it wasn't just in his head. He couldn't seem to breathe normally.

Then he opened his eyes.

They began to water, his coughing getting worse. What the hell? It was so dark. What was going on?

He covered his mouth with one hand as he spluttered. Why couldn't he seem to get enough air into his lungs? With his other hand he fumbled with the lamp on his nightstand, pawing at the cord until he found the switch and clicked it on.

There was smoke in the room.

Panic took hold and had him standing up in his boxer-briefs in a flash. Now he was awake, he could hear a beeping coming from somewhere in the building.

A fire alarm.

This couldn't be happening. There couldn't *actually* be a fire in the bar, could there?

He ran across the room to his apartment door. At the last second, he pulled his hand back from the lock and looked at the back of the door. Then he touched the back of his knuckles against the wood.

It was hot.

"Fuck!" he cried, snatching his hand back as tears sprung to his eyes. "Fuck, fuck, *fuck!*" He was so scared he couldn't think straight. What the hell was he supposed to do? He couldn't go out there. Who knew what state the place was in?

What time was it? How long ago had he locked up? His phone would tell him the time.

His phone. *Call 911,* a voice popped up in the back of his head.

Yes. He needed help, immediately. He fumbled his way back to his bed, already feeling light-headed. He snatched up whatever pair of jeans he found lying on the floor and shoved his legs through them. Whatever was going on, he didn't think being almost entirely naked was a good idea.

His hands shook as he yanked the phone from its charger cable. He swiped the screen lock open and tried dialing the number. It took him two attempts to hit the correct three digits.

"911, what's your emergency?" the woman on the end of the line said after a single ring.

"My building's on fire!" Kris yelled, followed by a series of hacking coughs. He lunged for the window and shoved it open. Why hadn't he thought of that before? Smoke immediately began billowing out into the night. He looked down at the sidewalk dozens of feet below. "I can't get out! It's the bar on the corner of Jefferson and Row."

He wasn't sure if it was his terrified imagination at work, or if he really could hear the crackle of flames now. He snatched up a towel from his bathroom. Stumbling, he made his way back to the apartment door, laying the towel down at the crack between the base of the door and the wooden floor. That went a small way to stopping the smoke, at least.

"Please, please help," he begged the dispatcher. "I don't know what to do!"

"Help is on the way, sweetie," the dispatcher told him firmly. "Stay low on the floor. Try and keep out of the smoke."

"Okay," Kris rasped. He dropped to his knees, sweat pouring from his skin. "Okay. How long until the firefighters get here?"

"A few minutes, hon," the dispatcher said. She had a very reassuring voice, but Kris was still trembling in fright. "Where are you? Is there anyone else in the building?"

"I'm in the apartment," Kris told her. He had to stop and cough again. "There's only one, on the third floor. It's above the bar. I don't think there's anyone else here."

For a terrible moment he wished he hadn't said that. If it was just him inside, would they really risk all those firefighters coming in to try and save him? But then the dispatcher's voice was in his ear again. Of course they would come. They *had* to.

"Okay, stay there," the dispatcher instructed. "Help is on the way. Don't move."

"I won't," Kris promised.

The line went dead.

He choked down a sob and howled, balling up his fists. What the fuck was going on? *How had this happened?* Was he going to die here?

No. He was not going to fucking die. He was going to be rescued by a hunky fireman and everything would be fine.

He couldn't say the same about his apartment, though.

"Tay Tay!" he gasped, making himself splutter again. The smoke was getting thicker, but in the lamplight, he could see his fish swimming around her tank, flicking her tail in agitation. "Shit!"

He knew the dispatcher had told him to stay on the floor, but he wasn't about to abandon his Tay Tay. So he crawled across the floor, pushing his crap aside as he did. His hand happened to land on a tote bag and he made a snap decision.

He grabbed the bag as he continued to crawl, chucking the phone he still had clutched in his other hand inside. It took less than a second to yank the charger from the wall and add that beside the phone. Then, only because it was in reach, he also grabbed his makeup bag. There was *hundreds* of dollars' worth of supplies in there. He wasn't going to let it all melt if he didn't have to.

Once he reached the bed, he used it to pull himself up next to the tank. He reached above the bubbling water to the shelf where he kept Tay Tay's supplies, including the large Tupperware box he used to scoop her out when he cleaned her tank.

He was coughing nonstop now and tears were streaming down his face. Not just from the fear, but also a reaction to the smoke in his eyes. The open window didn't seem to be doing anything much anymore to clear the air. Kris blinked rapidly and clung to the side of the tank, plunging his hand into the water with the bottom half of the plastic box.

"Come on," he cried as he tried to catch Tay Tay without bashing any of her long, flowing fins. But she was scared as well and flitting around in a state. Kris let out another sob. His head was killing him and it was getting harder and harder to take proper breaths. "Come *on!*" he yelled in frustration. The poor girl was too scared, though.

He stopped moving, making himself take as slow a breath as he dared. He was getting really dizzy.

"Come on, sweetheart," he whispered, holding the box still.

Tay Tay turned, her tail twitching. Then she cautiously swam toward his hand.

He let out a nervous laugh, his lip cracking as he smiled. He tasted blood. "Come up, little one," he urged as he gently scooped her up. "That's it. In you go."

His hand was shaking, but he slowly lifted her and the water inside the Tupperware up. More water streamed from his arm onto the floor as he grabbed the lid, jammed it on and dropped his body back down below the thickest layer of smoke.

His coughing wouldn't stop and he felt like he couldn't really catch his breath. Clutching Tay Tay's box to his naked chest, he threw the handle of the tote bag over his shoulder and hugged his few possessions to his belly.

It had occurred to him before that his room didn't have a fire escape outside. But he'd always idly thought if anything major happened, he'd scale a drain pipe or something.

There was no way he was doing that. There was maybe one pipe he could try and climb, but it was several feet away from his window. He was much more likely to slip and fall and break every bone in his body.

"Please. Please," he whispered as he lay down and curled into a ball, Tay Tay nestled between him and the tote bag. He could hear the sirens getting closer. Through the smoke, he tried to keep his gaze on the door, but it was difficult when his eyes were streaming so much. He didn't think the flames were actually at his room yet. He couldn't make out any bright light or flickering around the edges of the door. He could hear the blaze roaring, though.

He just had to hold on a little longer. When the firefighters got here, they would save him. That was what they did.

He screwed up his eyes and cursed as much as he could when he was coughing and spluttering. Talking took up too much energy, though, so he swallowed with a sandpaper-dry mouth and tried to save his strength.

It was too easy with his eyes closed, however. Darkness was enveloping him. He felt sleepy and sluggish. His breaths were too shallow. Was he drowning? What was happening?

He clung to whatever was in his arms for dear life. Maybe that would keep him safe? Lead him home.

There was wailing in the air, loud and piercing. It sounded sad.

Kris was sad. He didn't want to go. He wanted to stay. He wanted to sleep.

"Please," he murmured, hugging tightly to his box. "Please."

The darkness was too much. He couldn't fight it. All he could do was try and hold on as he slipped away, and hope it was enough.

4

REMI

Remi didn't even wait for the engine to fully stop before he yanked the door open. In all his time fighting fires and tending to medical emergencies, he'd been lucky enough to never know anyone personally involved in a serious incident.

So it didn't matter that he didn't know Kris Novak all that well. What mattered was that Leon's little brother was caught up in that blaze. Remi's best friend since kindergarten, Leon. Their moms were almost sisters. Remi and Kris had never had much in common or spent any real time together, but it was enough of a connection for Remi to take this call more personally than he should.

"Washington!" Captain Bishop called out as several more pairs of boots hit the asphalt. The sirens were wailing around them and flashing red lights illuminated the grisly scene. "Do we have a problem?"

"No, sir," Remi replied without hesitation. He could still do his damn job. He just wanted to do it fast. Christ, Leon would never forgive him if his baby brother got hurt.

Bishop seemed satisfied with his answer and was already looking back toward the building, assessing the situation. "Holby, Greg," he called out. "Get to the roof and cut us a vent." The truck was already winding up the ladder, angling it toward the top of the bar. Greg and Holby ran for it.

Remi was edging toward the front door. Although the flames were bad, the building's structure was intact for now and he was sure he could get inside. Sure enough, Bishop turned back to him. "Remi, Alondra, take the front entrance. Channing and Travis, check the back and sides for another way in or out."

"Yes, Captain!" Remi cried in chorus with the others, already running. Alondra was by his side. She might be smaller than him, but he didn't have to worry about her keeping up. For all her joshing about her ankle earlier, it was perfectly fine, and the woman was built like a tank.

Remi turned so his back was to the bar and kicked next to the handle of the door with his heel, forcing it to open inwards. The fire wasn't so bad by the entrance, but the inside of the bar was already looking bad with flames licking at the walls, particularly by the dance floor where some sort of fabric hung. Remi had never been inside before, but he could tell the blaze was already wreaking havoc.

"Fire department!" he bellowed at the top of his lungs, his mask firmly in place to protect his face and keep his oxygen flowing. "Anyone here? Call out!"

The 911 phone call had come from the apartment up top, but protocol was to check each floor as thoroughly as they could. This place was bigger than an average house, so Remi and Alondra were soon joined by guys from the truck.

"You take this floor," Remi instructed, heading for a door that looked to lead out back. "There's a balcony level, too. We're heading for the third floor."

"Okay, got it," one of the part-time volunteer guys called back, already pointing to his colleagues where to go.

Alondra looked behind the bar, not getting too near the flammable alcohol. "Clear here," she called out to the room, signaling they didn't need to check again. Remi was running for the door, trusting she would be right behind.

It was locked with a keypad, but they kicked and hacked their way through. Remi's instincts had been right. The door led to a stairwell. Some of the flames were clinging to the walls, but they could make it up the stairs. The fire could easily spread fast. They had to hurry.

There were no other doors until they reached the third floor, which took them to a single corridor. A visual check confirmed no one else was in the stairwell or the hall. Remi sprinted for the only apartment door, wasting no time turning and kicking the thing in. A lock splintered away from the wood at the force of his foot, but he encountered some resistance as he pushed his way through.

There was a towel lying at the base of the door, stopping the smoke from getting in.

Clever man.

"Fire department!" he yelled through his mask. "Anyone here? Call out!" Before he'd even finished speaking, he spotted the huddled shape on the floor. "Kris!" he yelled, dashing over.

As Remi dropped to his knees, he was already pulling off his glove. Kris was easily identifiable by his blond hair and purple tips, even in the murky gloom. He was huddled in the fetal position with something – or things – clutched to his bare chest. He wasn't moving, but as Remi jammed his two fingers against his throat, he was immensely relieved to discover Kris still had a pulse. His hand was damp enough that when he held it in front of Kris's mouth, he felt the breath right away.

"He's alive," Remi reported. He yanked off his helmet so he could remove his mask. As he covered Kris's face with it, he looked over his shoulder to see Alondra had shut the door and was holding it closed with her back. That wasn't a good sign.

"It's getting a little cozy out there," she said. "Unless you want to work on your tan, I think we need to take the window."

Kris murmured and twitched. Thank fuck. The oxygen was doing its job.

Remi shoved his hand back into his glove and put his helmet back on. Then he grabbed his radio, pressing the button down. "Bishop, do you copy?"

"Bishop, here," came the instant reply.

"We have the victim," Remi reported. "The stairwell isn't looking good. We need an evac through the window."

"You got it," Bishop told him. "Greg and Holby are back on the ladder. We're moving it to you now. Get ready!"

Remi looked to Alondra, still holding the door in place. She nodded. Remi coughed, the smoke getting to him without his oxygen mask. Kris needed it more than him now, though. He was half naked and shivering. As Remi maneuvered around him, he noted that although he was still a small-ish guy, Leon's little brother wasn't quite so young or little anymore.

"Come on, Kris," Remi said. He slid his arms under him and shook loose the things he was holding. "We gotta go."

"No!" cried Kris, suddenly snapping awake and snatching at the items in his arms. There was a bag over his shoulder, but he fumbled with some kind of large Tupperware filled with water.

There was a fish inside it, swimming about.

"Oh fuck," Remi said. Kris was still half in and out of consciousness, his heavy breathing fogging up the mask. But he was grappling for the damn fish box.

"Tay Tay," he muttered with a sob. Remi guessed that was the fish. Goddamn it. This wasn't protocol. Remi's priority was always the people, not their pets. But he plucked the Tupperware from Kris's trembling hands and slid it into the bag, keeping the handle looped over Kris's shoulder.

He was going to get a reputation for being Dr. fucking Doolittle at this rate.

With the bag on Kris's belly, Remi scooped him up like a groom carrying his bride over the threshold. Kris flung his arms around Remi's neck, holding on weakly.

"Please," he whimpered. *"Please."*

"I've got you, Kris," Remi assured him, moving to the window. "It's okay. I'm here."

"Remi?" Kris mumbled. Remi looked over from the moving ladder at him in surprise. Kris's eyes were closed, but his face was screwed up with a little frown. "Remi?"

Remi wasn't sure the kid even knew his name. Sure, he and Leon had been best buds since forever. But there was five years between them and Kris. The kid had fled anytime Remi had come halfway close. In truth, Remi wasn't even sure Kris liked him.

But here he was, moaning his name. He must have recognized Remi's voice on some subconscious level after all these years.

"I've got you," Remi promised. "We're almost out. Hold on."

"We gotta go!" Alondra yelled. "It's getting hotter!"

The ladder was just about level with the window now. Remi could see the guys had almost descended all the way down. "You first," he told Alondra. "I'll pass the kid out to you. He's pretty woozy."

"You got it," she said. As soon as the ladder touched the windowsill, she bolted, launching herself toward it. The door started rattling. The guys had obviously cut a vent through the roof, but the fire could still race in here at any second. This place could still go up like a box of tinder.

Once Alondra was down a few rungs, Remi eased Kris out, encouraging him to get his footing. Unfortunately, the mask was attached to Remi's tank, so he had to take it back. But he also took Kris's bag with the fish in.

"No," Kris moaned, fumbling on the ladder. Remi and Alondra were there to grab him, luckily.

"I've got your fish," Remi yelled over the noise of the fire. Ash was drifting all around them like demonic snow. "You need to move, Kris. We have to get away from the fire."

Kris smiled sleepily up at him, blinking his silvery-blue eyes at him. Remi was surprised. He'd had no idea they were that color. Why would he?

"I always dreamed you'd be my hero," Kris mumbled, his eyes already half closed again.

What? Remi was completely taken aback. Thankfully, Alondra had her head on straight.

"Come on now, sweetie," she said firmly, yanking at Kris's jeans to get him moving down the ladder. "This way. We gotta hurry."

The second he had enough room, Remi swung his leg out and got himself on the ladder. The three of them worked their way down as the truck slowly backed up, giving them space between them and the blaze. At the same moment, the crew around the engine let loose with the lines, pumping water over the building and dousing the flames.

They were in the clear. Providing Kris hadn't sustained too much damage to his lungs from smoke inhalation, they were going to be okay. Sure, Remi's captain was probably going to rip him a new one if he realized he'd risked bringing out a goddamned goldfish after the cat incident that afternoon. But in that moment, it felt worth it.

As soon as they reached the ground, Holby draped a blanket over Kris's shoulders and steered him toward the end of the truck. "Let's get some O2 in you, buddy," he said kindly.

Remi hopped down from the engine and jogged behind them. His heart was finally starting to slow down after all the action. He watched as Kris sat on the end of the truck and allowed Holby to slip the smaller oxygen mask over his face. Kris was blinking rapidly and looking about.

"What happened?" he croaked. He clutched the blanket around his shoulders and held the mask closer to his mouth and nose.

"You had a bit of a close call," Remi said as he stood in front of Kris and Holby. He took his own mask and helmet off, breathing the night air in deeply. The crew behind him was doing a good job finally putting out the flames in the bar. Remi dropped his bits of gear beside Holby, then turned to Kris. "I believe this is yours."

"Tay Tay!" Kris cried.

He shot his hands out for the Tupperware box first, then the tote bag Remi still had dangling from his arm. Remi purposefully ignored Holby's raised eyebrows as he handed them over.

Remi looked back up to find Kris gawping at him with a look of mild horror. "Remi?" he cried, his voice muffled from behind the oxygen mask. "Remi Washington?"

"Er, hi," Remi said with an awkward wave.

He guessed Kris didn't remember saying anything about Remi being his dream hero back up in the burning apartment. That was probably for the best.

So why did Remi feel so disappointed?

5

KRIS

Before Kris could get enough wits about himself, his mouth was off again.

"Sweet baby Jesus, what are y'all doing here?" he blurted at Remi through the oxygen mask. Wow, that air felt good. His words still sounded a little slurred to his ear but he was starting to feel a lot less light-headed. Then he shook his head at the stupidity of his question. "You're a firefighter, duh."

"Uh, yeah," Remi said, his ash-streaked face breaking into a big goofy smile. Fuck, he hadn't changed a bit. No, that wasn't true. Even under that big awkward suit, Kris could still tell Remi had bulked up even more since Kris had last seen him.

Remington D. Washington. Shit. Had there ever been a time when he hadn't taken Kris's breath away? For as long as he could remember knowing he was gay, he also knew he thought his older brother's best friend was the man of his dreams. Painfully straight, of course. For fuck's sake, the dude was a goddamned firefighter. It didn't get much manlier than that.

Feeling self-conscious, Kris used the hand that wasn't clutching

Tay Tay's box to try and pull more of the blanket over his bare chest. Fuck. He was glad he'd at least put a pair of jeans on. Had Remi carried him out of his apartment like this?

Oh lord, his apartment. For a second, he was able to forget he was half-naked and look up where the rest of the firefighters were still aiming a couple of different hoses at Bottom's Up, gradually getting the blaze under control.

"Is it all gone?" he asked Remi and the other firefighter sitting next to him. The guy was taking his blood pressure, so Kris guessed he was an EMT as well.

Remi looked back toward the charred remnants of both Kris's job and home. "Uh, no," he said, not sounding convinced. "I mean, there's probably going to be a lot of damage, and the stairs won't be safe to walk up anytime soon. But there might be some things you can salvage."

Kris bit his lip and tried really hard not to cry as the other guy took the blood pressure cuff off. It wasn't like Kris had loads of stuff. The only thing that *really* mattered was Tay Tay, and she was safe.

But how was he going to be able to buy a new tank for her? She could only survive in a bowl for a couple of days, maximum. All his clothes were gone. His shoes. His laptop.

Before he could completely lose his head, he gritted his teeth and took a deep breath of the glorious oxygen that soothed his raw throat. He had all his music and photos uploaded into the cloud. He had money in the bank. Not a lot, but his mom had pressed the importance of saving for a rainy day on him the second he started earning his own wage. He had a few hundred bucks, at least.

And he had his phone and his makeup. Realistically, he could take on the world with just those things.

Still, he wasn't exactly thrilled with his situation.

"Fuck me sideways on Sunday," he said angrily. Remi's eyebrows shot up. "Do y'all know how it started?"

"Um, err," Remi said. He ran a hand through his short, dark hair. "No, we won't know until we've gotten the scene under control and fire investigation can take a look."

"How are you feeling?" the other guy asked. Kris realized he had a name badge sewn onto his suit that read 'Holby.'

Kris pulled the air mask away from his face. It felt good, but he didn't really need it as much now and it was awkward talking through it. "Like my whole life just went up in smoke," he said glumly, shaking his head. "But I feel fine, I guess. My chest hurts a bit."

"That's normal," Holby assured him. He got Kris to look into a small flashlight he shone into each of his eyes. "Do you have somewhere you can go tonight? Maybe someone who can come get you?"

He nodded. His mom would have her cell phone off overnight. She still had this idea the thing would microwave her brain while she slept. But his brother, Leon, or Leon's girlfriend, Ava, would have a phone on vibrate between them. They were more likely to hear their landline, too.

It was only a temporary solution, though. Neither his mom or his brother had anything more than a couch to offer Kris. None of them were well off, and Ava was heavily pregnant.

Where he was going to live was a problem for another day, though. Right then, Kris placed Tay Tay carefully down beside him in the back of the firetruck and fished out his cell from the tote bag. Holby clapped him on the back and stood up to head over toward the other firefighters. But Remi stepped closer, that same goofy smile on his face as he pointed at the phone in Kris's hand.

"You know, we're really not supposed to rescue anything except the people," he said with a nervous laugh. For such a big handsome guy, he always was kind of dorky.

It was the main thing that made Kris's heart ache for him. He was just a big ol' teddy bear, sweet and fluffy under all those muscles. His light-brown skin and dark eyes were as beautiful as ever, despite the fact he was covered in soot.

Fucking hell. Of all the firefighters that could have pulled Kris out of the fire, it had to be Remi Washington. Kris's dumb crush had faded into the background over the past couple of years. It was true what they said. Out of sight, out of mind. But now it was back in full force, making butterflies dance around his heart, which had quite frankly been through enough already tonight.

Kris gave him what he hoped was a grateful smile and tried not to gush. "The phone is nice," he said. "Really, it helps me out so much. But thank you for rescuing my fish. I know it's silly, but she's my little buddy. It would have broken my heart to leave her behind."

He meant it. He got a lump in his throat just thinking about it. Tay Tay was the first living being, pet, human or otherwise, he'd been truly responsible for. He was sure he felt as strongly about her as other people did their cats and dogs.

"Hey," said Remi. He reached out, seemed to second-guess himself, then patted Kris once on the shoulder. "No sweat. It's my job, dude. I'm sorry this happened to you. But believe me, you can recover from anything so long as you're still alive to do so. You'll get yourself sorted again in no time."

He was sounding forcefully cheerful, but Kris appreciated it. After all, Remi must have pulled hundreds of people from fires and other accidents, right? He'd seen firsthand how people put their lives back together afterward.

"Thanks," Kris said quietly.

He did his best to smile. It only felt like a twitch, but Remi smiled back at him again in response. It made Kris's heart flip. Damnit, what he wouldn't give to have that smile directed his way every day.

He was being ridiculous. There were actual problems he needed to tend to right now, pretty damn big ones.

He held up his phone. "I better call Leon," he said apologetically. Ideally, he would have kept Remi talking to him all night if he could. But Remi had a job to do, and Kris needed to be picked up so he could get out of the fire crew's hair.

"Oh, yeah, sure," Remi said, nodding and stepping backward. His mask slipped off the side of the truck and dropped toward the ground, yanking Remi's upper body down with it and causing him to stagger as he fumbled to catch it. He laughed sheepishly. "So, uh, see you around?"

He gave that dorky wave again and jogged off back to his coworkers. The fire was pretty much out now. Just the embers were smoldering beneath the blackened remains of the bar. Kris sighed and bit his lip. Considering how fucked he was, he didn't feel too guilty about taking a little bit of joy from seeing Remi again.

Luck was on his side, which made a change for that night. Leon picked up after a few rings. "Kris?" he grunted sleepily. "What's going on? What time is it? Are you all right?"

Kris huffed and patted the lid of Tay Tay's box. "About three thirty. And no, not really."

He gave his brother the basics. But by the time he got to the whole 'rescued from a fire' part, he could hear Leon was already running for the door, grabbing his car keys and yelling to Ava that he would be back soon.

Kris smiled to himself, feeling incredibly grateful that he at least had family he could rely on. "Thank you so much, dude. I owe you."

"No, you don't, you jerk," Leon said fondly. "Just hang tight. I'll be there soon."

Kris hiccuped back a sob. "Thanks," he said thickly. "Bye."

Knowing his big brother was coming to the rescue threatened to make him cry again. Despite their differences, Leon *always* had his baby bro's back. He'd never once cared that Kris was gay, or twinky, or lacked life ambition. He just loved him, unconditionally.

Kris wished he could say the same thing about the rest of his family, but he definitely wasn't thinking about that tonight.

Lucky for him – or not, as the case may be – he was soon offered a distraction.

"What the fucking fuck is this fuckery!"

Kris leaned around the firetruck to see PJ step out of his car onto the sidewalk and slam the door so hard the whole vehicle shook. He shoved his hands into his brown hair and looked over his glasses in despair at what was left of the bar.

To be fair, a lot of the building itself was still intact. Kris was no expert, so couldn't judge if it was salvageable. But he wasn't feeling completely hopeless about their prospects of refurbishing and reopening. This *was* the town's only gay bar, after all. There would be a demand for them to open their doors again.

"Hey," Kris said. He offered PJ a wave that felt kind of pathetic. But he didn't have the energy for anything else.

PJ's expression changed from horror to concern in a flash. He darted over to the end of the firetruck and crouched in front of Kris. "Jesus, fuck, man. Are you okay? Were you in there?"

Kris shrugged and sighed. He was feeling sleepy again now the adrenaline was wearing off. "Yeah, but I'm cool. Me and my fish are in one piece, so the rest can be replaced, you know?"

PJ stood, nodding and biting his lip as he turned his attention back to what was left of his business. He was probably already thinking about what the hell he was going to do. Kris didn't know anything about insurance claims or how long it would take them to get back on their feet. Would insurance cover his pay or would he need to look for another job? There were about a dozen of them on staff. How would PJ afford their wages when there was no revenue coming in?

Once again, Kris found himself wondering what on earth could have caused such a blaze. An electrical fault? Even though it was illegal to smoke inside the bar, had someone dropped a cigarette and not put it out properly? How did fires just randomly start in the middle of the night?

He guessed he'd find out soon enough. In the meantime, he had to work out how he was going to manage with nothing but his beloved fish, a pair of jeans, a phone, its charger and his makeup to his name.

One way or another, he'd manage. He always had.

It just wasn't the most cheerful prospect. He huddled under his blanket, hugged his fish's box tightly, and waited for his brother to come rescue him.

The rest they could figure out in the morning.

6

———

REMI

emi was more than used to his shift pattern by now. He worked twenty-four hours on, then forty-eight hours off. The day after a shift was always a bit weird, depending how much sleep he had been able to get. After a shift like the one on Friday, where he didn't get any shut -eye at all, it meant the first day off was a write-off as he tried to reset his body clock and feel more human again.

But by the time he woke up on Sunday morning, he was still feeling out of sorts and he wasn't sure why. It was like he couldn't shake off his last shift, even after a run and a shower. It wasn't like there had been any loss of life. Those were by far the worst days to get over. They'd had a great shift. Leon had texted Remi to let him know Kris was doing fine after his narrow escape.

So what was it? Remi half wondered if it was his interrupted jerk-off session. It got him thinking how much better it would be to come *home* to someone. Or even just date somebody. Remi had been with a few girls during and since high school, but for one reason or another, all his relationships had fizzled out.

He got himself dressed and decided his best bet was distraction. This worked out quite well, as his mom had texted the day before inviting him over for a Sunday afternoon barbecue. She was hopeless at remembering his shift rotation, so she just tended to text him the day before any plans were happening and hoped for the best.

Sometimes it irked Remi because it highlighted the fact that he *never* really had plans these days unless it was a firehouse event. As much as he was thrilled that Leon had met such a wonderful girl as Ava, there were times when Remi felt the loss of his and Leon's close relationship.

He just needed to find himself a nice lady, too. It always seemed like an insurmountable task, though. Remi was on a couple of dating apps, but Hidden Creek was a pretty small town. There were times when he and Leon or one of their other old high school buddies took a trip into Houston on a Friday or Saturday night. But with his shift rotation, Remi always felt like he was held back from making any real commitment, even if he did hook up with someone cute.

Ah, who was he kidding? He could probably find a way to make the stars align for the right girl. Lots of people worked shifts, after all. But there was always something holding Remi back from trying that hundred percent, he knew.

He did some chores to fill the couple of hours before heading to his folks' place and tried not to muse over his single status too much. He finally took the clean laundry that had been piling up in his spare room and put it away, opened a few bills he'd been meaning to look at and emptied the trash. He knew he wasn't the most house-proud person, but it did feel good to sort a couple of things out in between shifts.

Just before he was ready to head out the door, a swish of a tail caught his eye in the backyard. He hadn't mowed the lawn in a while, but he was still able to see a familiar black furry face with green eyes moving through the grass.

Remi smiled. Even after the incident on Friday evening, he was still glad to see this little kitty again. She had been popping in and out of his yard for a few weeks now, and he'd taken to leaving some water and sliced turkey out for her when she came around. He knew he probably shouldn't, but she was skinny with no collar and it made him feel better to give her a little something.

"Good, kitty," he murmured, stroking her as she bound over to greet him and the bowls he placed on the patio. He guessed she was probably only about six months old. Hopefully, she had a home to go home to at night.

Time was creeping forward, so Remi left the skinny cat to her lunch and began his journey to his own food. He locked his door and swung his keys in his hand as he crossed his boiling-hot drive to open up his car. Even with a visor up to shield it from the sun, it would take the A/C a minute to cool the interior down.

As he waited, he thought about the snippet of conversation he'd caught in the early hours of Saturday morning between Kris and his boss, a guy called PJ. They'd said something about Bottom's Up being the only real gay club in the area, and how much it was going to affect the LGBT community.

Remi swung his keys around in a loop on his index finger. Here he was complaining how hard it was to meet a lady he connected with. It must be ten times harder for gay guys to meet other guys in a small town like Hidden Creek.

How did you meet dudes when you weren't in a place that told other dudes you were gay? Or bi? It wasn't like you could always look at a guy walking down the aisle in JJ's Fresh Goods and tell he was into men. Well, some people could, couldn't they? That was what they called gaydar, or at least they had back in the nineties.

But what if you were wrong? How could you know *for sure?*

Remi had often wondered.

He shook his head. A few years ago he'd come to accept the fact that, yeah, from time to time he ran into another guy that made his stomach flip and heart pick up the way it did when he met a gorgeous girl. He thought of the porn he'd found the other night and rolled his eyes. Yeah, there was a good chance he...wasn't quite straight. But he'd never felt strongly enough to go somewhere like Bottom's Up and test the theory. Not when he absolutely liked women as well. That was just the easier option, wasn't it?

Well, it wasn't like he was about to get the opportunity to test that anytime soon with the town's premier gay bar out of commission. But now that option was gone, at least for the time being, Remi couldn't help but wonder if he'd missed out. You only lived once, right? And it was the twenty-first century, for crying out loud. Maybe the next time he saw a guy that made his heart rate increase, he shouldn't be so afraid and go with it.

If seeing life-threatening situations on a daily basis had taught him anything at all, it was that people's time on this earth was too damned short. If he was lucky enough to be attracted to a wider range of people, surely he owed it to himself to think outside the box and go for it.

He grunted and pulled the now cool car out of his driveway. Yeah, right. What would people say? That he was going through a phase, probably. And that was if they were being nice or polite. He heard the words the guys at work used to insult each other and they almost always implied queerness in a derogatory way. Even though they were just joshing around, it made Remi uncomfortable. There was no getting away from the fact that people associated being gay with weak and effeminate and therefore bad.

It pissed Remi the fuck off. Although he'd obviously never come out – what would be the point? – he still felt the sting when people spouted homophobia. It was probably one of the reasons he loved Leon so much. Even before his little brother had come out, Leon had always been a more decent kind of guy compared to a lot of the dicks they went to school with. Remi had no time for people who were racist or homophobic or any of those other prejudices that were still sadly a little too common in a small town like Hidden Creek.

Remi's mind naturally wandered to thoughts of Kris. Leon had come to his rescue after the fire, so Remi had texted him yesterday to ask how he was doing. Although Leon's younger brother had grown up significantly over the past couple of years, Kris had still looked small and shaken to his core as he'd sat on the end of the firetruck, shivering under a blanket.

Blazes of that magnitude were unusual in Hidden Creek. Ordinarily, Remi was called out to grease fires in kitchens or barbecues gone awry. To see a whole building go up in flames was unusual, to say the least. Even after a couple of showers, Remi still caught the odd whiff of the smoke in his hair.

Thank goodness Kris had gotten out unscathed. But he was bound to be reeling from it still, despite Leon assuring Remi he was fine. Even if his things hadn't been burned, they were bound to be damaged and waterlogged. It was anybody's guess how long it would take before he could get access back into his apartment to inspect the situation. Thanks to the town's experience with Hurricane Harvey, at least they knew how to get industrial fans in there quickly to dry it out and stop the mold growing. But still, Kris had probably lost everything.

Remi knew there wasn't anything more he could have done to help. He still had a lingering sensation of guilt, however. The idea of Leon's brother being in a bad way niggled at him. Like a muscle ache that wouldn't go away.

Remi made up his mind to text Leon again once he'd gotten to his folks' house and said his hellos. Remi knew he and Kris weren't close, not by a long shot. But Remi cared about Leon, so Leon would understand that meant Remi cared about his little – or not so little – brother too.

Except when he parked the car and rang the doorbell at his parents' house, he realized he didn't need to text Leon.

Because Leon opened the door.

"Buddy," Leon cried with a sigh and a big grin. "Your mom was threatening to send out a search party." He laughed as the two of them naturally leaned in for a hug.

Leon wasn't much like his brother in appearance. If Kris was a flower, Leon was a tree trunk, much like Remi. Tall and solid with muscle. But they both had the same bright, welcoming smile Remi had noticed over the years.

"I'm not that late, am I?" Remi said. "Besides, what are you doing here? Not that it isn't great to see you."

"Come through before you let all the hot air in," Leon said, ushering Remi inside. He had stayed over at the house hundreds of times, so he was just as comfortable here as Remi and his sisters were. "Your mom just likes to fuss over things. You know that."

Remi certainly did. There was no business too small that Bettina Washington wouldn't stick her nose in, Remi thought fondly. His mom liked to know all so she could fix all because she always had an opinion on everything.

"No search party needed," Remi assured his best friend as they stepped into the hallway covered in family photos from over the years. "I just lost track of time a little. You here for the barbecue?"

Leon nodded as Remi followed him down the hall toward the kitchen. He picked up a half-finished beer from the counter, presumably where he'd left it, then fetched one out of the fridge for Remi without asking. "After the couple of days we've had, your mom insisted on dishing out a little TLC." Leon smiled affectionately at Remi, then stepped out into the backyard.

Remi could hear numerous voices before he stepped back into the sunshine. His dad had the grill going by the swimming pool and his mom had all the folding chairs out. Every one was occupied and the chatter over the music playing immediately became a chorus of cheers as the guests realized Remi had arrived.

"You made it!" Darcy, Remi's younger sister cried as she bounded over to throw her arms around him. Having finished college over the summer, she was now living in Houston and came home frequently. Although thanks to his shift pattern, Remi hadn't seen much of her lately. He smiled as he wrapped his arms around her small frame.

"Y'all are acting like I dropped off the grid," he said with a chuckle.

His mom tutted as she came over for a hug after Darcy. She was a large Black woman with natural hair and a big smile, her lips always painted ruby red. His sisters took more after her with their darker skin, whereas Remi was a little lighter because of his dad's fair complexion.

Remi clung to her and patted her back. "You should text if you're going to be late, Remington," she admonished. "I thought there might have been a car accident or something."

Remi resisted the urge to roll his eyes. Instead he waved over to his older sister, Jamila. She and her husband, Thom, were fussing over their eighteen-month-old daughter, Kendra, who was squirming around, getting more food on her dress than she was in her mouth. Ava, Leon's heavily pregnant girlfriend, was also sitting with them, tiredly rubbing her belly and sipping an iced tea.

"The man of the hour," Remi's dad announced happily, poking at the sausages he was currently grilling. In contrast to Remi's mom, his dad was tall, slender and blond, his hair cropped close ever since his days in the military way back when. "How you doing, son?"

"Great," Remi said with a nod. He noted his dad had placed the propane tank too close to the barbecue *again,* so Remi would have to stealthily move it in a minute.

That would have to wait a moment, however. "Oh, Remi," a tearful voice came from his right. He turned back toward the house to find himself immediately enveloped by another pair of arms. Stefania Novak let out a sob as she clung to Remi and buried her face in his neck.

It wasn't unusual to see Stef hanging out with his mom. But as Remi looked over her shoulder while they hugged, he saw someone that he wasn't sure had ever come to his parents' house before.

Kris.

7

REMI

It was probably because he wasn't expecting to see him, but the sight of Kris looking so small and tired in one of Leon's old shirts that was about five sizes too big for him knocked the air from Remi's lungs. Kris stopped at the threshold of the doorway of the house when he saw Remi, his eyebrows raising.

"Hi," Remi mouthed at him, then stroked Stef's hair. "Hey, hey," he said soothingly. He hugged her small frame as his mom rubbed her back. "Stef, what's wrong?"

The people around the barbecue watched with sympathy as Stef hiccuped and pulled away from Remi, wiping her eyes. "You saved my baby boy," she said. "Thank you."

Remi glanced awkwardly at Kris, who shrugged. "I was just doing my job, ma'am," he said. "But it was my pleasure. I'm damned glad we got Kris out of that fire."

"How many times do I have to tell you not to call me ma'am?" Stef chuckled, relaxing a little.

"Sorry," Remi said. It was just habit for him to be polite.

Kris shoved his hands into his jeans pockets and offered Remi a small smile. "Thanks," he mouthed. It was strange seeing him subdued. Ever since he'd come out in high school, he'd been larger than life. Even though Remi hadn't had much to do with him, it was always obvious when Kris Novak was in the room. He was the life and soul of the party.

Remi's mom stepped in and wiped Stef's mascara off her face with her thumb. "Now, now," she said firmly. She steered her over to a vacant seat and pressed a homemade mojito into her hands.

They had been best friends as long as Remi and Leon had. Remi couldn't even remember a time when their moms weren't close. He was glad Stef had someone like his mom to look after her. Even if she was a little overbearing, she cared deeply about the people in her life. After Leon's dad skipped out on his family several years ago, Stef didn't have her husband to rely on anymore. But with a best friend like Bettina Washington, she was in good hands.

"Everything's fine," Remi's mom insisted. "Don't you go stressing yourself out over what might have been."

"Damn right," Leon said. "We're all still here, thanks to Remi. I think that deserves a toast."

"Here, here," said Remi's dad from over by the barbecue. He raised his tongs while everyone else lifted their glasses and bottles. "You're a real American hero, son."

Remi didn't want to burst their bubble while they were being so sweet. That was the closest Clive Washington would ever get to sappy. But that kind of talk made Remi really uncomfortable.

"Honestly, it was a team effort," he said. He glanced at Kris again. Remi would hate Kris to think he pulled him from that blaze for the glory or anything like that. "We were just doing our jobs."

Kris placed his glass of cola down on the table and walked over to Remi with his hand out. He was still kind of on the small side, but having seen him half-naked, Remi now knew he was pretty compact under that oversized shirt. Remi wasn't sure why his brain felt he needed to remember that in this particular moment, but Remi coughed and tried to clear his mind as he shook Kris's hand.

"Job or not, honey bee," Kris said, "I'm seriously grateful." He had a firm shake despite his hand being a lot smaller than Remi's.

"Take a compliment for once, Remi," Jamila said with a laugh, bouncing Kendra on her knee. "Besides, aren't you happy you finally got to do something exciting for once rather than rescuing cats from trees?"

"We heard about that!" Darcy said gleefully. "Dad said Bishop told him you fell into a pool!"

As the party laughed good-naturedly at Remi's expense, he relaxed a little. For some reason, it was *really* important to him that Kris didn't feel like his traumatic experience was a fun day at work for Remi. But Kris was laughing as Darcy recounted Remi's kitten adventure for those that didn't already know.

Kris looked more like his usual self as he chuckled along with the story. The purple tips of his white-blond hair meant he always looked that bit extraordinary, but laughing brought the sparkle back to his eyes. It made Remi happy to see that despite going through a tough time, the fire hadn't burned away his spirit.

"Son," Remi's dad called out. "Come give me a hand with these ribs, would you?"

Remi's dad was the king of the barbecue, despite never caring that much about safety. Remi came over and moved the propane tank to an acceptable distance, hoping his dad didn't notice. While his dad never had much to offer in the kitchen, as soon as they lit that gas, he was the one in charge. 'Barbecuing is a man's job,' he had always told Remi.

Remi's dad was a big fan of men's jobs and women's jobs. Remi had thought he was just traditional growing up, but when Jamila had Kendra, their dad had jokingly complained a fair amount about ballet classes and everything being pink. He took every opportunity to drop hints that Jamila and Thom needed to get on with having a boy so Remi's dad would have someone to throw a football with in the backyard.

Remi had made the mistake of suggesting Kendra was probably capable of catching a ball only once. His dad had taken the genuine suggestion as a hilarious joke and moved the conversation onward.

Gender roles were a simple matter, as far as Clive Washington was concerned. He liked that his son was a firefighter and his daughters worked in offices. That suited his world view nicely.

So what did he think of Kris?

Leon was big and tough like Remi, so there had never been a problem with their friendship. But when it became common knowledge that delicate, arty Kris was gay, Remi's dad had scoffed 'no surprise there' and not mentioned the matter again. Remi glanced between his dad and Kris as they plated up meat from the barbecue.

Was Remi's dad comfortable with Kris's presence? Or was he okay with Kris being gay because he slotted into that acceptable effeminate category that had been so stereotypical in the media while Remi was growing up? Was Kris the 'right kind' of gay or did Remi's dad dislike him anyway and was just being polite?

Having Kris in their house made Remi desperately want to know. He suspected his dad had opinions on the issue, but Remi couldn't be confident what they were. In that moment, he wanted to know that his dad was okay with Kris. That his being gay, no matter how he presented it, was okay.

Because he suspected it wasn't. Deep down, Remi knew a big part of why he had shied away from expressing any bisexual inclinations was due to the fact that it would rile against his dad's notions of what it meant to be a man. Remi was a tough guy.

Tough guys didn't kiss other guys.

"That chicken's catching, Remi." His dad's voice cut through his thoughts. Before Remi could look down at the barbecue, Kris looked up, prompted by Remi's dad, no doubt. So Remi realized the same time as Kris did that Remi had been staring at him.

Shit. Remi felt his cheeks heat up as he hastily used the tongs in his hand to turn the chicken legs. "Sorry," he mumbled. "I'll have the burned ones."

Ava shook her head and raised her hand. "I love burned food right now. This baby has strange taste, I'll tell you that."

The group laughed, taking the focus off Remi. But he glanced at Kris again. He didn't want Kris to think…what exactly? Why *had* Remi been staring at him? Yeah, Remi didn't want to think his dad was a bigot, but it was something more than that.

"So, Kris," Jamila said as she tried to persuade Kendra to try a slice of tomato. "Are you going to be living with Leon until everything gets sorted out?"

Kris shot Leon and Ava a smile when they looked uncomfortable. "No, there isn't really room for three adults, not with the baby set to arrive any time now," Kris said. He shrugged and squeezed his mom's hand. "Mom let me stay on her couch last night."

Remi's mom tutted as she bustled around the patio, topping up people's drinks. "Stef, that apartment is barely big enough for you. Surely you're not suggesting Kris stays there in the long run? This could take months to sort out, right, Remi?"

Remi blinked in surprise. But he figured he actually was the authority in the group on the matter. "You mean Kris's apartment?" he asked, flicking his gaze between Kris and his mom. "Uh, yeah. It could be a while before the insurance all gets straightened out. The fire investigation team will need to determine the cause of the blaze. With such a big building and so much destruction on the lower levels, it might take a while."

Stef shook her head and patted Kris's hand. "I don't care if it's a tight squeeze. Kris doesn't have a job *or* a place to live right now. He can stay with me as long as he likes."

Kris nodded and sighed. "Honestly, I'm just glad to be alive right now," he said genuinely. "I don't really mind where I live. Plus, Mom has a great hair dryer," he added, making the ladies in the party laugh.

Remi should have seen it coming. His mom always had to fix everything, after all. But she spoke before Remi could anticipate her meddling.

"Nonsense. Remi has a spare room. Kris could stay there, couldn't he, Remi?"

Remi almost dropped his tongs. "What?" he asked.

His mom waved her fingers toward Kris, whose eyebrows had shot up almost into his white-and-purple hair. "You're not going to let Kris camp out on a couch when he could have a bed and his own room, are you?"

"Oh, no," Kris spluttered. "I wouldn't want to impose. Remi literally carried me from a burning building. I couldn't ask him for any more."

"Impose?" Remi's mom repeated with scorn. "Son, you and Leon are practically family. You could stay with us, but wouldn't you rather stay with someone your own age? Remi doesn't have enough friends outside the firehouse, anyway."

"*Mom,*" Remi growled, trying not to get flustered. "I have friends. But – uh – Kris, of course you'd be more than welcome." He actually thought it was a terrible idea. As much as he liked Kris and didn't want him to be couch surfing, the two of them had nothing in common. Living together would most likely be awkward as hell.

Remi's dad scowled. "I'm sure Kris has friends like him he could stay with, Bettina," he said, his eyes on the burgers he was flipping. "No need to put Remi out."

Remi bristled. *Friends like him?* In other words, other gays.

Remi still wasn't sure how his dad felt about Kris, whether he actually did have an issue with him because of his gayness. But Remi could take a wild guess and figure out his dad didn't want Remi to be associated with someone like Kris in case it tainted him. Maybe it was fine for *other* people to be queer. But Remi's dad didn't want his son associated with people like that.

"He wouldn't be putting me out," Remi said firmly, meeting Kris's gaze. "I think that's a great idea, Mom."

"That's really decent of you, buddy," Leon said. The relief was clear in his voice as he held his girlfriend's hand and Ava rubbed her expanded belly. "We really wanted to help, but it's hard."

Kris shook his head. "Oh honey, I know," he said to his brother, clearly flustered. "But I couldn't, Remi. You're the sweetest, but it's too much."

Didn't he want to stay with Remi? Or was he just being polite?

"Kris is fine to stay with me," Stef insisted.

But Remi had made up his mind. He could still see his dad shaking his head from the corner of his eye. However, it just spurred Remi on. Plus, his mom was beaming at him. She didn't care Kris was gay or what people would think of him staying with her son. As frustrating as her meddling could be, in this instance she was right. Remi needed to step up.

"No, Mom's right. Kris can have his own room. I don't want any rent, but maybe you can help out a bit with groceries."

"O-of course," Kris spluttered. He rubbed the back of his neck and bit his lip. "Goodness gracious me," he said, hamming up his Texan accent. "You really are my hero, aren't you, darlin'?"

Remi gave a one-shoulder shrug and tried not to feel embarrassed again. "It's the right thing to do, isn't it? I'm happy to help."

Yeah, he and Kris had nothing in common. Remi had no idea what they would talk about – if it would be awkward as hell or, worse, they would piss each other off within the first week. But damn it, he wasn't going to back out now. If his dad thought it was only manly to help people when Remi was on the job and their lives were in danger, that was his issue. As far as Remi was concerned, it was just as manly to open his home to someone who was practically family in a time of need.

And if some people got the wrong idea about Kris moving in with Remi because of Kris's sexuality, that was their problem.

It wasn't like there was anything between Kris and Remi. Kris didn't even know about Remi being kind of bi and if he did, he probably wasn't interested in Remi anyway. Just because they were going to be two queer guys living together didn't mean anything was going to happen. Remi didn't feel anything even remotely sexual about Leon's younger brother, in any case.

Sure. He was cute and had a hell of a lot of style when his clothes hadn't all been wrecked in a fire. But he was so different from Remi. Remi wasn't even sure Kris liked him all that much. But right now, he didn't need a friend. He needed a roof over his head. Remi would try his best and not put his foot in his mouth. Then hopefully the two of them would get along just fine.

The situation would only likely last a couple of weeks if they were lucky. What was the worst that could happen?

8

KRIS

What the hell was Kris doing? This was a terrible idea. And yet here he was, waving his mom goodbye as she drove away from the curb. He walked up to Remi's front door with a pounding heart and dry mouth.

Remi had a house. A *real*, two-story house with front *and* back yards. There was a damn mailbox out by the sidewalk. This was actual grown-up shit.

Kris knew not to look a gift horse in the mouth. The truth was, his mom had purposefully moved into a tiny apartment as soon as Kris had moved out to save a ton on rent. Leon and Ava's place wasn't much bigger and their spare room had already been turned into a nursery.

Chase had begged Kris to stay with him at his house, but Kris didn't want to intrude on his daughter Lyla's space. In fact, several of the friends Kris now knew through Chase had offered a spare bed or a couch, but there was something holding Kris back each time.

Gabe had moved in with his boyfriend, Orion, and Kris didn't fancy being a third wheel. Koby lived alone, but his spare room was stuffed with his metalworks projects and art supplies. Even Pete Miele, Orion's uncle, had offered Kris a room as thanks for Kris helping him come out recently. But Pete was still going through his divorce, and even though there wasn't anything between him and Kris, Kris didn't want to complicate Pete's life any more than it already was.

Remi was single and had a whole house to himself. Here, Kris would have a room of his own and Remi was insisting he just help out a little with groceries, maybe some bills, but no rent. Moving in here would mean Kris might not go totally broke while he got back on his feet.

All he had to do was act naturally around the guy he'd been pining for since he was thirteen years old. No big deal, right?

Kris rubbed his jaw and hugged his bag and Tay Tay's Tupperware box to his chest. Along with his phone, charger and makeup bag, Kris also had a couple of Leon's old T-shirts and a pair of his beat-up sneakers to his name. His mom had also taken him shopping for a toothbrush and deodorant. It wasn't much, but at least Kris didn't feel like he had nothing left in this world as he pressed the doorbell with his thumb.

This was the best option. It was *sensible.* Remi and he could be civil roommates, surely. He never had to know how Kris felt, and he *definitely* never needed to find out how many times Kris had jerked off thinking about him during high school. Kris blushed just thinking about it.

As the door rattled from the other side, Kris managed to calm down enough that he hoped he wouldn't give himself away when he greeted Remi. "Hi," he squeaked as the door swung inward.

"You made it," Remi cried, pushing the screen door outward for Kris to step inside. "I mean, obviously you did, you're here. Um, you wanna come in? *Mi casa es su casa.* Or it will be when I get you a key cut. I assume you'll want a key, right?"

"Oh, sure, hon," Kris said as he stepped in from the porch into the front room. "If that's okay? Thank you again. I super appreciate this."

"No sweat," Remi said, shutting the door. "And of course it's okay for you to have a key. I want you to feel at home. So, um, this is my place."

He held his hand out, indicating the living room, then let it drop to his side. Kris wasn't surprised he was kind of lackluster about his enthusiasm for the place. It didn't seem like he had a lot of people over.

There were the furniture basics. Coffee table, a sofa and a television. But there were also several cardboard boxes tucked into corners, the curtains were half hanging off the rail and a mirror was propped up against the wall rather than hanging off a hook.

"Sorry, it's kind of a dump," Remi mumbled, rubbing the back of his neck.

"Oh, no," Kris said quickly, shaking his head. "It's totally cute. Lots of potential. When did you move in?"

"Two years ago," Remi said with a sheepish look. "You, uh, want to see the kitchen?"

"Sure," said Kris, quickly. Two years? The poor lamb obviously had no clue how to make a space feel cozy. "I bet working shifts makes it hard to get around to DIY."

Remi made a noncommittal sound as Kris followed him through a door into the kitchen. "My grandfather left me and my sisters some inheritance money," Remi explained. "I put the money toward a down payment. It's nice to have somewhere to myself. But I've never really known what to do with the place."

The kitchen walls were a garish blue color. The cabinets were white and some of them had smudges and scuffs on them. It wasn't *bad,* per se. It just lacked any real personality or signs of love and care.

"You've got time," Kris assured him. He felt awkward, like he was tripping over his own tongue. Ordinarily, he would skip about the place and make interior design suggestions or at least throw around a couple of playful insults. But with Remi, he felt like he was under a microscope.

For fuck's sake. He hated reverting to this shy, insecure version of himself. Ever since he came out in the summer before his junior year at high school, he'd promised not to be this lesser model. For so long he had been too afraid of his own shadow to really live his life. He never wanted to go back to that.

But being around Remi, knowing that he had even less than usual thanks to the fire, Kris couldn't help but feel inferior. Remi owned a *house,* and he had a *career,* not just a job. Kris's greatest achievement was the goldfish he still had clutched to his chest.

Hopefully, once the shock of the fire wore off and he got more comfortable in Remi's house, he could act more like himself again. He hated feeling like he couldn't say whatever he wanted or flounce around for fear of how that would be received. As much as his other friends' offers of a couch weren't quite what he needed, Kris would have at least felt more comfortable living with another gay guy.

But he didn't feel like Remi was the kind of dude to be secretly homophobic. So far, he gave off nothing but friendly, accepting vibes. Kris needed to trust that Remi would be okay with him acting like his usual self. They just needed a few days to get used to one another.

Kris placed Tay Tay's box on the counter and his bag of possessions on one of the chairs at the kitchen table. Remi opened the fridge door.

"You want a beer?" he asked. "I'm not really hungry after the barbecue earlier, but I've got a few cans and some chip and dip if you'd like?"

Ah. Damn. They were at this point already. Kris tried to give Remi one of his cutsey, no-big-deal smiles he was so used to dishing out at the bar.

"Oh, no thank you, babe. I don't drink beer."

Remi just looked from the fridge at him, though, and gave him one of those dorky, lovely, lopsided smiles. "Oh, sure. I've got vodka and soda you could mix it with. Or I think Jamila got me some wine a while back."

Kris gritted his teeth and did his best to keep smiling. "Thanks, but that's okay. I don't drink."

Remi blinked at him. Kris braced himself for the usual 'But you're a bartender?' line.

"Like, at all?" Remi asked. But he didn't sound incredulous. More intrigued. "Are you teetotal?"

Kris licked his lips and tried not to get flustered. "No. I'll have something every now and again. Not that I think there's anything wrong with drinking. I just don't enjoy the way alcohol makes me feel."

Remi seemed to consider that. Then he nodded. "Cool," he said, half smiling again as he looked inside the fridge. "Well, like I said, I have a bunch of sodas or iced tea or plain old tap water?"

Kris was momentarily stunned. Really? Remi wasn't going to give him a hard time? "Uh, iced tea would be great." Remi nodded and withdrew from the fridge with two bottles. "Oh, I don't mind if you want a beer, really," Kris said. This was one of the main things about not drinking. It always made him feel like a killjoy around other people.

But Remi threw him a strange look. Like Kris was being cute. "Nah," he said. "I had a brew at my parents, but I'm not that big on drinking either, if I'm honest. I just tend to get involved because other people are doing it."

Kris was genuinely at a loss for what to say at that. Remi wasn't that into booze either?

Maybe the two of them did have something in common after all.

When Remi handed him the opened bottle, Kris managed a small thank you. Then he picked up his stuff and followed Remi back through the house to take a tour of the upstairs.

Every room was just as unloved and unfinished as the last. Kris could tell Remi was embarrassed as he showed him around. For a moment, Kris wasn't sure which was the spare room and which was Remi's – they were both so empty and filled with unpacked cardboard boxes.

"Sorry," Remi mumbled as Kris placed his small bag on the sofa bed in what he finally worked out was the spare room. At least the bed had been made up with clean sheets. Remi had most likely done that while Kris had popped back to his mom's to get his few possessions. "I don't really have people over. I kind of didn't realize how crappy the place looked."

"Hey," said Kris a little sterner than he meant to. "It's not crappy. It's..." He waved his hand about as he tried to think of the right word. "It's like a caterpillar cocoon. With a bit of help it can be a beautiful butterfly one day."

Remi smiled and placed his hands on his hips as he looked about the spare room. "Yeah," he said with a nod. "You're right. It could be a butterfly."

He directed that smile toward Kris and Kris felt something flip in his chest. What the hell? Remi was just being nice, he wasn't flirting. Kris must still be overemotional from everything. His poor heart was latching onto whatever little bit of sympathy came his way.

"Do you think I could borrow your computer at some point?" Kris asked, changing the subject and indicating the slightly beat-up-looking machine on the desk in the corner of the room. "My phone's pretty good, but there's some things I need to do that would be much easier with a proper keyboard."

"Oh, sure," Remi said. He nodded and darted over to the computer. He almost tripped on some sweatpants shoved into a pile of dirty laundry under the desk, but he managed to catch himself and style it out. Or at least he tried to. Kris was very proud of himself for not gasping too loudly. "Um, sorry," Remi said bashfully as he dropped into a chair that didn't look quite big enough to carry his large frame. "I forgot this was here. I'll run around and pick up all the mess tonight."

Kris shook his head. "Oh, honey child. Do *not* go to any extra trouble on my account. I am super grateful for everything you've done. I mean it. She is very hard to shock."

Remi frowned at him. "She?"

Kris felt himself begin to blush in embarrassment again, but he tried not to let it show too much. "Sorry," he said, pulling self-consciously at his brother's baggy T-shirt. He'd at least wanted to tie the damn thing into a crop, but he was trying not to be overtly gay. He didn't want to make anyone – namely Remi – feel uncomfortable. But the extra material felt like it was smothering Kris in that moment. "I mean me – I'm very hard to shock. It's like a thing some guys do. Refer to themselves as 'she.' It's stupid."

He hadn't succeeded in stopping his cheeks from going pink, he could tell.

But Remi's lopsided grin was back as he turned on the computer. "That's kind of cool," he said. "Like…another persona. Oh! Like how Beyoncé is Sasha Fierce?"

Kris couldn't stop his jaw from falling open. "You know about Sasha Fierce? Oh, baby. You just earned so many points." Kris clicked his fingers a couple of times and grinned, his embarrassment forgotten. "There's hope for you yet."

Remi's half smile became a full one. He sort of looked pleased, in a bashful kind of way. That was interesting.

The moment was interrupted as a loud thud came from downstairs. The two men frowned at each other. "What was that?" Remi asked.

Kris shrugged and followed Remi as he jogged back down to the kitchen.

Where Kris shrieked.

"Tay Tay!" he screamed, rushing forward to seize her box from where it had been knocked onto the kitchen tiles. One of the corners had come loose and the box had started leaking water. "You never said you had a cat!"

He didn't mean to sound so accusatory as he rushed over to the faucet to refill Tay Tay's box, but after nearly losing her once, Kris wasn't prepared to let his baby get eaten or suffocate.

"I don't!" Remi cried. But Kris turned and looked at the small, black cat that jumped onto the kitchen table and raised his eyebrows. "She's not mine," Remi spluttered. He scooped her up and hugged her to his chest, then glanced at the now open back door. "I must not have closed the door properly and she got in. But she's not mine. Well, I guess I feed her sometimes-"

"No wonder she thought she'd found a free snack," Kris said.

He tried to laugh, but tears were pooling in his eyes. What the fuck? It was just an accident, a misunderstanding. But after everything he'd been through, the idea that he might lose Tay Tay had pushed him over the edge and he couldn't seem to be rational about this.

"Sorry," he stammered. "I didn't mean…I, uh, she's all I've got left and uh-"

"No, I'm sorry," Remi insisted. He didn't seem to know what to do with the cat, who didn't have a collar, Kris now noticed. Remi walked over to the back door and let her out again before closing it securely. "She's never come inside before. I'm sure your fish will be safe." He gave Kris an uncertain smile. "You could maybe put her in a little bowl with a shipwreck and coral and stuff."

Kris bit his lip. "Uh, shucks. Sorry, I should have mentioned. I need to get my lil' baby boo a new proper tank. Small bowls like that kill goldfish. Is that going to be a problem?" Fuck, he should have asked this *before* Remi agreed to give him his spare room.

"How big a tank?" Remi asked with a slight frown.

"Uh, a few feet long," Kris said, embarrassed. "I'll put it in my room and take it with me when I go. Or I guess I could see if Leon could house her-"

"No, no," Remi said, waving his hands. "No, it's fine. I just, uh, well

I wasn't expecting that. But it's fine, totally. I mean, if the cat gets back in, it'll have a much harder time getting into a tank, right?"

Kris licked his lips. "Sure," he said. "Well, uh, I guess I'll go back to my room and get settled and stuff."

"Right," Remi said, nodding. "Oh, uh, let me finish setting you up on the computer, okay?"

Kris followed him back upstairs with Tay Tay clutched to his chest. There was an awkward silence as Remi set up a new profile for him to use. Kris didn't know what to say to make the atmosphere go away.

"There you go," Remi said, rubbing his hands on his sweatpants as he stood up from the desk. Then he swooped down and scooped up most of the laundry he'd piled up there, leaving a couple of odd socks behind. He hugged his clothes while Kris hugged his fish box. They stared at each other. "Well, uh, goodnight," said Remi. Then he fled the room.

Kris sighed and placed Tay Tay carefully down on the nightstand and closed the door after Remi.

This was going to be awful, wasn't it?

9

REMI

"*Y*ou're joking," said Channing as he munched his way through a bag of chips.

As usual, when their shift rolled into the evening, the team congregated in the kitchen at the firehouse. It had been a quiet day, with just a couple of call-outs for minor traffic accidents and a kid who got their arm stuck in a section of railing in Moore Wood.

Channing was sitting in one of the chairs with his boots up on the table, no matter how many times Holby swatted them down. Alondra was reading one of her NASA books. It looked like this one was about Mars from the cover. Remi loved how much of a sci-fi nerd she was and had been out-geeked by her during several late-night conversations about Star Trek over the past few years.

Remi frowned and concentrated on getting the water he had in a pan up to boiling temperature.

"No," he said sincerely in response to Channing. "I'm not joking. He's my best buddy's younger brother. When I realized he was homeless, I offered him my spare room."

He left out the part where his mom had basically steamrolled him into it. That made it sound like Remi was still a kid who couldn't make his own decisions. He was glad when Alondra looked up from her book and raised an eyebrow at him.

"How *old* is he?" he asked. "He looked like he was still in high school."

"He's twenty-one," Remi said quickly, aware he sounded a little defensive. But he didn't want anyone to think he was taking advantage of a victim or anything. "And he's not paying rent. I'm just helping him out in the short term. Plus, it'll be kind of nice to have a roommate."

Having lived at home when he'd trained at the academy, Remi had missed out on that particular life experience. It was already nice knowing someone else was in the house when he'd left that morning and that they'd be there when Remi got home. Even if they had gotten off to an awkward-as-fuck start.

For a second, while they'd been getting along, it had almost felt like hanging with Leon again, in a similar-but-different way. The two brothers had matching mannerisms and turns of phrase that were spooky at times. The main difference was that when he let his guard down, Kris got louder and campier, coming back out of the shell the fire seemed to have put him in.

But that damn cat had almost killed Kris's fish and the evening had never really recovered from that. Without the excuse of eating dinner, Remi didn't really have any reason to knock on Kris's door. So they'd both gone to bed without speaking again and Kris had still been asleep when Remi had left that morning.

Still, Remi hoped they could come back from this. He was starting to think he quite liked Kris when he wasn't clamming up or censoring his fabulousness.

He glanced up from his almost-boiling pot to where Holby was looking over at him from his tablet. "What?" Remi said.

Holby shook his head and went back to his game. "Nothing."

"So, y'all are like friends?" Alondra pressed, putting a ribbon between the pages and closing her book. "You said you knew who lived at the apartment when we got there, but I didn't realize he was an actual buddy?"

"Well, he's not," Remi admitted. "Or he wasn't. I dunno. Leon and I have been tight basically since kindergarten. But Kris was always this shy, tiny kid who stuck to his books. Then their asshole dad finally up and left and-" he made an explosion noise and fanned out his fingers "-it was like Kris just *arrived* in a shower of glitter."

He shrugged and picked up his packet of ramen noodles to check the instructions. He made these things at least once a week, but he always read the back of the packet each time, just in case he forgot a step.

"Leon and I had left high school by then," Remi continued as he carefully opened the top of the packet. "So I never really got the chance to know him when he quit being all closeted. I guess I will now – *shit.*"

His fat sausage fingers slipped, sending the brick of dried noodles skittering out of the packet and over the kitchen table. Holby automatically shot his hand out to catch the noodles while Alondra grabbed the packet of flavoring before it slid off the table and under one of the cabinets.

Channing guffawed and licked salt from the chips off his fingers. "So, having a gay guy in your space doesn't freak you out?"

Remi frowned as Holby handed him back the mostly intact brick of noodles. "No," he said carefully. "Why would it?"

Channing shrugged and fished out another handful of chips. "Dunno, dude. It's just…different, you know?"

Remi considered that as he added the noodles to the water and checked the time on his phone. "I guess," he said. "But my life isn't exactly a riot, you know. Maybe different will be fun."

A scoff drew their attention toward the sofa in front of the TV. Discovery channel was playing back-to-back shark documentaries and the watery scene on the screen was all bloody. Old Travis didn't bother looking over his shoulder at them, just wagged the remote by his head.

"So long as you don't wake up covered in lipstick and shit one morning – or worse." He chuckled to himself.

Remi's skin prickled. "Come on, dude," he said, folding his arms. "The guy's a friend and he's been through a lot."

Travis did look over at them at that. "Hey," he said. He scratched his round belly, then held up his hands defensively. "I'm just kidding. But, you know, he is one of *those* kinda guys, you know?"

"No," said Alondra, also crossing her arms and turning around in her chair. "We don't know, Travis." Remi was grateful for her support. He wasn't sure he liked where this was going.

Travis sighed and finally made the effort to turn ninety degrees in the permanently sunken dent his ass had made in that end of the couch. "Okay, so, the gays can get married now, right? Nobody's making a fuss over that."

Holby frowned. "I'm pretty sure a *lot* of people are still making a fuss over that," he said.

Travis scoffed again. "Not really. So, everyone can get married. That's great. Knock yourself out. What I don't get is all this goddamn parade shit and running around like fucking fairy boys." He affected a limp wrist and fluttered his eyelashes like he was having a seizure. *"Oh! Oh!"* he squealed. "You want to marry another dude, *fine.* Just act like a fucking man, not a goddamned teenage girl."

Channing snorted and shook his head. Alondra blinked and leaned back in her seat. Holby frowned even harder.

Remi clenched his fists. "Cut it out, Travis. That's not cool."

But Travis laughed at Remi, making his hackles rise. "Oh, come on!" he cried. He bounced on the sofa as he flung an arm out. "It's just kinda gross, you know? Like, why do you gotta shove all that queer shit in my face, dude? Act like a real man."

"What, so we're all just supposed to be exactly the same?" Holby asked.

Alondra smirked and shook her head. "I think you and I have very different ideas of what makes a 'real man,' *güey.*"

"I don't get what your point is?" Remi said. He was aware the pot was rattling behind him, but he didn't turn around to look. He just kept his eyes on Travis. "You don't like Kris because he's 'too gay'?"

Travis rolled his eyes and dropped back into the sofa to face the TV again. "Oh, come on, dude. Don't twist my words. I'm just saying, it makes me uncomfortable, is all. I would get sick of that shit in my house real fast."

"Well, it's a good thing Kris doesn't have to rely on a bigoted *asshole* like you then, isn't it?" Remi snapped back.

It was only when he noticed all four people in the room had turned their faces toward him did he realize he'd shouted. He swallowed and gritted his teeth. But fuck it, he wasn't backing down.

"No, seriously," he pushed, looking directly at Travis. "Are you saying that Kris deserves to be left couch surfing? That because he falls outside your narrow view of male gender presentation, I shouldn't help him out?"

Travis sneered and huffed. "Listen to yourself, man. 'Male gender presentation' – what the fuck does that even mean? Fucking millennials," he grumbled as he crossed his arms and sunk back in the couch to watch the TV. "Why don't you go rescue a puppy or something, Dr. Doolittle, instead of making up problems that don't exist."

"Yeah, you know what," Remi yelled at the back of his head. If he wasn't careful, Captain Bishop was going to come in here and read him the riot act. But in that moment, he didn't honestly give a flying fuck. "I *am* a fucking millennial. And we let go of all that caveman bullshit about what the fuck a man is 'supposed to be.' Kris is my friend and he's also now my houseguest. So it might be best you keep that homophobic crap to yourself in the future."

"Whoa!" Travis shouted back. He jumped to his feet and advanced toward the kitchen area. "I ain't no homophobe, kid. You take that back. I said they can get married, I can't help how I feel about *some* of them being all la-de-da. What more do you want?"

Remi shook his head. The rattling lid of his pot alerted him to the fact his noodles were boiling over. He turned away from Travis and snatched the pot from the stove and threw it all into the sink. "Nothing," he muttered, stalking out of the kitchen toward the corridor that led to the break room. "The great Travis Murphy graciously says the gays and lesbians can get married now. *Halleloo!*" He threw his hands in the air like his grandma did at church. Fuck, her thinking was more progressive than this hillbilly.

"Remi," Channing called after him through a mouthful of chips. "Come on, man. He's just kidding!"

"No, he's not," Remi said, stomping through the doors into the quiet of the corridor.

Remi knew he needed to cool off. He'd probably have to swallow his pride and apologize to Travis because he knew hell would freeze over before Travis made amends with him. There could be a call any minute and the two of them might have to rely on one another to save a life. Feuds were never a good idea in this job. But Remi was going to need a bit of time to calm down if he was going to make any apology sound genuine.

The trouble was, he thought as he dropped into one of the bunks in the break room and shoved his hands behind his head, he'd gotten so irrationally angry on Kris's behalf. Sure, it pissed Remi off too, knowing what he did about his hidden sexuality. But Kris didn't deserve to be talked about like that. He was spunky and sassy and full of fight. Jerks like Travis saw one aspect of him and just judged the hell out of him. It was bullshit.

"You okay, man?" Greg asked in the gloomy light. He poked his head above the partition of one of the bunks down the line. Damnit, Remi must have stormed in here making more noise than he thought.

"Yeah, sorry, dude. I'm fine."

Alondra scoffed as she pushed her way through the door. Technically, she had her own private bunk area, but she often came into the guys' area anyway. "This one's on fire," she said, nodding her head toward Remi and grinning. "Mad respect. Put it there, *mi hermano.*"

She held up her hand for a high five. Remi couldn't help the slight smile on his lips as he slapped it. "Thanks, Lonny."

"What I miss?" Greg said. "I always miss the good stuff."

Alondra winked at Remi. "Washington here put Travis in his place for being a homophobic douche. It was sexy."

Remi was fully aware Alondra had a boyfriend. But knowing she felt secure enough with him to flirt a little just reinforced the strength of their friendship. "Thanks," he said again, quietly this time.

"Ah," Greg said with an appreciative nod. "Nice. Good one, dude."

He dropped back down on his bunk, presumably to sleep. Alondra gave Remi a wave. "I'll let you know when Travis has cooled off. Channing said he's got some pizza rolls you can have if you want, instead of your noodles?"

Trust Channing to prioritize the food. "Yeah, thanks," Remi said gratefully.

When it was quiet again and he was by himself in the bunk, he took a moment to go over what had just happened.

That was the first time he'd tried to shut down any homophobic shit. And come to think of it, it *always* came from Travis. Sure, Channing had tried to brush the whole thing over, but the other guys kind of felt like they were on Remi's side about Kris.

Did that mean they might be on his side about *him?*

The thought made something warm blossom in his chest. What if he *did* come out as bi? Maybe it wouldn't be the total disaster he'd always envisioned.

He didn't try and sleep. But in the quiet of the break room he smiled to himself for a while.

Maybe, just *maybe,* coming out might be a tiny bit awesome. Lucky for him, Remi had a new gay almost-friend he could potentially ask. What if he came out to *Kris?* Who better to understand what Remi was going through?

He grinned even broader in the dark. Yeah, that could be pretty damn fantastic.

10

KRIS

Kris stood and looked at the options in the fried chicken joint he'd stepped inside. Ordinarily, he quite enjoyed shopping trips. But when it was for the very bare necessities and he had no money to spare, it kind of lost its appeal. He should probably not waste money on fast food when he could go to JJ's and get some real stuff for the rest of the week. In that moment, though, he just wanted some damn comfort food. Plus, the A/C in Randy's Chicken Shack was just what he needed after traipsing up and down Victory Boulevard all morning.

He wasn't the only one. There was a fair-sized line, considering it was a Thursday before noon. But Kris wasn't the only person who worked shifts, and Randy's did a mean bucket of legs.

He sighed and wiped his forehead, looking down at the few bags in his hands. At least the pet store had carried some of the gear Kris needed to sort out Tay Tay's new tank that had arrived that morning. He'd forked out a hundred bucks for a new aquarium from eBay. The damn thing was ancient, but the guy had taken pity on Kris and knocked twenty bucks off to have it couriered from Louisiana in a matter of days. It meant Tay Tay would finally have some room to swim again and proper clean water.

Since Remi left early for work, Kris had spent the first part of his morning messing around setting the tank up as best he could in the spare room. Even though he was only sleeping on a pull-out bed, Kris was kind of starting to feel at home there now.

Or less awkward, in any case. Remi's shifts were even crazier than Kris's had been at the bar. Where Kris tended to work late and rise late, Remi did a whole twenty-four hours at a time. It had meant he'd come home and slept half of Tuesday, so Kris had kept himself as busy as he could out of the house so as not to disturb his host. But there were only so many times he could walk around Moore Wood.

Wednesday had still been kind of strained. Kris definitely got the impression Remi felt like he had to entertain Kris while he was in his home. Kris was hoping that would die down soon enough. He didn't want to be a burden. He was capable of looking after himself.

The truth was, Kris liked Remi's company more than he knew he should. Even if conversation was stilted between them and they didn't really have anything in common. Remi was one for rambling, starting to talk about something, then changing his mind halfway through what it was about. He did it several times during the day. Kris couldn't help but find it adorable. However, he did also wonder if Remi had something on his mind he wanted to discuss.

Naturally, Kris worried it was something to do with him being a more acceptable guest, especially after that cat incident. Maybe Remi wanted to ask Kris not to be too gay around his neighbors or something? The thought saddened Kris, but he wouldn't be surprised or really blame Remi if he did want to request something along those lines. Kris was fully aware of how extra he could be at times. Especially now, when his whole life was up in the air.

He would be less antsy if he knew what was going on with the bar and his apartment. But every time he called PJ, he just got more irritated with Kris. Yesterday evening he had snapped that he would let Kris know as soon as anything changed with the insurance or the fire investigation report, but until then, he should quit bugging him. All Kris had really been able to glean was that there had been several more anonymous messages on social media gloating about the bar's demise. It wasn't that surprising, but it still hurt to know there were people out there who were happy about what had happened.

Kris was used to being busy. His lack of funds meant he felt guilty even thinking about going to the movies or anything else fun. Living above his job meant he hadn't needed a car and he wasn't about to get an Uber into Houston. So he was stuck in Hidden Creek without its only gay bar to entertain him.

Being idle had left him worrying more and more about his situation. His mom and brother were trying to help him out as best they could. But the thing was, he only had a couple of pairs of underwear, the one pair of jeans and a few old, oversized T-shirts to work with. One of them he had at least cut up into an off-the-shoulder crop, but as of yet he'd been too shy to wear it when he wasn't home alone. That only irritated him further. When was his confidence going to fully come back?

So, yes, damn it. He was going to waste a couple of bucks on a damn bucket of chicken, fries and slaw. He might even go all out and get some corn, too. If he added some vegetables, even covered in butter, he might feel less guilty about treating himself to lunch.

His phone rang and Kris answered it as quickly as possible before he subjected the whole shop to the full chorus of Britney's 'Toxic.'

"Chase!" he cried happily. The woman in front of him in line threw him a look over her shoulder. Kris smiled, popped his hip and ran his hand through his purple-tipped hair, hoping to aggravate her further. By the way she tutted, it seemed to work. "How's it going, baby?"

"Good, good," Chase said.

They hadn't been friends long, only a couple of months. But Chase and his new *gorgeous* boyfriend, Hunter, had become regulars at Bottom's Up in that time. They sat so often at the counter and chatted with Kris, it had only been a matter of time before they swapped numbers and started hanging outside of work. Kris suspected they felt a little sorry for the baby gay, but Kris didn't mind. Chase had been through more shit than Kris had with an even crappier dad. They had a lot in common. Plus, Chase's kid and Hunter's dog were both frigging *adorable*. It might have started as a bit of pity, but they were definitely genuine friends now.

"You at work?" Kris asked. JJ's was on the other side of town, but Kris didn't have much else to do. He could maybe swing round and say hi.

"Yeah," said Chase. "Just on a break. I wanted to see how you were doing."

Kris sighed as the line shuffled a bit. It seemed like there was only one poor person on the register and they were struggling somewhat. Kris wasn't in any rush, though. He was happy to wait his turn. "I'm fine," he said. "Bored, broke, but fine." He pressed the back of his hand against his forehead and swooned, even though Chase wasn't there to see his dramatics. "She'll survive!" he joked. The woman in front tutted again.

Chase laughed. "Well, how do you feel about some cheering up? Gabe made a delivery yesterday and he mentioned that brunch we never got around to organizing. How does ten o'clock on Sunday at Rocket sound?"

They'd been talking about this for a while. Chase joked that they'd sort of started a kind of twink club recently, with a few friendships merging together. Kris had been all for a decadent day of food and gossip. However...

Kris bit his lip. "Oh, honey, that sounds great. But..." He sighed heavily. "I don't think I can afford anything like that right now."

He felt so shitty. Here his buddies were, trying to brighten up his crappy situation, and he couldn't even afford some pancakes and orange juice. Maybe if he was super strict about what he ordered, he could make it work? But he'd feel so guilty going out when Remi wasn't charging him rent. In fact, the thought made him glance sheepishly up at the menu he was about to order from.

"Um," Chase said. "Hunter and I might have talked about it last night, too. He said he'd give me some money to pay for you. Actually, he absolutely insisted. He said seeing friends is really important for recovery after a traumatic experience."

Kris had to close his eyes as the tears threatened to spring free. "Hunter's not even coming," he said around the lump in his throat. That was such a kind offer, but he couldn't accept it. "I thought the plan was for him to go see Axel and Orion?"

"Yeah," said Chase. Kris could practically *hear* the smile in that one word. The boy was so in love it was sickening. Kris adored how gross they were together. "But you know what he's like. He's worried you might, you know..."

Kris tried to blink the tears back once more. "Need cheering up?" Kris supplied.

He knew Hunter was all too aware of the effects of PTSD and was probably concerned for Kris. Kris was fine, though. Sure, he'd had a couple of nightmares since the fire. Who wouldn't? Still, he was touched by their concern.

"Thank you, sweetie," Kris said, dropping the over the top attitude. Chase was someone he could be authentic with. "I won't lie, this whole thing sucks," he added in a small voice. "I really appreciate the thought. It means a lot."

"So you'll come to brunch?" Chase asked, the eagerness clear in his voice.

Kris huffed, but there wasn't any bite to it. "Hale *did* mention it again last week," he said. He and Hale hadn't been close at school until Kris had come out as the *other* gay kid in their class in junior year. They'd reconnected again once Hale had gotten his life back together after that crazy business with his cousin and started seeing his boyfriend, Austin. He definitely qualified for their sassy twink brunch club and had been eager to get to know Chase better.

Chase clearly felt the same. "Awesome," he gushed down the line. "Koby's in, too, and I think Gabe wants to bring Cas. We'll have a blast."

Kris shook his head. He *hated* the idea of relying on his friends for charity. But this was an extreme situation, after all. "Fine," Kris conceded, rolling his eyes, even though he was grinning. The grumpy lady in front of him shot him another glare, then went back to harassing the poor server for being too slow. "I'll be there. God, you're such a drama queen."

Chase chuckled, knowing he was teasing. "Takes one to know one. See you there, dude. Don't be late."

Kris hung up the call and couldn't help but smile a little to himself. He really was lucky to have such good friends. He looked up at the ceiling fans and blinked back the tears so he wouldn't smudge his eyeliner. He may not have any decent clothes right now, but at least his makeup was on fleek.

"See, miss. That really wasn't so hard, was it?" the grumpy woman in front said to the cashier. The woman managed to sound both exasperated and smug at the same time. But at least she finally moved away to wait for her order, allowing Kris to step forward.

The poor cashier took a deep breath as Kris stepped up to the counter and forced a painful-looking smile. "Hi," she said. "Welcome to Randy's Chicken Shack. I'm so sorry for the wait. Can I take your…"

The server's eyes went wide. Likewise, Kris faltered a second as he realized he knew the cashier. It was Harrison, from the night the bar burned down. Only at the moment his nametag read 'Jessabelle.'

Harrison looked like he might pass out. But Kris quickly gave him his brightest, most genuine smile. "Hey, how you doing?" he said. "Don't worry about the wait. I can see you're slammed. I'd like to order the four-piece bucket with a side order of fries, slaw and corn. I'll take some barbecue sauce while I'm at it. Oh, and an orange soda."

Harrison blinked then slowly smiled, the tension leaving his chest. There wasn't much he could do either way with the delightful red-and-yellow employee shirt he had to wear, but it looked to Kris like he was still wearing his binder. Good for him.

"Sure," Harrison said. "That'll be nine ninety-five."

Kris handed over a ten and forced himself not to wince. This was his treat. He could live off ramen noodles for a week if necessary.

Harrison glanced at Kris a couple of times while he rang up the order. Kris wasn't in a hurry to stand by the grumpy woman while he waited, so instead, he hung by the till. Harrison looked like he maybe wanted to say something more to Kris. He wasn't looking so relaxed again. But the mom behind Kris in the line dragged her wailing toddlers up to Harrison and rattled off an order while sounding like she might burst into tears before it was done.

Kris looked Harrison over while he waited for his order. Thankfully, grumpy woman left with her food and the poor mom made it through her order without bawling herself. The kids even calmed down at the prospect of fries.

Kris moved slightly down the counter to give them some space when he got an idea. Like Kris, Harrison might be stuck with some crappy clothes options thanks to his uniform. But there was always makeup.

Quickly, before his number was called, Kris whipped out one of his receipts from shopping earlier and grabbed a crayon from the kids' area. Trying not to get wax all over his fingers as he used the bright green stick to write, he scrawled a couple of addresses down for online video tutorials he'd come across. He couldn't remember the specific video names, but he knew the vloggers. Harrison could navigate his way from that.

He finished writing just as his food was ready. He took it from a girl about his age who looked equally as harangued as Harrison, smiling at her before she ran back into the kitchen. Kris caught Harrison's eye and moved back beside the register before he started serving his next customer. Luckily, the toddlers were wailing again, so it covered Kris's words a little bit as he handed the receipt over to Harrison.

"In case you're interested," he said with a wink.

Harrison frowned, then looked down at the two tutorial links. One was for a more masculine brow shape, the other was how to use contouring to create more male facial definition.

"They're both really subtle," Kris said quietly. "Drop me a line if you ever want to talk." He'd noted down his cell number, too.

Harrison opened and closed his mouth, glancing anxiously at the next customer that was waiting impatiently. "I owe you for those cranberry juices," Harrison said in a small voice. But the joy on his face from the video links was clear.

Kris shook his head. "Oh, honey bun. That's the least of the bar's worries," he said with a laugh as he stepped away from the line to let Harrison do his job again. "I'm serious. Call or text if you want. Love you, darling! Bye!"

The man in a suit waiting to be served glowered at Kris, but he didn't care as Harrison gave him a big smile as he left. He walked back out into the Texas sunshine with a spring in his step. Suddenly, he didn't feel so bad about accepting Hunter's charity if he could pay it forward. It felt fair to allow him to help Kris if Kris could help someone else.

He really hoped Harrison would try out those makeup tips. It wasn't something Kris had particularly done himself, but he'd watched the videos out of interest and they'd looked good. If a bit of contouring could help Harrison with his body dysphoria and make him look more like he felt on the inside, Kris would be over the moon.

He stopped and squinted in the sunshine, pulling out the sunglasses Remi had loaned him from his pocket. Remi had done so much for Kris, just because he was his best friend's little brother. It wasn't enough that he'd pulled him from a burning building. Remi was giving him a place to stay and even feeding him.

Kris had been feeling overwhelmed, thinking about how he might be able to pay that back and try and defuse the awkward atmosphere that permeated the house. But he had been thinking too literally – paying with *money.* Maybe there was another way, though?

He glanced at the time on his phone. He had eighteen hours until Remi got back from his shift. Kris was already in town, so he could swing by the thrift store and see if they had anything useful for dirt cheap he could grab to help him put his plan into action.

He ate his food as he walked in the direction of the Goodwill. Maybe this was kind of nuts, but the lightness in his heart that hadn't been there since the fire told him he was doing the right thing.

It was time to thank Remi for all that he had done.

11

REMI

When Remi pulled his car into the driveway on Friday morning, he was astonished he was still able to keep his eyes open. He was bone tired and drained from a grueling shift. All he wanted was to collapse into his bed and sleep all day, but he knew he couldn't if he wanted to keep his body clock running properly. He could only afford a few hours shut-eye at best.

After killing the ignition, he leaned back in his seat and stared at nothing for a while.

He hated the days where they couldn't save everyone.

There had been a nasty pileup on the interstate. Remi would have to do his best to wipe the images he'd seen from his mind and move on. This was just the way it was in this line of work. After a few days, he would be able to assure himself of all the people they had helped, the lives they *had* saved. But for now, it was all a bit too raw.

Funnily enough, the one thing that had cheered him up on the drive home had been remembering the house wouldn't be empty when he got there. Just knowing that Kris would be around when Remi stepped through the front door somehow helped Remi to feel lighter. Things remained a bit stilted between them. They were still getting to know one another, after all. But Kris was starting to relax more, and he had been thrilled to get a new tank for his fish yesterday morning.

It was sweet how much he loved that little pet. Remi had never thought about fish having personalities before, but she absolutely did. He was stunned at how much food she ate and the way she came to nibble at Kris's fingers was adorable. Remi had overheard Kris talking to her over the past couple of days, too. He put on such a flashy, sassy persona, but Remi was starting to suspect Kris was a sweetheart underneath all that.

It was like they were dancing around, each afraid they were going to upset the other. It was clear Kris still felt like he was an imposition and Remi wasn't sure how to assure him that wasn't the case at all. Maybe they needed to do something together, like buddies would – watch a dumb movie with popcorn or play a video game. The trouble was Remi wasn't sure what Kris would like to do. Did they even enjoy any of the same stuff?

Remi sighed and stretched in the car seat, fiddling with his keys. At least living together was making him more domesticated. He'd gone around the whole house on Wednesday and picked up all his laundry, done a load and made sure all the dishes were washed, too. When there was someone else sharing the same space, Remi found he was suddenly far more conscientious of being less of a slob.

There had been several times on Wednesday Remi had tried to broach the subject of coming out to Kris, but each time he had chickened out. No matter how he looked at it, every time Remi felt like he was somehow *using* Kris. They weren't good enough friends yet for him to come out just because he wanted to. It was painfully obvious to him that he wanted to talk to Kris about this situation simply because he was also a queer man. That didn't feel right.

But after such a shitty shift, Remi discovered that he was really looking forward to seeing Kris *specifically*, not just because he happened to be the person living with him at the moment. Kris was sweet and kind and a good listener, or so Remi had experienced so far. Even if he wasn't in the house right then, Remi felt like he'd want to give Kris a call and chat with him anyway.

So perhaps they were on their way to a real, solid friendship, like Remi had with Kris's brother, Leon. He hoped so. He wanted to talk to Kris about what was on his mind.

Not so much the crash. Kris didn't need to know the details of the aftermath of the accident Remi had witnessed last night. But he did want to talk to him about Travis and what their argument had highlighted for Remi. Namely, that he might finally feel confident enough to come out.

There was still another niggle of hesitation bothering Remi, he thought as he wasted more time wiping dust off the car's dashboard. He'd read enough online to know that some gay guys thought bisexual people weren't really gay enough, or that they were just straight people going through an experimental phase. Remi bit his thumbnail and looked at the front door leading him inside to Kris. It might just break his heart if Kris thought he was 'less than' or something. Remi's gut, which was usually pretty intuitive, told him that Kris wouldn't be like that. But Remi wanted to make sure before he wrecked their friendship before it even got a chance to bloom.

At least things with Travis were tolerable. Neither of them had apologized, but Remi took the fact that he hadn't *had* to apologize as a victory. In the meantime, they'd gotten through their shift yesterday being civil and professional. No doubt Travis would take another jab soon enough. But for now, Remi felt like he'd won this particular battle.

With that thought buoying him a little, Remi finally got out of his car, stepping onto the driveway already radiating heat in the mid-morning sun. He'd had to work an extra hour to get everything in order after such a bad call so late in the night. But it was worth it. He could leave all that behind him for a couple of days.

He was excited to think he and Kris might get a chance to hang out again. Perhaps *this* time it would be less stiff. Kris was at something of a loose end while the fire investigation was still pending on his job and home. Maybe they could go out for dinner later or catch a movie. Everyone liked doing that, right? It would be a Friday night, after all. Remi liked to make the most of those when he could.

He pulled the bug screen toward him, turned his key in the lock and pushed the front door inward, stepping inside his front room. Then he stopped, stepped backward, and checked he had the right house number.

How was this his place?

"Oh my god, you're home!" a voice cried. As Remi slowly stepped back inside his house, Kris came sliding out from the kitchen looking frazzled. His hair was standing up at all angles and the shadows under his eyes suggested he might not have slept all that much. Remi wouldn't be surprised. He had apparently stayed up all night decorating Remi's living room.

Or not decorating, exactly. The walls hadn't been painted. But there wasn't a cardboard box in sight. The curtains were properly hung. There were pictures and mirrors fixed on the wall, some which he recognized and some he didn't. There were candles on tables and his DVD collection had been displayed on a bookcase he had been meaning to construct for about six months. There were family photos that he thought might have been printed off Facebook standing in frames.

The carpet had been vacuumed and the table top polished. There was a plant in the corner by the TV (which had been dusted) that definitely hadn't been there before. The comic book postcards that Remi had been collecting for a while were all arranged artfully on a cork board.

Kris grabbed his hair and looked like he was going to cry as Remi covered his mouth and stared in wonder. "I'm so sorry," Kris moaned. "I just got carried away. I only meant to do a bit to say thank you for everything, but then it was four in the morning and it occurred to me that it might be a serious overstepping of boundaries. But I'd had so much coffee by then I just kept going and it was only when dawn came I realized I'd opened so many boxes and you might not like it, and, oh, god, I'm so sorry! I really hope you're not too mad. I had good intentions, but you know what they say about *those,* and if you want me to put it all back or move out, I totally understand-"

He ground to a halt. Probably because Remi had sniffed quite loudly.

He was fucking tired and it had been such a shitty shift and this was one of the single nicest, most thoughtful things anyone had ever done for him.

"I love it," Remi said, dropping his hand to his chest and doing his best to blink back tears. His dad always told him 'real men don't cry' but damn it, he was overwhelmed by emotion. "It's incredible. It looks like a *home.* You did all this in a day?"

Kris dropped his hands from his hair, a hopeful smile creeping onto his lips. "Uh, yeah. You like it? It's okay?"

Remi shook his head. "Dude, no. I fucking *love* it. It's amazing. You really didn't have to do anything like this. I…honestly, this rocks so hard. Damn."

Kris bit his lip and grinned. It was only then did Remi appreciate he was wearing one of Leon's old T-shirts with a pair of jeans. But he'd cut the bottom half away to make it a crop top and opened up the neck so it hung off his right shoulder.

Remi was momentarily taken aback by what the sight of so much toned skin did to him. Wow, he really must have been tired. This was Kris Novak. Remi remembered when he was a tantruming toddler, a shy gangly teen. He wasn't either of those things anymore, though. He was a grown man, and a cute one at that.

Remi shook himself mentally, refocusing on the here and now. It must be the incredible gratitude, but his heart was aching with happiness. And it was all thanks to Kris.

"Uh," Remi said, his own grin growing as he continued looking around the room. "Wow. Sorry, I feel like crap, but after a nap, I'll definitely tell you how much I love this all over again."

Kris looked bashful but slightly excited, too. "You want to see your bedroom?" he asked.

Remi barked out a laugh and rubbed the back of his neck. "You did not do this to my room as well?"

Kris turned his knee in a coy gesture and pretended to twirl his hair. "Maaayy-be," he said, fluttering his eyelashes.

Remi shook his head and laughed again. "Show me!" he commanded with a grin so big it was hurting his cheeks. He held his hand out to the stairs. "Lead the way!"

Kris gave a little wiggle, then dashed up the stairs with Remi right behind him. Remi's heart was racing already. Despite feeling beyond tired, he was suddenly giddy with excitement.

Again, Remi recognized several items in his room from stuff he'd had lying around or that had been sitting in boxes for the past couple of years, like the lamps on the bedside dressers. There were things his mom had given him when he'd moved out and stuff from his old room back at the family house. But there were also numerous pieces, mostly the photos frames, that Remi had definitely never seen before.

He looked around in awe at his room. Once again, there were candles arranged on shelves and the windowsill. Remi's old Hidden Creek High Bears jersey was framed and hanging on the wall, and one of the old footballs he'd once thrown around with his dad was standing on a little plinth on top of his chest of drawers. There was a collection of ticket stubs in a glass jar with a cork lid.

Remi covered his mouth again as he took it all in. "Did you buy all this new stuff?" he asked, feeling guilty. Kris didn't have the money right now to be spending like that on him. Or at all. They didn't really know each other. Yet.

But Kris shook his head and smiled. Remi detected a hint of pride and he couldn't blame him. Kris had done an incredible job.

"I recycled a surprising amount of stuff," he said. "A lot of this was junk from your garage. There was a couple of boxes that looked like they might have even belonged to the previous owners?" he said, posing it as a question.

Remi shrugged. "Maybe," he admitted. "I've never really gone through everything in there."

Kris nodded, looking around the room again. "There is some stuff I got from Goodwill. So, yeah, a few bucks for a few newish frames. But the rest was just elbow grease, honestly." He peeked at Remi through his lashes. "Does she like it?"

Having Kris call Remi 'she' did something strange to Remi. As if Kris had included him in a secret. It felt like a badge of acceptance, a token of affection.

Remi turned back to Kris and couldn't stop the smile that felt like it was glowing on his face. "This is above and beyond, I swear," Remi said. "Thank you. I love it."

Kris bit his lip and smiled back. "You're welcome," he said softly.

The moment stretched between them as they held each other's gazes. All of a sudden, Remi became aware that they were standing alone in his bedroom.

That was crazy, though, right? There wasn't anything fizzing between them. Not Remi and his best friend's younger brother. But there they were, looking at one another as the silence stretched on.

Remi was consumed with the reckless notion that now would be the time to blurt out his secret. He *burned* to tell Kris he was bi. Because…well, his overly tired brain seemed to be suggesting good things might happen if he did. Instead, he shook himself, as if waking from a trance, and a nervous laugh bubbled up his throat.

"I seriously need a shower and some sleep," Remi said. Then he winced internally. Kris didn't need to know how gross he felt. "Uh, you feel like maybe getting some takeout tonight, or I dunno, grabbing a burger somewhere?"

He thought he saw Kris's eyes light up. But before Remi could be sure, Kris's face was back to neutral again. However, he did nod. "Sure," Kris said. "I might have to have a nap, too. The caffeine seems to finally be wearing off and I think I've run out of rooms to make over."

Remi opened his mouth to ask if that meant Kris had re-vamped the spare room as well. But Remi was certain he had. He'd enjoy seeing that later. For now, however, his body was crashing fast and he needed to crawl onto his mattress.

He nodded. "Sounds like a plan," he said. "So, I'll see you in a couple of hours?"

"Great," Kris said. There was a pause, like he maybe wanted to say something else. But then he nodded one last time. "Goodnight," he said, then vanished into the hall.

"Night," Remi murmured after him.

Something was stirring in his chest. He wasn't sure what it was, but after some sleep, he might have a better clue.

For now, he wanted to enjoy his new room – his new house. The whole place felt brand new. As if Kris had breathed life into everything like a Disney character come to save the day.

After a quick shower, Remi drifted off to sleep immediately, a smile lingering on his lips.

12

—————

KRIS

*T*here were probably better places around town to have brunch, but Kris wasn't the only one of his friends who had a soft spot for Hidden Creek's retro pizza diner. During the day, the blue-and-yellow-neon lights weren't so obvious as he walked up to the front entrance. But the mint-green Cadillac parked out front was gleaming in the summer sunshine and there were a few people hanging around taking photos as usual. It probably constituted as one of Hidden Creek's only tourist attractions.

The bell tinkled as Kris pushed his way in on Sunday morning, sighing as the blissfully cool air hit his skin. He was a little early. Remi wasn't noisy when he got ready for work, but Kris was a light sleeper so he'd been awake since about seven thirty. He had been eager to get out of the house and make the walk across town to spend some time with his friends. He figured their table would already be available at this time of the morning even if it was before their reservation.

However, it seemed he wasn't the only eager beaver.

As he fanned his T-shirt away from his chest, his attention was caught by the hand waving in the air from a table at the back. Kris grinned, heading over before a server could come to greet him. Kris wound his way past the red leather booth seats filled with families and the jukebox playing 'Rock Around the Clock.'

Chase jumped out of his chair to hug Kris hello. "Dude," he enthused. "It's so good to see you. How are you?"

He held Kris by the shoulders and studied his face. Kris rolled his eyes and huffed. "I'm *fine*," he insisted. Although he couldn't help but admit that having Chase fuss over him was nice.

The last few months had been kind to Chase. Since he'd been granted full custody of his daughter after her mom's tragic passing, Chase had really stepped up. He was a top-notch dad, doing everything he could for Lyla. Kris suspected falling in love with a handsome hunk hadn't hurt either. Hunter treated Chase like a prince, as he should.

As a result, Chase had put on a little weight and his face was quick to smile. Kris was glad they'd gone from being acquaintances at the bar to real friends.

Urgh, the bar. He tried not to think about it. He was slightly concerned the fire investigation report hadn't come back yet. But then, it might well have and PJ was just neglecting to tell him. It wouldn't surprise Kris. PJ didn't generally think about his underlings at the best of times.

Today wasn't about that, though. Kris was here to forget his woes and have some fun. He was glad only Chase had arrived so far. It would be good to have a few minutes to catch up, just the two of them.

"You look *gorgeous*, darling," Kris said, deflecting the attention away from himself. Besides, it was true.

Chase grinned at the compliment. "Thanks," he said. He was

wearing a new-looking shirt and his tennis shoes were scuff-free and expensive looking. It made Kris feel a little self-conscious in Leon's old T-shirt, but he had tied it at the back to make it more fitted and taken the time to do a full face of makeup. Nothing too over the top for daytime wear, but enough to make him feel like he'd made an effort for his buddies.

"How's Lyla?" Kris asked as they sat back down at the end of their six-seater table.

Kris picked up one of the rocket-shaped menus to glance at the options for shakes. There was a raspberry one he normally liked getting when he visited here, but he might go nuts and try the banana one this time.

Chase nodded and sipped at the ice water they already had on the table. "Great. She actually has a playdate today with Gena Miller, her best friend. Little League is over right now, but they've been getting into swimming over the summer." He shook his head. "She's so fast, I can't keep up with her."

Kris could feel himself grinning at his friend. His pride was infectious. Kris wondered what it would feel like to have your whole life revolving around someone so important.

"So, Hunter's out too?" Kris asked. Then he cackled at Chase's blush. Even after several months, he was still like a teenager with a crush.

"What?" Chase asked, pretending to look at his menu.

Kris shook his head. "Nothing." He winked. "You're too precious, baby."

Chase grumbled something under his breath. Kris suspected he was telling him to fuck off in the nicest possible way. That just made Kris snicker more.

"Yeah," Chase said. "Hunter and Orion have gone over to Axel and Fox's to play video games. I'm so glad he's made some friends of his own from the gym. As much as I love doing everything together, it's nice to have different news to share sometimes."

"Gossip, you mean," Kris said, waggling his eyebrows.

But Chase shook his head. "Not much gossip from all us happy couples," he said slyly. He nudged Kris's leg with his foot under the table. "That's where you single guys come in."

For a brief second, Kris was proud of Chase. He'd been so painfully in the closet until he'd met Hunter, he never would have dared played footsie with a male friend before. But Kris's pride was hastily replaced with several emotions at once.

"Nope, sorry, no gossip here," he said quickly and brightly. Then he purposefully buried his face in his menu. "Do you think the peanut butter cream pie would count as brunch? I could add cherries to it to make it healthy."

The truth was, the mention of video games brought him right back to thoughts of Remi. They had both slept most of Friday, but, as promised, they had grabbed burgers and fries in the evening and eaten them outside while the sun had set. Then yesterday, after spending a couple of hours sorting out the last few bits of Remi's 'new' house, they had indulged in a video game marathon, racing cars and blowing up aliens.

Kris still couldn't get over just how much Remi had freaking *loved* the makeover. By the time the front door had opened on Friday morning, Kris had convinced himself he had made a terrible mistake and grossly overstepped his boundaries. But Remi had nearly fucking *cried* over it.

Kris wasn't used to straight guys who showed emotion like that. It was goddamned refreshing. But after the burgers and games and just hanging out for almost thirty-six hours, it left Kris wondering.

Was Remi a hundred percent straight? The last couple of days had felt awfully date-like to Kris.

He tried telling himself that thoughts like that were merely wishful thinking. But he couldn't deny there were moments that felt like something was going on between them. Moments that seemed to stretch out while Kris's heart danced a jig in his chest before they were abruptly broken.

"What?" Chase gasped, his tone scandalous.

Kris glanced up from the menu. "What?" he repeated.

"You have a look on your face," Chase hissed in delight and leaned in closer. "You ho! Spill!"

Kris was glad his vocab was rubbing off on his friend, but he wasn't about to cave. "A lady doesn't kiss and tell," he teased, miming a hair flick.

Chase kicked his foot, making Kris jump. "You're no lady," Chase told him with a giggle. "Spill the T!"

"Ohh, there's T?" a new voice cried.

Luckily, Kris was saved by the arrival of an excitable redhead in the petit shape of Hale McMillan. He skipped up to the table and threw one arm around Kris before he even got the chance to stand up. The other arm had a large grocery bag swinging from it.

Kris laughed. "No, darling, no T. She's an angel, I swear." He let Hale go and crossed his heart then pressed his hands together in prayer. "Chase was just trying to start gossip, the minx. Chase, this is Hale. Hale, Chase." He waved his hands between his two friends. "Play nice."

There had been a time Kris had idolized Hale when they'd been in the same class at school together. Hale had never really tried keeping himself in the closet and had been out more or less since freshman year. Kris remembered how he'd been green with envy as several older girls doted on Hale as the 'only' gay kid at Hidden Creek High. But Kris had been too terrified to come out himself until junior year.

He and Hale had enjoyed their last couple of years at school together, even tried dating for a hot minute. But they were better as friends. After graduating, they'd drifted apart, both kind of lost trying to find their place in the world. But since getting back in touch this year, it was like they'd never been apart. Kris was excited for Hale and Chase to meet and expand his friendship circle.

They were quickly immersed in introductions. Kris had told Hale about Chase and Hunter's awesome three-legged puppy, Trooper, so Chase soon had his phone out showing them both pictures. At which point, Koby Duvall also appeared at the table.

"Oh, he's grown, hasn't he?" Koby commented on the picture of Trooper that Chase had up for Hale.

Koby was probably the least twinky of their little group and several years older than Kris. But he still fit in just fine from what Kris had experienced so far. Koby's mom, Shelly, was Hunter's next-door-neighbor and the breeder whom they'd got Trooper from. Shelly had apparently tried to hook Hunter up with her daughter, but when she'd discovered Hunter was with Chase, she'd settled for introducing them to her gay son instead.

It amused Kris that she'd treated them like children needing play-dates, but as it turned out, Koby was pretty awesome. He had studied art at college and was now a semi-famous metalworks artist. Kris suspected Chase had hoped Koby and Kris would hit it off, but there hadn't been that spark between them. As friends, Kris had warmed to Koby immediately, however. He was edgy in that give-no-fucks kind of way, as illustrated by his goth-inspired look and disregard for gender presentation.

"Ohh, looking like a queen, hon," Kris cried as Koby gave them a twirl. Despite the heat outside, Koby was sporting black army boots, a knee-length black pleather skirt, like a kilt, and a black mesh vest under an open black fitted jacket that went well with his dark hair, lip ring and pale skin.

He too was a holding a tote bag. Kris frowned and glanced under the table. Sure enough, Chase had a bag with him that Kris hadn't noticed before. Was he supposed to bring a change of clothes and they hadn't told him?

Before Kris could bring up the question, Koby leaned down to kiss his cheek and hug him. "Hello, beautiful," he murmured, rubbing Kris's back. "Happy to see you."

He spoke with such sincerity, Kris got a lump in his throat he had to swallow. By the time he did, Koby had kissed Chase and introduced himself to Hale, who he hadn't met yet either, then sat down.

Koby had a way of taking up more space than his slender frame should. He leaned back in his seat, draping his arm over both his chair and Kris's, then stretching his long legs out between Hale's feet. It could have been easy to interpret it as arrogance, but Kris knew it was just Koby showing how comfortable he was with them.

"This place is hideous, isn't it?" Koby commented warmly, his tone making it clear he loved it just as much as Kris and Chase. "Are we waiting on anyone else?"

"Gabe and Cas," Chase said with a nod as he checked his phone.

"But they've said they're happy to share a round of Bloody Marys and mimosas with us, so to go ahead and order drinks."

Kris licked his lips and glanced down at his menu again. He'd forgotten he was with people that didn't know him all that well. But Chase just tapped the milkshake section and smiled when Kris looked up at him.

"I love the raspberry one," Chase said. "Have you had that?"

Kris glanced at Hale and Koby, who didn't blink an eye. "I thought I might live wild and try the banana," Kris said. Then he batted his long lashes, always eager to make a joke to defuse any potential tension. "You know I love a hard, curved banana."

Hale snorted. Koby licked his lips and grinned. "Good choice, darling," he said smoothly. And like that, it was fine. Kris relaxed a little bit.

It was good to be among friends again.

13

KRIS

They made chitchat until their waitress, a girl in her late teens with a nametag that read Tammy, came over. It turned out she was the older sister of the girl Chase's daughter was best friends with.

"Oh hey, Mr. Williamson," she said cheerfully as she noted down their drinks. Then she noticed Koby and went crimson. "Oh, um, I'll be right back with your order," she mumbled, then scuttled away.

"What was that about?" Chase asked with a grin.

"Aww," Kris said, clutching his hands to his chest. "I think the little duckling has a crush." He fluttered his eyes at Koby and wriggled his eyebrows.

"Wait, was that Tammy *Miller*?" Hale asked, his eyes going wide. "Her cousin is *Jason* Miller. Y'all hear about that? He's qualified as an *astronaut* over at NASA in Houston. How insane is that?"

Kris felt like that was pretty damned impressive as far as he was concerned and Chase seemed to agree. But Koby just hummed and began discussing pancake options. Maybe as an artist, he just wasn't all that interested in science. But Kris had to admit, surrounded by cheesy fifties-style rockets and little green men from Mars, there was a childish side of him that was fascinated.

"I'm so sorry we're late, y'all!" Gabe's voice carried over the din of the restaurant. "We were grabbing a few things."

Kris and the others looked over to see him and his friend Caspian pause as one of the other servers dashed around them. They were both on the smaller side so didn't take up much room, but both looked uncomfortable getting in the way of the staff.

Now it was getting closer to lunchtime, the place was pretty packed. Kids were squawking and crying and people competed to have conversations over one another. Kris liked the bustling vibe. He felt connected with people in a way he hadn't since he'd worked his last shift at the bar. He was surprised how much he'd missed it.

Then he noticed that both the newcomers were also holding bags full of stuff.

"Okay," Kris said probably a little harsher than he meant to. But he hated feeling out of the loop when his life was already so up in the air anyway. "Have I missed something? Are we going out afterwards?"

Five faces turned to him as Gabe and Cas took their seats. "What do you mean?" Chase asked.

Kris bit his lip and waved his hand at the party. "You've all got bags. Was I supposed to bring something?"

To add to his paranoia, the guys all exchanged smiles with each other. But Chase leaned forward and gripped Kris's hand before he could cross his arms. "Now we're all here, we have a surprise for you."

The other guys nodded and reached under their seats to pick up their bag. Gabe hadn't put his down, so he rose and walked back to Kris's end of the table. "Chase said you lost everything in the fire," he said. His voice caught just a fraction. Kris didn't know Gabe all that well yet, but his emotion still caught Kris by surprise.

"Um," said Kris, hesitant to take the bag. "I don't know. It's more that I can't get up to my apartment. I'm hoping there's some things that are salvageable."

Koby gave Kris a lopsided smile. "Stop being so tough for one second and just let us be nice, you drama queen," he said fondly.

"We went through our wardrobes," said Hale, also holding out the bag he had brought. "We can't have you looking like your *brother*, can we? He's so painfully heterosexual."

That got a chorus of laughs from the table. But Kris was too stunned to laugh. He watched as five bags of clothes were placed in front of him, taking up the whole end of the table. He could see all kinds of vests and shirts and shorts and even belts and hats. Despite biting his lip hard, he couldn't stop the tears from pooling in his eyes.

"Oh," he said softly, reaching out to touch one of the tops in the nearest bag. "Y'all. You didn't have to."

Gabe hugged him from behind. He smelled comfortingly of warm earth and flowers. "But we wanted to," he said, then kissed Kris's cheek. "You of all people should not be fashion deprived in a crisis."

"Oh, I wouldn't go so far as to call this fashion," Kris teased with a laugh, picking up a dorky T-shirt that had probably belonged to Hale. That got a laugh from the table. "But, fuck. Y'all are going to make me cry, aren't you? Just when I went and put *all* this mascara on." The table laughed. "Um, thank you. Even if all these bags mean I have to get an Uber home, that's really kind of you."

"You're such a brat," Chase bemoaned. But he grinned and nudged Kris's foot with his own.

Kris wasn't quite sure how to process all this kindness. Hale was the only person he'd known for any length of time. The rest of the guys were either new friends or people he was only just getting to know. Yet they had just given him all this stuff? There had to be a whole wardrobe full of possessions here.

He was too shy to go through the bags in front of them, but he could even make out the soles of some shoes in a couple of the bags. The particular brand of makeup remover he liked was poking from Koby's bag and Gabe's had a damn houseplant nestled in it. Kris chewed his lip and blinked back the tears that were still threatening to fall.

He was one lucky little snowflake.

Before anyone noticed him wiping his eyes, Cas's phone pinged. He had left it on the table, so everyone heard it. "Ohh," said Gabe in a conspiratorial tone as he hurried to sit back in his seat. "Who's that, Caspian Grey?"

Cas's cheeks went pink as he snatched up the phone, as if someone might swipe it off him. "No one," he mumbled.

"Has Cas got a *boy?*" Hale asked in a singsong voice.

Kris both appreciated Hale steering the conversation away from him as well as how well he was already getting on with everyone. Cas and Gabe both knew Koby as they all moved in the same artsy circles and had stalls at the farmer's market every Saturday together. But although Hale might have met some of them in passing before, this was essentially their first time all hanging out. Kris was glad Hale was fitting in just fine.

"Is it Mr. Mysterious Text Friend?" Gabe asked, clearly goading Cas. Cas scowled at Gabe, who just grinned cheekily back at him.

"None of your business," Cas said, opening the message he'd received as close to his chest as possible while still being able to read it.

"Kris has a mysterious boy as well," Chase announced to the group.

Kris spluttered on the water he was sipping as once again all five faces turned to him. For fuck's sake, he'd just gotten himself out of the spotlight. "No," he said firmly. "No, I haven't got a boy."

"Look how red he is," Hale cried gleefully. Kris glanced around to see if Tammy the waitress might be about to rescue him. But sadly, she looked to be taking a large order from a kid's birthday party.

"Oh, Kris," drawled Koby. "Come now, fess up. Who is he?"

"The guy you're living with?" Chase asked.

Kris gritted his teeth and busied himself putting all the bags of clothes on the floor around his feet. He wasn't kidding. He was going to have to grab a cab back to Remi's.

"You're living with a guy?" Cas asked. He was probably relieved the attention had been drawn away from him.

"It's nothing," Kris insisted. "My brother's friend had a spare room that he's opened up to me while I don't have a place."

Hale slapped his hands on the table. "Not Remi Washington?" he asked, devilment in his eyes.

Fuck. Kris had forgotten how perceptive Hale could be. Kris might have mentioned his crush on his brother's best friend once or twice when they were back in school together. *Damn* Hale for remembering.

Kris neatened up his knife and fork. "Okay, so what if it is?" he asked.

"You were crazy for him!" Hale cried back triumphantly.

"So there *is* a man," added Chase with a grin.

"One who is still very much straight," Kris said pointedly.

He had to give his friends credit. They gave him sympathetic nods and changed the subject to what food they were going to have. Chase congratulated Gabe on securing his first landscaping job the day before at a retirement center. They all knew there was no point pining over a straight guy.

Except...

Koby leaned over to murmur in Kris's ear. "Are you *sure* he's straight?" he asked.

Kris glanced at him and tried to keep his expression neutral. "All evidence seems to say so," he said.

Koby licked his lips, tugging briefly on the piercing at the corner of his mouth. "Maybe you should double-check. Just to be sure," he suggested. There was a wicked edge to his tone. He winked then turned to join in discussing ornamental garden features with Cas and Gabe.

Thankfully, Tammy finally came back with their drinks, full of apologies for the delay in their service, eager to take their order now.

Kris didn't want to give Koby's words space in his head. But they were there now, taking root and refusing to be moved.

Would it *really* hurt to see if Remi was even just a little bit queer?

Fuck, Kris's cock twitched in his jeans just thinking about it. He knew what he'd felt the past couple of days. There were definitely moments when the air hung between them like charged electricity.

Almost like those seconds before a kiss might happen.

Kris shook his head and did his best to push the train of thought from his mind for the rest of brunch. There was no sense dwelling on it now. He could just wait until Remi came back from work tomorrow morning.

Until then, there was nothing he could do but wonder.

14

REMI

"Okay, boys and girls," Captain Bishop called out.

Remi looked up to see him emerge from his office with a slightly pudgy man in a gray suit with gray, wavy hair and black framed glasses. It had been a slow Sunday shift so far, but after the pileup on Thursday night, Remi wasn't complaining.

Most of the team were sitting around watching more sharks on the Discovery Channel. Travis had passed Remi a bag of pretzels an hour ago. He hoped that meant their feud was officially put to bed.

The captain pointed the pen in his hand toward the gray-looking fella. "This here's Mr. Epstein from the fire investigation team over in Houston. Y'all might remember him from that business back in April."

Oh, yeah. Now Bishop mentioned it, Remi did kind of recognize the guy. That had been so crazy with the explosions around town. That was some shady CIA business, he was sure. They'd never officially heard back on those reports. Remi assumed it was above his paygrade.

Epstein took his glasses off and rubbed the bridge of his nose, shaking his head. "This damn town," he muttered.

"Epstein and his team have concluded their findings on the Bottom's Up fire," said Bishop. It looked like it pained him every time he had to say the bar's name. Remi glanced at Alondra and they both suppressed a snicker at his discomfort.

His next words wiped the smile off Remi's face, however.

The captain sighed. "It looks like it was arson."

"Arson?" Remi repeated. Immediately, his thoughts flashed to Kris. Jesus, fuck. He could have been *really* hurt if someone had set that fire on purpose.

Epstein nodded and slipped his glasses back on. "It seems we have a town of fire starters!" he cried in disbelief.

Remi thought that was taking it a bit far. On the whole, Hidden Creek was usually a calm and quiet sort of place. This guy was bound to think differently, though, if the only reason he came was to investigate suspect blazes.

"I need someone to take Mr. Epstein over to the bar so he can discuss the matter further with its owner, Mr. Maddox," Bishop said. "Any volunteers."

Ordinarily, Remi and the guys would do anything to get out of babysitting duty. What if they missed a call while they were out? But today, Remi stood and raised his hand. "I'll do it, sir," he said.

He felt like Travis might have twitched below him. But he was slightly out of Remi's eyeline. He was probably already lining up jokes about Remi looking out for his 'boyfriend's' job. Well, fuck him. He could make jokes like that all he liked.

The truth was, Remi *was* concerned on Kris's behalf, and he wanted to learn everything he could on the matter. Especially if some fucker had torched the place intentionally.

"Excellent, thank you, Washington," the captain said. "You're in safe hands with Remi, Mr. Epstein. I'm here if you need anything further."

Epstein nodded and strode over to Remi. "Thank you kindly," he said. "Please lead the way."

Remi wanted to ask the guy more about the investigation on the drive across town. But Epstein spent the entire journey on the phone alternating between his wife and teenage son, from what Remi could catch. It sounded like his son had gotten in trouble at summer camp.

Remi felt sorry for Epstein as he pinched the bridge of his nose under his glasses and sighed. "I know, I know, Tommy," he said. "But...please. Can you just try? If not for me, for your mom." There was a pause while Remi made a right turn. "Thank you. That's all I'm asking. Okay, I'll see you soon, okay?"

He closed the call and Remi tried to pretend like he hadn't heard any of it. But Epstein sighed again and looked over at him from the passenger seat.

"You got kids?" he asked.

Remi glanced at him and gave him a sympathetic smile. "No, sir," he said. "Not yet, anyway."

Epstein rubbed his gray, stubbled jaw and slipped his phone back in his breast pocket. "The thing is, Tommy's a great kid. He really is. He's just suddenly gotten so angry."

"I think all teenagers get angry at some point," Remi offered. Epstein nodded and gave him a half smile in return. Remi suspected his words weren't much comfort, but he did truly hope the guy's kid worked out what was making him lose his shit.

They pulled into the empty parking lot beside Bottom's Up. The building looked charred and sad in the daylight. A husk of what it had been before.

Remi recognized Kris's boss, PJ, as he stood looking up at the damage with a couple of guys in hard hats. Contractors, Remi guessed. They were probably giving him a quote for the restoration. PJ squinted through glasses in the afternoon sunshine at Remi and Epstein as they got out of Remi's car. He lifted his hand to block out the glare and walked closer to them.

"Can I help you gentlemen?" he asked pleasantly enough.

Epstein nodded and did up the middle button on his gray jacket. "David Epstein," he said, offering out his hand as they came together.

"PJ Maddox," was PJ's reply as they shook.

Epstein nodded, apparently expecting that, then released his hand. "I'm with the fire investigation team out of Houston." He nodded toward the remains of the bar. "I believe you've been informed this was a deliberate blaze."

PJ shrugged. "Yeah," he said. "They told me you guys had all the evidence you needed and I was good to go ahead with the rebuild. I'm losing money here."

Epstein blinked, then nodded. "Yes, that's correct," he said.

Remi's eyebrows shot up over his sunglasses. "You don't seem all that surprised it was arson, Mr. Maddox?"

PJ shrugged again. "Don't get me wrong," he said, shaking his head. "It fucking sucks. But we've been getting regular threats for a while now. Nothing specific, so I didn't go to the police. But this kind of place? Nah, I'm not all that surprised. I just thank god whoever did it waited until everyone had gone home, you know? And then my guy made it out, too." He shook his head and whistled. "It's a damn miracle. This could have been a hell of a lot worse."

Remi had to agree with that. He counted his blessings they were dealing with arson here and not a terrorist attack. The mere thought sent chills down his spine. It was almost too awful to think about something like that happening in a town like Hidden Creek.

"A place like this?" Epstein repeated.

PJ nodded. "A gay bar. There are some folks who really take offense to that, as I'm sure you're aware. I'm not part of the community myself, but I was proud to run this place for the LGBT folks." He looked back at the building. "Will do again, soon."

"Huh," said Epstein, nodding. Remi was relieved. For a second, he'd worried Epstein might have not taken that news well. Perhaps reacted like Travis with the attitude that it was 'only a gay bar and maybe if they didn't prance about so much, people wouldn't light the place on fire.' But Epstein just scanned the remains of the bar's exterior with a look of concentration. "Threats?" he asked, getting right to the point.

PJ nodded. "Mostly direct messaging on our social media accounts. I can put them all together and email them over, if you like?"

"Please," Epstein said. "Is there anything else you can think of? Any unusual activity or anything you might have seen that was out of the ordinary?"

PJ shifted from foot to foot. He already looked like he wanted to get back to his contractors who had tape measures and calculators out as they slowly paced in front of the bar. It was going to be a pretty substantial restoration, Remi guessed.

"I left the place right after closing," PJ said. "If anyone saw anything, it would be the guy that closed up, Kris Novak." He glanced at Remi. "He's the one that lived above the place, too. You guys pulled him out?"

"I pulled him out myself," Remi said. He wasn't sure why he was feeling so defensive. "He was asleep when the alarm went off. Not sure what he might have seen."

Epstein was writing in a small notebook he had produced from somewhere on his person. "He could have noticed someone suspicious hanging around the bar when he took out the trash," he said. "Something like that. You never know. I'd like to speak to him at some point, if you have his contact details?"

PJ sighed and gestured towards the bar. "Somewhere in there, I guess?"

Remi hesitated. He wasn't sure how this would look, but he wasn't comfortable with obstructing an official investigation. Besides, Kris didn't have anything to hide. Remi didn't need to worry about him talking to Epstein. He seemed on the level.

"He's a friend of the family," Remi said, pulling out his cell phone. "I can give you his number."

Epstein smiled at him and nodded. "That would be great, thanks. Any idea of an address?"

Remi smiled back at him, telling himself this was no big deal. "Actually, he's staying with me. So, yeah, I know my address. Obviously," he added, feeling dumber by the minute. Epstein didn't appear to mind, though. He just copied down the details Remi told him.

What was Remi really worried about here? That these guys might assume something about him?

About him and Kris?

So what? Remi was psyching himself up to come out of the closet. Soon, if he could manage it. They would be correct if they thought Remi might date someone like Kris. He would have to get used to the idea that not everyone would be happy about that.

It was kind of a lot to wrap his head around as he let PJ and Epstein talk. Remi zoned out and looked at the blackened walls of Bottom's Up. This was the kind of hate, prejudice and intolerance he would be facing when...or if...he came out. No, when. He didn't want to hide this part of himself anymore. But it wasn't going to be easy, he had to admit. Looking at the evidence of the lengths people would go made that very clear to him.

Maybe he should wait to come out when he found a great guy? Someone to stand by his side and make it all worthwhile? Otherwise, he'd be opening himself up to this kind of crap unnecessarily.

But then...people like Kris didn't have the luxury of that choice. There was no hiding their sexuality from the world. It didn't seem fair that Remi should get that option and they didn't.

He chewed on his lip and made up his mind. He was going to wait for the right moment, sure. But he promised himself there and then that he would come out as soon as he could when the time felt right. When the person he told felt right.

Remi couldn't help that when he thought of the 'right' person to come out to, his mind still supplied an image of Kris. Maybe it was time to stop fighting it and just go with his gut instinct that Kris might be who he trusted the most with this.

His heart warmed with the thought. Yeah, Kris might just be the one he needed.

15

KRIS

ris couldn't breathe.

There wasn't enough air in the room. It was dark and he was reaching out, but he couldn't move. It was like he was frozen.

He coughed, desperate for oxygen, trying to call for help. There were tears running down his face even though his eyes were closed.

No, no, he didn't want to be here. He couldn't stay. He had to get out. But he was all alone, there was no one around to help. He tried to call out again, to scream, but he couldn't get the air into his lungs.

It wasn't fair. This shouldn't be happening. He had so much he wanted to do, so much he wanted to see and feel. He wasn't ready to leave it all behind. He was crying hard now, sobbing and still trying to scream. But his mouth felt like it was full of cotton.

"Remi," he whimpered.

Remi would save him, wouldn't he? Fuck, there was so much Kris wanted to say to Remi. He knew he couldn't, but it seemed cruel that he should be forced to go before he could even *try*.

"Remi," he cried again, fumbling with his hands, kicking his legs. He was still stuck, going under in the smoke and darkness. He tried one last time to take a breath, to fill his lungs and call out for help.

He wasn't going without a fight.

"Kris!"

Kris screwed up his eyes and tried to find the voice. But he was too far under. He tried to yell, but he was coughing too much.

"Kris? Kris, wake up!"

Firm hands took hold of his shoulders and shook, hard. Kris gasped, finally filling his lungs as his eyes flew open.

He was soaking wet with perspiration. The bed sheets clung to his naked body as he thrashed, blinking against the morning light streaming around the curtains. The hands were still holding him tight.

Remi's hands.

Kris choked back a sob, horrified. He pawed at his face, trying to wipe off some of the sweat and tears and rub the sleep away.

"Remi?" he asked. Reality was coming back to him now. He was in Remi's spare room, on the fold-out couch. Remi had been at work last night. He must have just come back off shift. "Wha-?" Kris stammered, his voice a hoarse croak.

"I think you were having a nightmare," Remi said. He was dressed in his firehouse polo shirt and sweatpants. He smiled, his face warm and full of concern. "You were screaming. Here."

He let go with one hand to reach for a glass of water that hadn't been on the nightstand when Kris had gone to sleep. Remi passed it over. He must have grabbed it before coming in to see why Kris was screaming bloody murder.

Kris accepted it sheepishly. "Um, thanks," he said, taking a few gulps. The cool water felt good on his sore throat. He clutched the glass with one hand and tried to make sure the sheets covered his modesty with the other. *Fuck.* He was really *naked* under here. Remi did not need to know that. "Sorry," he mumbled, feeling horribly exposed. "Yeah, it was a nightmare, I guess. I didn't mean to freak you out."

Remi shook his head before finally, mercifully, letting him go and sitting back a little on the bed. He was still close, but not so much that Kris was worried about accidentally exposing himself anymore.

"You didn't freak me out," Remi assured him. "Are you all right?"

His brown eyes were fixed on Kris in concern. Even though he'd worked a twenty-four-hour shift, he still looked fairly bright and alert. Maybe he'd had the chance to sleep? Kris realized he was staring. He blinked and refocused on Remi's face, trying to remember what he'd said.

"Uh, yeah," he said. He swallowed, his throat still tight. So he took another gulp of water. "I just…the fire…"

He trailed off in embarrassment. He'd been so proud of how well he'd been doing. After all his assurances to the guys at brunch the day before, what had happened at the bar had still managed to creep up on him.

He didn't want to let this thing have a hold on him anymore. Or at all. It was just something that had happened and he'd gotten out fine. Thanks to Remi. He didn't need to be going over and over it again.

But he knew he had been when he'd been falling asleep.

Remi nodded and looked at his hands before glancing back at Kris. "Did, uh, Epstein call you? The guy from arson investigation?"

Kris nodded. "We talked a bit," he said. "He said it was set on purpose. But I didn't see anything strange, so…" He shrugged and looked away.

"Oh, hey, no worries," said Remi. He patted Kris's knee gingerly through the bedsheets. "I think Epstein was just covering all the bases. He didn't expect you to solve the case or anything."

He smiled at Kris, but that just made it worse. Kris could feel the lump swelling in his throat. "It's, uh, not that," he managed to say. He couldn't look at Remi for more than a second, though. He kept darting his gaze back to Tay Tay, swimming around in her tank.

Out of the whole house, this was the room Kris had done the least work on with his makeover. Aside from sorting her aquarium, he'd basically just tidied it. It felt like if he did any more than that, it might seem to Remi like he was getting comfy here. Moving in. Kris would hate for him to think he was imposing any more than he already was.

Remi chewed his lip and rubbed the back of his neck. "I guess talking about the fire probably brought it all back for you, huh?" he said to Kris. "No wonder you had a bad dream."

Kris shrugged. His eyes were filling with tears. If he spoke, he knew they'd spill. Jesus Christ, he just wanted to disappear. But, of course, Remi was looking at him with even more worry and apprehension now.

"Shit, dude. I had no idea you were struggling so much." He flapped his big hands. "We have counseling services. Everyone freaks out after a big blaze like that, it's totally normal. I can get someone for you to talk to, if you want, I-"

"No," Kris managed to utter, shaking his head. The tears spilled down his cheeks and he let them drip from his chin. He held himself tightly, lifting the sheets so they covered his chest somewhat. "It's – it's not the fire, not really. It's…"

God, he didn't want to confess this to Remi. It felt too raw. But something was screaming at Kris that he could *trust* Remi. That it would be okay. And besides, he didn't think he could stop the words from spilling out any more than he had his tears.

"It was on *purpose*," he managed to whisper. "Someone set fire to the bar *intentionally*. Because it's a gay bar. And…and it just…*it feels like Pulse all over again.*"

The sob tore from his chest and he buried his head in his hands.

He didn't know a single queer person who hadn't felt personally attacked when Pulse in Orlando had been the victim of a terrorist attack. Gay bars were supposed to be the one place LGBT people felt truly *safe.* It was where you could hold hands and dress how you wanted and not be stared at like in the outside world. The horror of that sanctuary being violated was too much to bear.

Kris knew he'd been coping because he kept telling himself that the fire had been an accident. Some electrical fault or something. But to discover someone had tried to hurt the town's safe space, to tear it down just like they had with Pulse, it made him feel raw and helpless in the worst possible way. He felt attacked a hundred times over. Knowing this was arson on the gay bar was somehow worse than the fact his own apartment had been above it.

The sobs wracked through his chest and he tried to curl up as small as he could. The weight on the end of the sofa-bed shifted. Thank god. If Remi was awkward enough to leave, Kris could be embarrassed about that later. It was mortifying that Remi had to see him like this. Kris knew it would hurt to hear the door close, to know he'd humiliated himself in front of the man he had been crushing on for years. But what did he expect? He wasn't Remi's problem. It was good if he-

Strong arms suddenly wrapped around him, pulling him against Remi's firm chest and encouraging Kris to bury his face against Remi's neck.

"Hey," he said softly, rubbing Kris's bare back. "Hey, it's okay. It's okay."

Kris found his fingers making fists with Remi's polo as he clung onto him tightly. He cried out all his fears and horror, all while Remi rubbed his back and rested his cheek on top of Kris's hair. He kept making soothing noises until Kris was able to catch his breath. Even then, it was a few more minutes before Kris felt able to look up at him.

"T-tissue?" he asked. He wanted to mop up before Remi saw him. He knew he looked a mess with no makeup and red, blotchy eyes. But honestly, he felt so much better for a good cry.

"Oh, uh, sure," Remi said. He let Kris go and, from the sound of it, ran into the bathroom. Kris let out a little laugh and covered his face with both hands. God damn, the man was so sweet and dorky. It just wasn't fair.

He hadn't abandoned him. He'd hugged Kris, even though it must have been really uncomfortable for him to do so. Despite how wobbly Kris was still feeling, knowing that brought warmth to his heart.

Remi returned with a wad of toilet paper which Kris took gratefully. He wiped his eyes and blew his nose, then took a deep breath and looked back up at Remi. "Thank you," he said.

Remi shook his head. "No problem," he said. "Man, I knew it had to be tough that you lost the only gay bar in town. But I feel bad. I didn't really think about it like that." He bit his lip and ran his hand through his dark hair, mussing it up. "It must feel like whoever that asshole was, he was attacking your way of life. Not just a building."

Kris blinked, his eyes feeling sore. But his chest inflated a little with pride. He was impressed. "Yeah, yeah," he said, nodding. "That's exactly what it feels like."

Remi tutted. "Fucking piece of piss jerkwad," he grumbled with a scowl. He grabbed Kris's knee again and squeezed. There was a light in his dark eyes. "Well, fuck him, right? You're still here and the bar will open up again, better than ever. No one can take that away from you."

Kris was dumbstruck for a moment. But Remi's words lit a different kind of fire in his chest. A flicker of defiance sprung to life. "Yeah," he rasped. He cleared his throat and nodded. "Fuck whoever set that fire. We're here and we're queer and we're not going anywhere."

"Exactly," Remi enthused. He grinned at Kris. For a crazy second, it was like he included himself in Kris's 'we.' But he was just being supportive, right?

Before Kris could dwell on that too much, their conversation was interrupted by a flash of movement by the door. Kris couldn't help but jump at the unexpected intrusion and he wasn't the only one. It would have been amusing to see big, tough Remi startle at the sight of a small furry animal. But Kris wasn't laughing as that same damn skinny cat leaped up onto the table where Kris had perched Tay Tay's tank.

"Shit!" he hissed and almost lunged to shoo her away. But then he remembered he had no clothes on and didn't want to show his ass to Remi. So he held his breath as the cat twitched her head, looking at Tay Tay.

"Hey, no!" Remi called. He leaned forward and waved at the black kitty. "Away from there!"

The cat completely ignored him, dancing around the outside of the tank. Kris was pretty confident she couldn't get to Tay Tay unless she climbed up the glass and dropped into the water. But still, he watched on anxiously as she pawed at the aquarium.

Tay Tay couldn't seem to care less. In fact, she swam provocatively past the cat, swishing her elegant fins as if to say 'come and get me, you dumb kitty.'

Remi stood and scooped the gangly kitten up in his arms. She allowed him to hold her as he sat back down, but she twisted so she could still watch Tay Tay taunting her, flicking her golden tail as she nibbled on the stones at the bottom of the tank.

"Can you pick locks or something?" Remi asked the cat incredulously. He shook his head, then looked sheepishly up at Kris. "I'm so sorry," he said.

Kris was quick to shake his head back. "No, it's fine," he said as his heart rate slowed down once more. "I know it's not your fault. I might see if I can put a lid on that tank, though."

"I can do that," Remi said brightly. "How would a sheet of plastic with some holes drilled into it be? Something you could remove easy enough to feed her and stuff?"

Kris blinked, warmth blossoming in his chest. To be fair, after all he'd done for Remi's house, a favor like that wasn't much to expect in return. But Kris hadn't wanted anything. For Remi to offer to do something so thoughtful was priceless.

"Thank you. That sounds great," he said with a smile. "Not just for the tank, but…well, for getting how I feel about the arson attack and reassuring me about Epstein." Obviously, the reality that the bar had been targeted for arson still hurt. But right then, with Remi beside him, Kris didn't feel so persecuted.

"Hey, no problem, man," Remi said, scratching the black cat behind her ears. "Don't worry. Epstein is a great guy. He'll work out what happened. And we saw your boss, PJ, on site yesterday. He seemed eager to reopen real soon. I bet you the bar will be back on its feet in no time."

Kris managed a proper smile at that. He blew his nose again and ruffled his hair where it had gotten stuck to his head. "Phew! I bet I look like a horror movie," he said, trying to muster up some of his usual sass.

Remi snorted. "Don't worry," he said, rolling his eyes and patting Kris's leg. "You're still pretty."

Pretty?

"Weren't they building an LGBT center this summer?" Remi said with a frown, moving the conversation on before Kris could dwell on the compliment too much.

"Oh, uh, yeah," Kris said. "I think they're still working on it."

"Will that have a bar?" Remi asked. "If that gets finished first, maybe y'all could hang there?"

Kris sighed. "Maybe," he said. "Not that a lack of bar would bother me. I think it'll have a café and rooms for meetings and stuff." He chewed his lip. "People do like to party, though. They come to drink and forget their troubles or celebrate or dance. But…"

Remi raised his eyebrows. "What?"

Kris shrugged. "Well, I've thought for a while now that the bar could be a bit *more* than just a drinking hole."

What the fuck? He hadn't mentioned this to Chase or Hale or any of his other friends. Why was he telling Remi? But yet again, he couldn't seem to stop himself.

"In what way?" Remi asked.

Kris shifted in the bed. He'd kind of forgotten he was naked under the covers, but it didn't bother him so much now. "Well, I don't know if you know, but outside of Houston, Hidden Creek is the biggest gay scene for the surrounding towns by quite a long shot. People would come from all over to go out at Bottom's Up. I can't help but feel we could offer more than just a night out. Or we could offer different kinds of nights out, as well as daytime stuff."

Remi shifted his weight and raised his eyebrows. "You mean, like social activities?"

Kris nodded eagerly. "Between us and the LGBT center, I bet we'll have a lot of room for all kinds of activities. Obviously, Bottom's Up is a bar first and foremost. But during the day, you could have craft classes. We could have drag acts come and perform – not just at night. I've seen queens who do story time readings for kids."

He thought about the kid Harrison he'd met a couple of times now and smiled.

"We could offer make up classes, too. Not, like, just drag makeup, but regular makeup tips for guys who are interested." He giggled and swirled a hand around his face, unable to stop himself winking at Remi. "What, you think all this gorgeousness happens by magic?" he asked.

"Naturally," Remi replied with a laugh. Kris found he didn't care so much about his naked, tear-stained face when Remi was smiling and joking around with him like that.

He bit his lip. "And there's makeup you can do for trans men to look more masculine," he said, only slightly nervous. Remi was cool with him being gay and fem, but 'trans' was such a hot-button word these days. Kris would be heartbroken if Remi had an issue with someone like Harrison.

But Remi just raised his eyebrows. "Really?" he asked, seemingly genuinely interested. "You can do that?"

Kris nodded, relief making his chest feel like it expanded. "Obviously, it's not easy for trans people, men or women, to go into any old store and ask for help, though," he explained. "Even if it was just one or two people interested in that, it would be worth it. And, well, safety *is* an issue for us queers," he continued. "So we could run a self-defense class once a month or every quarter. Bingo nights, alcohol-free evenings for over-eighteens. In bigger cities there are LGBT sports clubs. We could do fundraiser nights for soccer teams and maybe even sponsor the uniforms. There's so much we could be doing for our community."

He took a breath and realized he had gone on a complete rant.

But Remi was nodding. Kitty had rolled around in his arms and now he was absently stroking her belly. "You know," he said. "I was wondering how the hell y'all meet without a bar." He was? Why would he be thinking about that? Kris didn't interrupt, though. "It's kind of simple, when you think about it," Remi said. "Just pick something you like doing, then make it LGBT. Then you can find other people with similar interests."

Kris grinned. "There's a rock climbing club over in Houston. And a lesbian knitting circle that just starting accepting all queer people. I just...I think that's awesome. We're kind of spread out, but groups like that make it so much easier for us to come together and find one another."

Remi clapped Kris's shoulder. "Dude, you're on to a winner. Have you talked to your boss about it?"

And just like that, Kris's bubble burst.

"Nah," he said, pulling at the edge of the duvet. "PJ would never go for all that. He's straight and he just sees the bar as this one thing. He wouldn't get the community side to it."

Remi frowned. "Have you asked him?" Kris shook his head. He was still so new at the bar, he hadn't dared. "Well, okay." Remi bounced on the sofa-bed, making the springs squeak. "When Alondra wanted to redo the shower facilities at the station – after years of just guys, you can imagine how gross it had gotten – she put a proposal together before going to the captain. That way, she had answers to a lot of his questions already. It helped him see her point and I'm sure that's why he signed off on it."

Something fluttered in Kris's chest. He tried not to get too excited, but it was difficult. What Remi was saying actually kind of made sense. "So…you're saying I should do some research and put a plan together to take to PJ?"

Remi nodded. "Now's the perfect time, while you're rebuilding. You can rebrand for the grand reopening! It's worth a shot, right?"

Kris bit his lip and scrunched his nose up, but he couldn't stop himself from grinning at Remi. "What's the worst that could happen?"

Remi whooped and punched the air, startling Kitty somewhat. "That's the spirit. All right, do you mind if I grab a couple of hours' sleep? Then we can do some work on it later. I'm not bad with a budget."

It felt like Kris's body rinsed hot and cold all at the same time. "You – you'd want to help me?"

"If you like?" Remi asked.

Remi lost a bit of his sparkle, so Kris quickly waved his hands at him.

"I'd love that!" Kris cried a bit too loudly. Fucking hell, could he make this crush any more obvious? He was lucky he wasn't sporting a boner under the sheets. "Thank you."

Remi stood and squeezed Kris's shoulder, the bounce back in his step. "Don't even mention it, man. This sounds awesome." He moved to the doorway. Kitty noticed Tay Tay again and tried to wriggle free from Remi's grasp, but Remi held on tight. "Hey, I'd understand if you want some more sleep after a shitty dream like that. But if you're hungry, I swung by JJ's on the way home. Help yourself to groceries if you want breakfast. I got that yogurt you like."

For a moment, Kris just stared at him. There it was again, that warm crackle between them, charged like a wildfire about to spark. "Uh, thank you," he managed to stutter before it became too weird. "That's so nice of you. Thanks."

Remi nodded. "No problem, man. My pleasure."

Kris watched as he left, pulling the door to behind him.

"The pleasure's all mine," Kris murmured to himself.

16

REMI

Remi had always loved his job. Yeah, there were days it tore his heart out and shifts that dragged for hours. This also wasn't the first time things had been a bit tense with Travis. But on the whole, Remi counted himself fortunate that he was lucky enough to look forward to heading into work.

For the first time in a long time, however, he'd been a bit reluctant this morning. And the reason why scared him a little.

He and Kris had spent the last couple of days going through all the possibilities for expanding the bar's mission statement in preparation for his meeting with PJ tomorrow. The guy was kind of an ass and had been wary to schedule anything. But Kris had firmly insisted it was in the bar's best interests and eventually gotten a time locked down.

Remi was proud of him. But it had come as a bit of a shock when he'd felt a slight pang leaving him on Wednesday morning. They pretty much hung out all the time now when Remi wasn't at the firehouse.

And yet Remi still hadn't come out to him.

Which was crazy. Because now when they talked about ideas for all these LGBT groups and clubs and activities, they just said 'we' all the time. Like it was both their community. Because it was. Kris just didn't know that yet.

What was Remi so afraid of? Was it rejection still? That didn't really fly. Kris talked about all kinds of queer people with the same amount of respect. Perhaps it was because he was kind of a girly guy himself. Fem, Remi thought he'd called it. Gender obviously wasn't a clear-cut thing to him, not like it was to people like Remi's dad.

Yesterday he'd said neither gender nor sexuality were as binary as people liked to make out. Remi had asked him to explain a bit more, and what it came down to was gray areas. Which was funny, for such a colorful guy. But the way Kris told it, things like gender and sexual preferences weren't just black and white. They could be in a messy gray area in the middle. His eyes got kind of misty when he talked about it. He obviously liked the gray area and wasn't afraid to get things messy and complicated.

So why was Remi being such a coward over this? Surely being bi fell quite nicely into that gray area. Was he really so scared Kris would treat him differently?

"Oh my god," Holby said. He'd just walked in the common area with Alondra and they both immediately changed course to veer toward the kitchen area. "What the hell smells so good, Washington?"

Remi grinned. He wasn't sure why, but the cure for feeling blue about leaving Kris at home was apparently cooking. On a crazy whim, he'd woken up early so he could swing by JJ's before his shift and pick up everything he needed to make a vat of macaroni and cheese for everyone for dinner.

"It's my mom's recipe," he said proudly. He'd forgotten just how much he loved making this. Actually, he'd forgotten how much fun cooking was in general. What better way to show people you cared about them than a delicious, hot meal made from scratch?

He had spread himself across the whole counter. The macaroni was bubbling away in a pot, and then he had bacon, chives, nutmeg and shredded onions all sizzling in a pan on the stove while he grated several types of cheese. He also had a bowl of beaten eggs ready for the sauce and a buttered casserole dish for when he put it all together in layers, kind of like a lasagna.

"This doesn't look like my mom's mac'n'cheese," Holby said in awe.

Remi chuckled. "Nothing against your mom," he said. "But ain't nothing that beats Mama Washington's recipe." He took the pan that had been cooking the bacon and slid the meat onto a plate to let it rest a minute. Then he dropped more butter in, watching it melt quickly so he could sprinkle flour into it to thicken it up for the base of the sauce.

By this point, Greg had wandered over from the TV. When there wasn't baseball to watch, they had moved on from shark documentaries to a nonstop Sharknado marathon. Remi wasn't sure how people could watch such ridiculous movies, but Greg seemed pretty into it. It was impressive that he'd pulled himself away.

As if hearing Remi's thoughts, he wagged his finger at them. "I ain't missing the good stuff today. You making enough for everyone, Washington?"

Channing scoffed as he skipped into the kitchen. "And the third watch, too, by the looks of it," he said with a chuckle. He reached over to snag some cheese from the pile Remi had made. Remi smacked the back of his hand with a spoon.

"Uh uh," he said with a grin at Channing's indignant look. "You sit your ass down and wait."

"Fine," Channing said with a roll of his eyes. He stalked off toward the TV and dropped down beside Travis, who had not moved from his dent or shown any interest in the commotion in the kitchen.

Remi didn't care. If the old grump was keeping to himself, that was better for them both at present.

Once the flour was mixed into the bacon-flavored butter to a smooth consistency, Remi began stirring in whole milk while he prodded the other simmering pans as well.

"So, it all goes in the same dish?" Holby asked dubiously.

Remi nodded. God, he couldn't remember a time when his mom hadn't made this for them. She always made a vat for church events, family birthdays, barbecues. It made a mean side dish for when Dad cooked steaks on the grill or even as a cold salad for later in the week with meatloaf.

"This here's for the cheese sauce," he explained as he poured the beaten eggs in after the whole milk. Then he added some chili sauce for kick before sprinkling in all his different cheeses. "I'll just stir the pasta into this, then take the bacon and onions I sautéed, then sort of layer it all up. Oh shit," he said happily, looking around his workspace. "I need to season. Where did the herbs and spices box go?"

A loud tut from near the TV made him and the others turn their heads. Alondra folded her arms. "Something to say, Travis?" she asked.

Travis didn't bother to look around but waved his hand by his head. "Nah," he said.

Remi shrugged. He couldn't summon the energy to care anymore what some old fart thought of him.

"So now the roux is done, I just dump it on the pasta and start layering it all up," he said as he sprinkled the crispy onions and bacon in his buttered pan to begin.

Another scoff came from the other side of the room. "Okay," Travis snapped. He dropped the remote on the coffee table with a clatter and deigned to turn around to face them. It was like he was glued to that damn sofa. "This is what I'm talking about!" he cried, gesticulating toward Remi.

Alondra dropped her head back and let out an exasperated sigh. Holby shook his head. "What, exactly, are you talking about?" he asked.

Remi could feel his anger threaten to start boiling. But he wouldn't let it. He wasn't going to allow Travis to spoil something he'd not been brave enough to do in all the years working at the station. This was his mom's special recipe and he wanted to share it with his other family.

Travis rolled his eyes. *"Sautéed* and *roux,"* he said with air quotations, like they were dirty words. He stood in indignation and came around the sofa. Wow. Remi was honored. "Not even two weeks with a gay in your house and you're talking all poofy like."

"I think that's just French," said Greg with a frown, crossing his arms.

Remi shrugged, spooning out creamy, squelchy macaroni and cheese over the onions and bacon. Fuck, it smelled good, even if he did say so himself.

"You know what, Travis," he said calmly. "If a man cooking makes you that uncomfortable, I pity you. If it makes you feel any better, you don't have to have any of this. You can make yourself a sandwich with that dry, tasteless beef you like so much. But I don't give a fuck if you think this is girly or if using the proper words to describe something is gay." He sprinkled the last of the chewy bacon on top of the last layer of pasta, then coated the whole thing with parmesan cheese. "Because, the thing is, there isn't one *fucking* thing wrong with being gay. Or effeminate. Or different. I'm done trying to convince you otherwise."

He yanked open the oven door, slotted the baking dish inside, closed it and set his timer for twenty minutes. Then he grinned at Travis, who was frowning at him.

"And as for 'the gay' living in my house, his name is Kris. He's got more heart, more color and more courage in his heart than you'll ever have. More to the point, he's now my friend. Not just my best buddy's little brother. My actual good friend. So by disrespecting him, you're disrespecting me. So knock it off."

Travis blinked and crossed his arms. Then he dropped them to place on his hips. Then he folded them again. "Why the hell do you care so much about the gays all of a sudden?" he said sullenly.

"Because I'm a human being," Remi said. He was calmly tidying up the mess he'd made while cooking. His mom had taught him to take pride in his workspace. It felt like he'd forgotten that over the past few years. But thanks to Kris, Remi was starting to remember that was the kind of guy he really was again.

Travis scoffed and shook his head. The rest of the team were looking between them like they were watching a tennis match.

"Maybe *you're* one of the queers, too," Travis said, a challenging tone to his words.

Remi knew he was clearly meant to take it as bait. His heart rate sped up. But not because he was goaded. But because he felt brave.

"So what if I was?" he said, amazed by the steadiness in his words.

He turned away with all his dirty dishes and utensils piled up to drop them in the sink. He heard Travis splutter before he turned the water on.

Fuck. His heart was like a goddamned jackhammer in his chest.

But the world didn't end.

"Yeah," Alondra said in a slightly scathing tone. "My friend from college is gay and married to another woman, so what?"

"So's that tennis guy," said Holby, clicking his fingers. "Here in town. Tyler Florman. He came out a while back, right?"

"And that chick, Peggy, at the auto shop," added Channing with a snicker. "She's a total-" He cut himself off so abruptly Remi glanced over. Channing cleared his throat and nodded. "Lesbian lady person," he said.

Remi suspected he had been about to use a less than appropriate term. But the fact he had stopped himself was kind of a victory in its own right. Let alone that he was defending Remi's side of the argument.

Good god. Had he just come out? Sort of. He felt light-headed.

He shifted his gaze from Channing to Travis. "I get this is hard for you," Remi said as sympathetically as possible. "Back in your day, men were men and women were women. But the truth is, queer people have always existed. This isn't a craze or a trend. We've lived in a society for the past several decades that likes to make everything out to be black and white." Remi smiled at him. "Welcome to the gray area."

Travis didn't seem to have anything to say to that.

Whatever Sharknado movie was playing came back from a commercial break, drawing Greg back in. Alondra and Holby started talking about whose turn it was to restock the paper towel dispenser. Channing popped some gum and flicked through a magazine before remembering he had his tablet right in front of him and started playing a noisy game.

Eventually, Travis turned and slunk back to his spot on the couch, leaving Remi to do the dishes in peace.

He was dizzy with happiness. This was it. This was what he needed to kick his ass into gear. He had *almost* come out to his coworkers. So now he wanted to come out for real.

To Kris.

Man, he was lucky to have such a great friend in his life. It wasn't like Remi was replacing Leon for his younger brother. But Kris was something else to him already, even after only a short amount of time. He hoped he would be proud of how Remi handled himself just now. It was funny how Kris was the first person Remi wanted to tell his news to these days.

He grinned the whole way through doing the dishes, thinking about how his victory with Travis would make Kris smile.

He loved it when Kris smiled.

17

KRIS

On Thursday afternoon, Kris stared up at the husk that used to be both his place of work and his home. It looked even more awful in the daylight when the sunshine highlighted every charred brick and broken pane of glass. He sighed and chewed his lip. There was a lot of work to be done.

Which was probably why PJ had insisted on meeting here, rather than at Grind for a cup of coffee like Kris had suggested. Kris had wanted to make this a proper meeting with trivial things like a table and some chairs. But if this was the best he could manage, then it would have to do.

Kris looked up to the third floor where his apartment still stood, in theory. He wondered how much of his stuff was still salvageable. It was pointless, because the stairs weren't going to be safe to get up anytime soon. There was no way to tell how long it would be before he could even think about getting inside there again. Still, Kris squinted through the sunglasses Remi had given him and allowed himself a moment of sadness. It may not have been much of a place, but it had been all his. His own tiny slice of peace and quiet.

He could lick his wounds over that and whatever fucker had taken it upon themselves to scorch his home later. Right now, he had a job to do.

Butterflies danced around his stomach as he walked up to the front doors. He had done this a thousand times. Except, when he had walked inside Bottom's Up in the past, there hadn't been the taste of ashes floating through the air.

Inside, where the main bar area used to be there were several floodlights set up as there weren't any windows to the outside world. A number of guys in hardhats were walking around with purpose, measuring things and clearing debris away. Kris was glad he had worn boots and one of the nicer button-down shirts Chase had given him. But he still felt small and fragile as he looked around at the carnage left behind by the blaze.

Without asking, one of the contractors placed a hardhat on his head, then winked when Kris looked at him in surprise. "Got to keep that face pretty," said the guy in a friendly, flirtatious manner.

He was gone before Kris could get a good look, but he wondered if he might have been a regular at the bar. Kris had served a couple of thousand customers each week. He knew people were more likely to recognize him than he was them, so he tried not to feel bad. In any case, the anonymous guy's compliment and care gave him the little boost of confidence he needed as he looked through the room for PJ.

Kris really didn't need to be nervous. When it really came down to it, he was *excited*. There were so many avenues that he and Remi had looked into for genuine expansion for the bar. This way they could reach so many more LGBT people than just the young, gay crowd.

While Remi had been at work yesterday, Kris had taken himself into town to meet with Chip Carter, the guy in charge of the LGBT community center project. He had been delighted at the prospect of teaming up with the bar to maximize the impact they could have on the queer community in the area and had offered several ideas of his own.

Kris had stayed up almost all night typing up his plans on Remi's computer, printing everything out in triplicate to present to PJ today. It had been a while since Kris felt so energized about anything. But this meant a lot to him. It meant he had slept late that morning and missed Remi before he went to bed. But hopefully they could celebrate when Kris got home.

It was crazy how quickly Kris had slipped into a domestic routine with Remi. It was dangerous, really, how easily it could feel like this was normal.

Like they were a couple.

Kris needed to be grateful for the friendship they had. Remi had been by his side throughout this whole process when Kris's family hadn't been able to. They did what they could, but between hectic jobs and the pregnancy, they only got so many minutes to call and check in.

Kris's own friends had busy lives too. But with Remi's shifts, Kris had found himself someone to hang with almost every other day.

Someone he cared very deeply for.

He shook the thought away. It was just a crush, nothing more. And seeing as there was no chance Remi would feel the same, Kris would take their new friendship with grace and sincere appreciation.

"Hey, PJ," he called out as he picked his way over the blackened remains of the dance floor. There were a few areas that had been marked off as structurally unsound and already there were several steel support beams in place. But this area looked to be okay, for now. Kris still felt nervous. "How's it going?"

PJ sighed and pushed his glasses up his sweaty nose. "I'm roasting inside the disaster area that used to be my business," he said waspishly. "How do you think I'm doing?" He pointed at one of the guys as he walked past. "Hey? What happened to getting some fans in here? It's summer, for Christ's sake."

The guy's eyes went wide. He nodded, mumbling something about getting it sorted and ran away.

Still a ball of fucking sunshine, Kris thought to himself. On the outside, he smiled. "Oh, honey," he said, batting PJ's arm lightly with the folder he had slipped his proposals into. "This is fine. The insurance will cover it. We'll bounce back bigger and better than ever."

PJ scoffed and shook his head. When he didn't say anything, Kris popped his hip and batted his eyelashes. Knowing PJ was more than a little straight-laced, Kris had kept his makeup to a minimum. Just enough so he felt confident without being too showy.

"About that. I've been having some thoughts about when we reopen-"

"If," muttered PJ, looking up at the balcony where a couple of guys were laughing as they used laser pens to measure something or work out the level. Kris wasn't sure. He was stuck on what PJ had said.

"If?" he squeaked.

PJ shook his head. "Look, kid. I don't know what to tell you. I won't know if it's commercially viable until the insurance money comes in. There's only so far a niche market can go." He shrugged and pulled out his phone to fiddle with.

Kris was flummoxed. "B-but," he stammered, "the town needs an LGBT center."

PJ frowned but didn't look up from his emails. "Aren't they building one?"

Kris shook his head. "A bar. We need a gay bar. It's important to the community."

"And it's my money," PJ snapped. He sighed and did Kris the courtesy of looking up at least. "I'm sorry. This is a fucked-up situation. I'll do what I can. But if it's not worth it, I'm packing up and heading back to Houston. Someone else can open a gay bar."

Kris tried not to take it personally. But it felt like PJ couldn't care less about a place that was so important to so many. Kris thought about young Harrison, coming along and being brave as his true self for the first time. He thought about Chase and Hunter, how their love had blossomed during their date nights here. He thought of the gaggle of bi girls from the local community college who played air hockey tournaments on the tables that were now crumbled away. Not to mention the guys who wanted to make a connection with someone, even if it was just for a one-night stand. Yeah, there was Grindr. But nothing could beat the thrill of *actually* grinding with someone, feeling that spark on the dance floor as hands wandered and lips met.

This bar was vital. Kris had to make PJ see that.

"If it's money you're worried about," he began, "that's actually why I came to see you." He pulled out one of the copies of the proposal he and Remi had worked on and presented it to PJ with a flourish. "I've been thinking about ways the bar can expand."

PJ was reading his emails again. "What?" he said irritably, not looking up.

Kris gave a tiny huff and waved the several stapled-together sheets of paper in front of his nose. "Ideas. For stuff we can do. Not just serve drinks."

That did make PJ look up. Unfortunately, it was with a borderline sneer. "What the fuck else would a bar do?" he asked.

Kris did his best not to flinch. *Just keep smiling,* he told himself. "Well, you already have the games tables. Or had, at least. But those will be easy enough to replace. I was crunching some numbers. If, when you do the remodel, you put an actual stage by the dance floor area where the curtains used to be," he pointed at the end of the room on the right, "people can dance on it on regular nights. But that gives us opportunities for talent shows and drag shows and so on."

PJ didn't react, so Kris just kept going.

"And, you know, this place isn't just a bar. It's a safe space."

"Safe space," PJ muttered with a roll of his eyes. "First my gym, now you. What's everyone's obsession with this idea right now?"

Damn. Kris knew what PJ was talking about because Remi had picked up a leaflet from Lift, the gym, to show Kris. He was excited they were introducing classes for people to feel at ease in, and that included queer people. He thought they could tie that into Kris's proposal, a suggestion that made Kris weak at the knees for its thoughtfulness. It was so damned typical that PJ didn't understand. Or worse, greeted the idea with disdain.

"When people, like the LGBT community, feel vulnerable, it's good to know there's somewhere you can go with other people who are like you," Kris explained cheerfully. "And that doesn't always necessarily involve clubbing." He cleared his throat and PJ grunted. Kris took that to mean he was listening and carried on. "Karaoke nights, bingo afternoons – in fact, I have a whole page here on senior citizen activities. There is a real lack of community services for the older LGBT generation."

That had been Chip's suggestion. Apparently, his aunt was very interested in something like that. But PJ still didn't take the proposal from his hand. Kris took a slow breath and tried to remember what else he had wanted to say.

"We could run makeup tutorials," he said, getting his flow going again. "Dance classes, maybe even theater productions. This could be a space for actual queer plays to be put on, even if they're small and run by amateur drama companies."

PJ was shaking his head again. "I'm sorry. I thought these were all things the new center was going to be providing. I went to that meeting. They were saying all these ideas as well."

"Yes," said Kris, doing his best not to get thrown. "Well, no. We've come up with a ton more exciting ideas as well. I spoke to Chip-"

"You did what?" PJ asked. He raised an eyebrow.

Again, Kris refused to be intimidated. He and Remi had gone over and over this proposal and he *knew* there were so many good ideas inside.

"Chip. He's in charge of the LGBT center development. We're proposing to run schedules in tandem. Obviously, Alcoholics Anonymous couldn't run here. That's ideal for the center. But we could run a Queers Without Beers night, for over-eighteens who want to socialize but can't drink yet."

PJ pinched the bridge of his nose. That wasn't a good sign. "And how much money would I lose on a fucking nonalcoholic night, exactly?"

Kris felt strongly about this, though. "The gay community has, en masse, a drinking problem," he said as confidently as he could. "By offering a night where people could enjoy themselves without booze, we would not only be giving a chance for younger queer people to enter the community in a safer environment, but it would also show our regular patrons they don't have to get shit-faced to have a good time."

PJ jabbed his phone so it locked and shoved it into his pocket. "I'll skip the part where, yet again, you seem to have missed the point that this will lose me a whole night's revenue because, guess what? Fucking cola doesn't cost a fraction of the whiskey you add to it." Kris went to open his mouth, but PJ shoved a finger into his face. "Let's get to the part where I have a bunch of baby gays running around my bar. Who's going to protect them?"

Kris scowled. "From what?" he asked. "They're old enough to be in relationships."

"Have sex, you mean," PJ sneered. "Yeah, I'm sure all the thirty-something leather daddies would fucking love that."

Kris felt like he'd been slapped in the face. "It's not just about sex," he said.

"Says you," PJ shot back scornfully. An icy sensation slid down Kris's guts.

"This isn't about me," he said. He heard his voice waver and cursed it.

"No, it's not," PJ agreed. "I'm here trying to save an actual fucking business. You come skipping in here trying to convince me to encourage minors into an adult environment and waffle on about a bar not serving *alcohol*. Has all that bleach in your hair seeped into your brain? Look," he said, holding up his hand, "I'm sure you mean well, twinkle toes. But you don't even fucking drink. You have no idea what you're talking about. So – consider yourself free of the obligation. Go get another job, and *if* I manage to salvage this tinderbox, I'll call you about coming back. All right?"

Kris willed himself not to cry. How had this become about his sex life and sobriety?

"You're firing me?" he asked in a small voice.

PJ already had his phone out again, typing furiously on it with one thumb. "There's nothing to fire you *from*," he said, barely pausing tapping as he spoke. "You don't have a job here anymore anyway. Look, we can't even think about reopening until the insurance gets sorted out, and that could take months. Trust me, I'm doing you a favor."

His phone rang, jumping to life in his hand as it lit up in the gloomy room. PJ didn't even give Kris another glance. He just answered the call with a loud "Talk to me, Bob!" He turned and walked away from Kris, his hand on his lower back as he yelled at whoever Bob was and looked up at the wrecked ceiling of the bar.

Kris couldn't believe this was happening. He'd come in with a cheery 'what was the worst that could happen?' attitude.

It turned out, this was it.

18

REMI

Kris was asleep when Remi got back to the house after his shift and gone when Remi woke up. He wasn't too surprised, but he had hoped to see Kris before his big meeting with PJ. He'd just wanted to wish him good luck.

At least, that's what Remi kept telling himself.

He was full of restless energy. He scrubbed the bathroom and put in a load of both his and Kris's laundry. Then he made a meal plan for the next several days and decided to take himself off to JJ's to stock up on groceries. After the success of his mom's macaroni and cheese at work, he figured he could maybe cook a few more things. Besides, wouldn't it be nice to have something good for Kris when he came home?

There was only so long Remi could distract himself watching recipe videos online. Eventually, he got in the car to head to JJ's, alone with his thoughts for the drive. Even the radio turned up loud couldn't drown them out.

Everything kept coming back to Kris. Remi had known it yesterday evening at the firehouse and he knew it now.

There was a *painfully* obvious reason why Remi wanted to come out to Kris. Why he wanted to tell Kris all his news first and was planning special meals for him and staying up late working on his proposal with him and worrying about his meeting today.

Remi *liked* Kris. Leon's little brother, Kris. His baby bro. The kid he'd known since he was pretty much a baby. Where Leon had been, Kris had been in the background, singing Disney songs wrapped in a feather boa or crying with a skinned knee or cramming for a trig test.

Remi remembered Kris coming out of the closet after his and Leon's asshole dad left. Remi had always wanted to ask him why he'd waited until then to burst like a butterfly from its cocoon. But now he understood. Kris and Leon's dad would never have accepted someone as fabulous as Kris under his roof. He had been ten times the jerk that Travis was.

The idea that anyone would hate Kris for being so fearless and fabulous made Remi's heart ache. How could they? Kris was dazzling and inspiring and made Remi's heart sing just by being close to him.

Remi sighed and finally picked up one of the lettuces he'd been staring at for several minutes. An older lady tutted as she leaned over and plucked one from the display herself, muttering about young people with nothing to do all day. Remi ignored her and tried to concentrate on what was next on his list. But it was as if his mind wouldn't rest until he'd tackled the subject of Kris.

Remi had a crush on Kris. He wasn't in the background anymore. As far as Remi was concerned, Kris was now the star of the show. This wasn't the excitement of making a new buddy. This was that dizzy stage of realizing you really liked someone. That you wanted to kiss them.

Maybe find out if they'd like to get naked with you.

The mere thought brought heat to Remi's cheeks. Jesus. His bisexuality had always been theoretical until this point. An acknowledgment that his heart fluttered around certain guys or his tongue got tied. But damn. The more he thought about Kris sashaying around in his little booty shorts his friends had given him, or those cute crop tops he'd made himself, the more Remi's cock woke up. He wanted to run his hands over that smooth creamy skin.

He wanted to taste it.

He cleared his throat and stomped off to the freezer section. A few minutes looking at ice cream with the door open calmed down the excitement in his pants and he was able to think straight again. Or, not, ironically.

The problem was, now he'd worked out why he'd been going so crazy over Kris, what the hell was he supposed to do? Flirt? That didn't seem right. Kris was a guest in his home. He didn't have anywhere else to go. Well, he probably did. He had a lot of friends. But for some reason, he had chosen to take up Remi's offer for a place to stay and Remi wasn't about to make him regret that decision. If he told Kris he liked him, it could backfire if Kris didn't feel the same, and then it would be awkward and uncomfortable.

What if he does feel the same? a seductive voice whispered at the back of his head. How would Remi know unless he asked?

"I always dreamed you'd be my hero."

That was what Kris had said to Remi when he'd pulled him from the fire. Remi was quite convinced Kris had no idea he had said that. But...did he mean it?

Kris flirted with everyone, though. It was just his language. He hugged people and kissed their cheeks and told them they looked gorgeous. Since they'd gotten closer over the past week or so, Kris would drape himself over Remi when he was tired or smack his ass when he was being playful. How could Remi tell if that was just Kris being Kris or if it was an invitation for more?

Still, those seven words played in Remi's mind. What if Kris was interested in Remi from before the fire?

He looked down at his basket and realized he'd finished his shopping. He sighed. He would have to concentrate on the drive home. Otherwise he was going to have an accident.

He made himself read the trashy magazine headlines while he waited in line to pay for his goods. By filling his head with nonsense gossip about who was pregnant and who had gotten fat, he left little room to worry over Kris. That was, until he reached the checkout.

"Oh, hey," the guy said as he started scanning Remi's things. He was kind of small with dark hair and green eyes that had gotten wide at the sight of him. Remi had seen him around the store a lot over the past couple of years, but he didn't think they'd even spoken. "You're Remi, right? Kris's friend?"

Remi blinked and looked around the store. But no one else was paying attention to them. Why would they? Still, having been so preoccupied with thoughts of Kris, it was a little eerie to hear his name spoken aloud by someone else.

"Uh, yeah," Remi said, nodding.

The clerk smiled, bagging up Remi's veggies. "I'm Chase," he said. "Kris's friend from the bar."

"Oh," said Remi in realization. "You guys had brunch the other day, right?"

Chase nodded. "Does he like his new clothes? He's still living with you, isn't he?"

"Yep," said Remi. He wondered if he was blushing. The simple question had made him feel fluttery. But the idea that Kris could be living with him like they were a *couple* popped into his head, and he almost knocked over the magazine stand with his elbow. "Uh, yeah, yeah, he loves the clothes, thank you. There weren't exactly many things me or his brother could offer him."

Chase chuckled. "Yeah, you're Leon's BFF, aren't you? Nice of you to help him out so much, dude. Me and Kris's other friends really appreciate it. He's lucky to have you."

Chase's gaze lingered a little too long on Remi as he packed some more boxes. He had this small smile playing on his lips. "Uh, yeah," Remi said awkwardly. "Well, Kris is a great guy. I'm happy to help."

"He is one in a million," Chase said knowingly.

Remi frowned and did his best to smile back. Was there something he wasn't getting here?

"You probably already know," said Chase casually as he bagged the ice cream and other final items, "but Kris is definitely single. Just FYI."

"Huh?" Remi spluttered.

Chase grinned and called up the total with a *ding* on the cash register. "That'll be twenty-three seventy-five."

"Oh, right," Remi said. He fumbled in his pockets for some bills, pushing them into Chase's hand. In a flash, Chase had his change and was helping Remi gather up all his bags.

"You have a great day now," Chase said. He waved at Remi, then turned to the next customer behind him.

Remi felt like he had no choice but to take his groceries and head back to his car. What had Chase meant by that? Why would he point out that Kris was single? That was obvious, wasn't it? Remi had been living with him for a couple of weeks now and there was no hint of a boyfriend. Why would Chase bring it up?

Had Kris said something about Remi to him?

His heart skipped a beat as he made his way across the boiling parking lot back to his car. Was Chase trying to tell Remi Kris was single so he could take a shot?

"Oh, hey, man," a voice called out.

Remi looked up as he placed his bags on the roof of the car to retrieve his keys from his pocket. He expected it to be one of his buddies from the firehouse or school. But instead, it was the guy that ran the vegetable stall for the Miele farm. Remi had bought carrots and strawberries off him several times. From the large box in his arms, it looked like he was making a delivery to the store.

"Oh, hey," Remi said in confusion. "Um, am I in your way?" He wasn't sure why the guy had made a point of saying hello to him.

But he shook his head. "No, you're fine," he said. "I just wanted to ask if you'd say hi to Kris for me. I hope his work pitch went well today."

Remi blinked. "You're...Kris's friend?" he asked dubiously.

The guy nodded. "I'm Gabe," he said. "You're Remi, aren't you?" He winked. "We've heard a lot about you." Before Remi could think of anything to say, Gabe shifted the weight of his box. "I'll catch y'all later. Have a nice evening," he called over his shoulder as he headed inside JJ's.

Remi realized his mouth was open and closed it with a click.

Warmth rushed over his skin, but it wasn't entirely unpleasant. Kris *had* been talking about him. Gabe was another one of his brunch buddies. Remi was sure he'd heard that name mentioned before. And he and Chase had both made a point of saying hello to Remi.

He could feel his heartbeat picking up. Did this mean he might actually have a chance? That Kris might actually like him, too?

After almost driving off with the groceries still on the roof of the car, Remi had to concentrate *extra* hard as he made his way back home. Kris still wasn't there when Remi let himself in. Good. He had some more thinking to do.

It was no longer a case of *if* he was going to come out to Kris, but *when*. And with that now came the added pressure of finding the right way to hint that Remi thought Kris was just great. Awesome. Cute.

Delicious.

"Hey, Kris," he said out loud as he peeled potatoes. He could hear the nerves in his voice. "So, uh, you feel like eating a film later while we watch dinner…no, wait." He gritted his teeth. "Hey, Kris. You know how we've hung out a ton and did all that romantic stuff. Well, I think I was accidentally dating you. Or trying. It's not a date without a kiss, right?!" He cleared his throat and hit his palm against his forehead a couple of times. "Uh, would you maybe, uh, like to Kris me – *kiss* me? Damn it-"

The key turned in the door just as Remi started dicing some chicken. Remi's heart rate shot through the roof.

"Okay," he whispered to himself. "This is it. Showtime." He washed the chicken off his hands as the door creaked and wiped them on a towel. "Don't fuck it up."

19

KRIS

Kris got an Uber back to Remi's. He couldn't afford it, really, but he wasn't trudging all the way over town in this heat while he was doing his best not to cry. He sniffed enough times that the Uber driver looked in his rearview mirror and asked if he was okay. When Kris struggled to reply, the driver pointed to the box of tissues in the back pouch of the driver's seat. After blowing his nose a couple of times, Kris at least felt less of a mess.

Who had he been kidding? He didn't know anything about business. PJ was right. He was just some silly twink who had big dreams and nothing to back it up. What kind of Disney nonsense did he have in his head if he thought he could waltz in there and tell his boss how to run his bar? He was an idiot.

He rubbed his nose and sighed heavily. PJ was right. The new community center could take care of all the classes and groups. It didn't need Bottom's Up to help it. But Kris couldn't shake the idea that there were certain things a bar *could* offer that nowhere else could.

It didn't matter now, anyway. PJ had made his position abundantly clear by *firing* Kris. Fucking hell, he was screwed. He needed to find another job, fast. One he didn't need a car to get to. He scoffed. Yeah, right. Like those kinds of positions just grew on trees.

"Thanks," he said as the driver dropped him off outside Remi's. How long would Remi be willing to put up with him when he couldn't even pay for the few things he had been? He would go broke so quickly now.

He hugged the stupid proposals to his chest as he trudged up the front path and fumbled to get the key out of his pocket. Despite the A/C in the car, the bar had been stifling and he felt gross in his formal pants and button-down shirt. It was a completely unnatural look for him. That alone should have convinced him he couldn't pull this off. He couldn't play pretend that he could hold his own with people who actually worked in business.

As he pushed the door inward, his heart managed to somehow leap and sink at the same time. Leap because Remi's cheerful voice called out to him from the kitchen, and hearing that never failed to warm Kris's heart. But it sank because of what Remi asked.

"Hey! How did it go?"

Kris shook his head, even though Remi couldn't see as he shut the door a little more forcefully than he meant to. "I have to get changed," Kris called back. "I'll be down in a minute."

There was a pause for a second or two. "Sure!" Remi called back. His happy tone sounded forced.

Shit. How did he know Kris well enough already to work out when he was bullshitting? Kris didn't dwell on it. Instead, he jogged upstairs, throwing the proposals so they skimmed off the bed and scattered on the floor on the other side. He grabbed his towel and decided a quick shower would be a good idea.

It might wash away some of his sense of failure.

As much as he wanted to dawdle and put off the inevitable, he also didn't want to be a dick and keep Remi waiting. So he turned off the water quicker than he would have liked and walked back to his room wrapped in the towel.

After the suffocating feeling of the pants and shirt, Kris deliberately picked out a provocative pair of booty shorts and a low-cut muscle shirt. God bless his friends for giving him some clothes he actually felt like himself in. He moisturized, swiped a candy-flavored lip gloss over his mouth and rubbed a bit of oil through his hair. That would have to do.

He felt a wild urge to throw himself under the comforter and stay there until he forgot how miserable he was. The only thing that stopped him was how rude that would be to Remi. Kris at least owed him an explanation. So he forced himself out the door and down the stairs, his heart in his throat.

He hated the idea that Remi was going to be disappointed in him. That Kris had let him down. Shame washed over him like waves on a beach.

He paused at the threshold of the archway into the kitchen. Remi looked up from where he was preparing some kind of chicken dish at the stove. Over the past week, he had gone mad with grocery shopping. Before the cupboards and freezer had been filled with instant meals and easy snacks. Now there was an abundance of fresh produce and Remi seemed determined to cook every meal himself. Kris wasn't sure what had come over him.

Remi looked up at Kris with a grin. But as soon as he saw his face,

Remi's expression dropped. He flicked off the stove, wiped his hands on a dish rag, then stepped toward Kris. "What happened?"

Kris gritted his teeth. "I – it wasn't good," he admitted. Remi crossed his arms and raised an eyebrow. Kris swallowed and exhaled loudly. It would be better to say it quickly, like ripping off a Band Aid. *"I got fired,"* he said in one rushed breath.

"What!" Remi exploded, flinging his arms out. "What the fuck? No, no. You can't have been fired."

Kris shrugged, turning and dropping into one of the chairs at the kitchen table. "Basically," he said, scratching at the grain in the wood, "PJ hated all my ideas and said I should get another job until he reopens the bar. *If* he reopens it."

Remi shook his head as he sat down. "I don't understand," he said. "Did you explain how much extra revenue such an expansive events program would bring in?"

Kris nodded miserably. "I tried to, at least," he said. "I told you, PJ didn't want to hear. He's so...*narrow.*" Kris held his hands a few inches apart and sighed. "I don't know what I'm going to do for money. I – I understand if you want me to move out."

Remi was frowning over toward the stove, although Kris suspected he might have just been staring into space. Then he blinked and jerked his head back toward Kris. "What? No, what the hell would you suggest that for?" he admonished firmly. "You're welcome here as long as you like. What kind of guy do you think I am? I'm not going to throw you on your ass when you're in trouble. Fuck that."

A small sliver of warm happiness fluttered in Kris's chest. "Thank you," he whispered. He continued to scratch at the table, the unpleasant vibrations jolting through his nail and up his fingers.

All of a sudden, Remi's large hand clasped over Kris's. Kris assumed it was to stop him from scratching, but Remi held it gently and rubbed the back with his thumb. Kris frowned and looked up at Remi in confusion.

"Don't give up," Remi urged, squeezing Kris's hand. "Don't let them win."

That was all a bit too much for Kris. What was Remi doing? Kris slipped his hand free, although he left it resting on the table. "Thanks," he said, shaking his head and biting his lip. "But, really – what was I thinking? I'm just a silly bartender." He gave Remi a rueful smile and mimed flicking back his hair. "I'm just here to look pretty. No one wants to hear what I think."

Kris looked into Remi's eyes as he frowned. Then Remi reached determinedly forward and took hold of Kris's hand again, this time cradling it tenderly between both of his big, slightly calloused hands. "*I* want to hear what you think," he said firmly. "You're so much more than just a pretty face."

The air whooshed from Kris's lungs. That was the second time Remi had called him pretty. Did he know what he was doing?

Did he know that he held Kris's heart in his hands as well?

Blinking, Kris looked between their connected hands and Remi's face. "You think I'm pretty?" he asked in a small voice.

Remi looked utterly panicked. Kris almost took the words back. But slowly, Remi nodded. "Uh, yeah," he uttered. His light brown skin had lost some of its color, but he still clung onto Kris's hand. "I do, actually."

Kris's heart was so loud he thought maybe it was going to explode. "I think you're pretty, too," he rasped, his words barely audible.

Fuck. A guy like Remi didn't want to hear he was pretty! What the hell was Kris thinking? He should have said handsome or gorgeous or-

"Yeah?" Remi replied. He sounded hopeful. His eyes lit up.

No. This couldn't be happening. There was no way on this earth that Kris was that lucky. Remi was not saying what he thought he was saying.

But he liked that Kris thought he was pretty. Where their skin was touching, palm to palm, felt like it had volts of electricity running between them.

"Remi, I…" Kris said. But he was lost for words. He was too afraid of saying anything that might burst this bubble.

"I'm an idiot," said Remi with a nervous laugh. The sudden break in tension shocked Kris. But before he could panic, Remi lifted up his hand between his own and held it to his chest. "Oh my god. You've been here the whole time. Like, literally forever." He laughed louder. It sounded like relief. "Kris. You're not stupid or silly or any of that crap you were saying. You're amazing. You're one in a million and…I, uh, fuck."

He bit his lip and cast his eyes around as if he was searching for the right words to say. He closed his eyes and took a breath.

"I like you, I think."

A wave of dizziness washed over Kris. "You like me?" he asked. He had to be sure about this.

Remi peeked between one cracked eyelid and grimaced. "Like…*like* you, like you. Yeah, I think so. But if that's not cool, just forget I said anything. You're a guest here and I would never want to make you feel, uh-"

"I like you, too," Kris confessed before he could chicken out. His mouth was dry and his pulse was hammering in his ears. Again, he had to be crystal clear on this. "It doesn't bother you that I'm a man?" he asked. Because under all the makeup and sparkles, he was still very much a man. Was Remi fully aware of what he was saying?

Remi took a deep, steadying breath. When he released it, he gave Kris a semi-confident smile. "No," he said clearly. "It doesn't bother me. I'm...I'm fully aware of that fact."

Kris rubbed his fingers against Remi's hand. On a sudden impulse, he stood, walking around the corner of the table and clasping his other hand over Remi's, holding them in front of his belly. "Have you done this before?" Kris asked.

Remi looked up at him, clearly unsure. He seemed to know that Kris meant with a guy, though. "No," he said softly. "I wanted to, someday. But there wasn't anyone...there wasn't anyone before you."

Kris's breathing hitched. "Me?"

"Yeah," said Remi. He looked up at Kris, those big brown eyes full of hope and sincerity. "You're pretty awesome, Kris. Like, seriously. I just didn't really see what that meant."

"Oh, uh," said Kris breathlessly. Despite the ceiling fan moving the cool air over their heads, he was just as hot and bothered as he had been out in the Texas summer sunshine. "So, what *does* it mean?"

Remi grinned, then gulped as worry clouded his features again. "That I'd like to kiss you. A lot. It's pretty all-consuming right now, actually. So, um, if that's something you'd like-"

Kris threw caution entirely to the wind and flung his leg over Remi's lap, straddling him as he let go of his hands and grabbed the back of his neck instead.

Remi squeaked.

Kris raised his eyebrows. He couldn't remember the last time he'd been so terrified to make a move on anyone. But this was *Remi.* Kris remembered the first time he saw him topless at the local pool. Remembered him and Leon taking their dates to senior prom. Remembered him over at his family home a thousand different times, playing video games or chucking a football around the garden.

All those times, Kris had felt entirely invisible.

Now, there was no way Remi was going to miss him. Slowly, Remi slipped his hands over Kris's hips, holding him gingerly. Like he was worried Kris might break. Fuck, Kris was desperate to show him how unbreakable he was. His hands felt *incredible* holding him like that. The denim of Remi's jeans rubbed deliciously against Kris's bare legs. The growing bulge in Kris's shorts bumped up against the matching firmness between Remi's legs.

He was turned on. There was no denying that.

He wanted Kris.

What if it was awful? What if it was amazing, but Remi got freaked out? Was he bi? Gay but closeted? Some other spectrum of queer?

Enough. Remi had asked Kris if he could kiss him. There was no outcome from this where Kris said no. He took a slow breath in. "Will you kiss me?" he whispered.

In a flash, Remi's hands flew up to splay over Kris's lower back and the back of his head. He pulled Kris to him, their mouths crashing together in a collision of lips, teeth and tongues.

If Remi was unsure about making out with a guy for the first time, he wasn't showing it. Passion simmered through him, his skin hot to the touch. Fuck, Kris wanted to touch it *all*.

After all these years, he couldn't really believe he was kissing Remi Washington. It was even better than he had ever imagined. Remi was warm and spicy and he moaned into Kris's mouth as his fingers dug into his skin. He wasn't sloppy or overly aggressive like so many bigger guys Kris had kissed. He was fiery and confident and knew just how to nibble on Kris's lip while his tongue lapped into Kris's mouth, making him wild.

How could Kris have been feeling so blue only a few minutes ago? Right now, it was as if he had tripped and found himself on cloud nine.

"Oh my god," Kris gasped as Remi's mouth attacked his neck, sucking and kissing and biting. "Holy fuck, yes."

Remi stopped and looked up at him, his brown eyes blown wide with lust. His hands rubbed Kris's back and hair with tenderness. "Can I take you to bed?" he asked, like he couldn't quite believe his own nerve.

Joyous delight and relief rushed through Kris. He still wasn't entirely sure what this was between them. But it was more than he'd ever hoped he would get in his wildest dreams. He bit his lip and grinned, resting his forehead against Remi's. Feeling devilish, he rolled his hips over Remi's lap, grinding their erections together. When Remi gasped in shock, Kris couldn't help but giggle.

"Yes," he hissed. "God, *yes.*"

Remi stood, wrapping his arms around Kris, keeping him safe. Kris crossed his ankles around Remi's bulky waist and held onto the back of Remi's neck. Kris looked down at him, Remi's chest visibly rising and falling as he panted.

"Are you sure?" Kris asked. This would be the last time he pumped the brakes, he swore. But he didn't want there to be a single ounce of regret between them.

In response, Remi leaned up and kissed him softly. It set fireworks off in Kris's belly. This wasn't like the frantic kisses before. This was sweet and simmering with desire. "You might have to teach me a couple of things," Remi mumbled into Kris's mouth.

Kris grinned, their lips still touching. "Oh," he said as Remi began to walk them out of the kitchen. "I'd be happy to."

2 0

REMI

Remi couldn't believe this was actually happening. Kris felt so perfect in his arms and around his waist as they stumbled their way from the kitchen to the living room. Remi was tempted to drop Kris right there on the sofa and get to business. The only thing that kept his legs moving was the box of condoms he had in the nightstand by his bed.

"Uh," he said between frantic kisses. Fuck, Kris tasted like candy and smelled like sunshine and it was driving Remi wild. "We, uh, need condoms, right?" Obviously neither of them could get pregnant, but there were other health issues guys still had to think about, he was sure.

Kris nodded against his lips. "Probably best to be safe," he mumbled into Remi's mouth. "Can talk later, about that, if want. Now, now is sex."

Remi laughed at his half-formed sentences. Kris was clinging to Remi like a monkey, digging his fingers into Remi's flesh and tightening his legs around his waist. Remi could feel Kris's erection rubbing against his stomach, demanding attention. Remi was amazed at how not freaked out he was by that.

He had always wondered how he would react if he was ever confronted with another guy's cock in a sexual situation. All his life, he'd been surrounded by the idea that a man's dick was his pride and joy. But any hint of being interested in another dude's junk was *gay* and obviously gay was bad.

But right then, Remi was salivating. Kris's prick was nudging him, desperate to be touched and petted and...sucked? Could Remi suck it? He liked going down on girls plenty. It drove him crazy to see them go wild as his tongue and lips worked their magic. Would Kris like that, too?

Okay, yeah, any residual doubt about him being bi was evaporating faster than a puddle in the Texas heat. He was so into this.

He was so into Kris.

"Fuck, you're gorgeous," Remi uttered as he carefully walked them upstairs. It was slow going because he wasn't letting up on kissing Kris at all. But they would get to the bedroom soon enough. He didn't want to waste a second that he could have his lips on Kris's. No matter how many times they banged into the wall or the banister. "So cute and fucking feisty."

Kris grinned like the Cheshire cat. "You haven't even gotten me in the sack yet," he said wickedly. Remi groaned.

"Holy fuck," he panted. Somehow, they made it up the stairs. Remi managed not to crash into anything on the landing. Then finally, mercifully, they were in his bedroom. The one that Kris had taken such care to redecorate. It already felt like he belonged in there with Remi.

They tumbled on top of the covers in a tangle of limbs, grinning too much as they tried to keep kissing while pulling at each other's tops. "You've really never done this before?" Kris asked breathlessly as he lifted his arms and allowed Remi to yank his muscle shirt off. As soon as it was over his head, he lunged for Remi's T-shirt.

Remi laughed as it got stuck around his ears and they both had to tug at the thing to get it over his head. "No, but, it's kind of the same basic principle, right? Get naked and…" He paused. Actually, what did two guys do, exactly? Obviously, he'd indulged in all that porn. But it was a little different in practice. What was he supposed to do now?

Kris must have sensed his hesitation. He pushed Remi over onto his back and lay on top. A part of Remi's brain noted the lack of boobs, but the rest of him was reveling in the sensation of feeling so much warm skin pressed against his chest.

"What do you *want* to do with me when you've gotten me naked?" Kris asked, his voice low and sexy. Remi's cock was already straining in his jeans, but that just made it harder. Kris bit his lip then began kissing down Remi's chest.

Remi was still stunned by the fact that Kris was attracted to him as well. Having been so unsure, Remi was starting to think his worries had been completely without foundation. He obviously *had* meant what he'd said about dreaming of Remi. Kris was desperate for him.

Remi was desperate for Kris, too. When he locked his lips around Remi's nipple and sucked, Remi cried out, a purely animalistic sound. He felt feral. He could smell Kris's musk under his after-shave. It was male and earthy, and *damn,* Remi wanted to lick his entire fucking body.

"Anything," Remi said, finally answering Kris's question. "I said – need help. What do you like?"

Kris left the nipple and made a quick trail of kisses down Remi's belly before jumping back up the bed. He was a little *firecracker.* "You got lube as well as condoms?" Remi nodded. Kris licked his lips, then bit Remi's lower lip between his teeth, releasing it slowly. "You wanna fuck my sweet, tight ass?"

Remi's brain almost short-circuited. He managed to nod again. "Y-yeah," he stammered. "That sounds good."

It also sounded easy enough. Having sex with women basically involved putting his dick inside them, once he'd warmed them up, of course. He felt like he could cope with doing the same for Kris.

But he was starting to appreciate he wasn't in charge here. Kris grabbed Remi's crotch through his jeans and squeezed his sensitive bulge. Remi cried out and arched his back in pleasure. "Can I ride you?"

"R-ride?" Remi repeated.

Kris giggled and nibbled at his ear. "Sit on you like this with your cock up my ass."

Remi swallowed, then gasped. "Wow, yes, please, that sounds, uh, real swell, thank you."

Kris dissolved into peals of laughter and flopped beside him on the bed. "Oh my god, you're adorable," he said. He cupped Remi's cheek and gave him a look so sincere it took Remi's breath away. They weren't just playing around here. This was a little deeper than that. "I can't believe this is happening."

Remi felt a twinge of doubt. He placed his hand over Kris's on his cheek. "Is this okay?" he whispered. There was a part of him that was still anxious he was taking advantage of Kris.

But Kris grinned. "Oh, baby," he said, that sass back in his voice.

He darted forward and smacked a big kiss on Remi's mouth. "This is *so* okay. Can we get nakey now?"

Remi laughed, too. "Yes, naked, good," he managed to rasp.

Kris shimmied away from him and with a flick of the wrist, his booty shorts were gone. He wasn't wearing underwear underneath.

"O-ohh," Remi stuttered.

It wasn't a bad reaction. More…well…there it was. Kris's cock. It wasn't that different to Remi's. A bit redder and smaller, but Kris was paler than he was generally and smaller all over. He was also extremely groomed. There was just a short length of hair in a neat strip above his cock, nothing down his legs or on his balls, unlike Remi.

He liked it.

"Can I touch it?" he asked, then immediately felt stupid, a flush blossoming on his face. But Kris just tossed the shorts on the floor and rolled back beside Remi.

"That's the idea," he purred. "I'd love you to."

Remi kissed him again because that seemed safer. Then he curled his fingers around Kris's shaft and stroked.

They both cussed into each other's mouths. Remi felt like he was handling hot, hard velvet. He loved it. Kris obviously liked it a bit, too.

"God, yes, squeeze it," he commanded. Remi did as he was told. Kris inhaled through his teeth, then attacked Remi with desperate kisses.

It didn't last long before Kris was fumbling with Remi's fly, trying to get him out of his jeans. Remi was glad he was barefoot, because once the button was open, he slammed down the zipper and kicked his way free of both jeans and briefs in the time it took him to draw breath and go back to kissing Kris's pretty, candy-floss-pink lips.

Their cocks were bumping together, sending sparks through Remi's body. He wondered what Kris thought of his junk – if it bothered him it was hairier. But Kris didn't seem to care as he rutted against him.

"What do I do?" Remi asked.

Kris shook his head. "The supplies are in this drawer here?" Remi nodded as Kris pointed to the nightstand. "Then, baby, you do nothing. Just lay back-" he pushed Remi's chest, encouraging him to fall flat on the bed "-and enjoy the show."

Remi watched, his chest rising up and down, as Kris preened, straddling Remi's hips with his cock pointing to the ceiling. He used his hands like Vanna White on Wheel of Fortune, showing off as he pulled open the drawer and retrieved the packet of condoms and pump of lube. Remi bit his lip. He'd used that with a few of the girls he'd dated over the past couple of years, sure. But he'd also fingered himself with the help of what was inside many times.

Kris didn't know that, obviously. He dropped one of the condom foils within easy reach, then pumped a couple of dollops of shiny lube on his fingers.

"Don't worry, honey," he said. He kissed Remi while he reached back behind his own ass. "This'll just take a few minutes. I can entertain you until then."

But Remi frowned. From what he could tell, Kris was fingering himself, stretching himself out ready for Remi's cock slide to inside him.

Remi felt drunk. He knew he wasn't, but he had that same dizzying high. Also, that same reckless abandonment of the tongue.

"Can't I do that?" he asked, slightly petulantly. He felt like Kris was denying him something. But as soon as he said it, he felt stupid. He didn't know what he was doing. Yet he wanted to shove his fingers up the most personal, intimate place a guy had?

Of course Kris just grinned and snorted, darting down for another kiss. "You can if you want," he suggested with a saucy air. "When did you last cut your nails?"

Remi would never have thought of that, but he thanked his lucky stars he'd actually trimmed them just a couple of days ago. Thank fuck he'd become more interested in self-care recently. Kris grinned when Remi showed him his hands. Then he dropped beside Remi on his belly and wiggled his ass.

"Play all you like," he invited, batting his eyelashes.

Well, damn it. Remi wasn't going to back down now. He grabbed the lube and pumped it a couple of times over his fingers. Then he scooched up beside Kris, spooning him.

"Hi," Kris said cheekily.

"Hi," Remi replied softly.

Kris leaned over to kiss Remi's lips gently. It gave him the courage he needed to slip his fingers in between Kris's ass cheeks where it was already slippery and stroke his hole. Here was totally hairless too.

Kris moaned into his mouth. "Feels good," he whispered.

"Yeah?" Remi asked. He couldn't stop the little smile that played on his lips. God, he wanted to make Kris happy. "How about this?"

He pushed his middle finger inside. It was so different doing this on someone else. Kris hummed and nodded, his eyelids fluttering closed.

Remi cuddled closer to Kris's body. The arm underneath Remi felt awkward, so he pulled it out from under his body and slid it under Kris's neck, giving him a pillow.

"Oh, baby," Kris mumbled, snuggling down and kissing Remi's bicep. "Fuck, your body is phenomenal."

Remi smiled at the compliment and kissed the tip of Kris's nose. "So's yours."

Kris scoffed. "Not really," he said. "I'm skinny."

"You're gorgeous," Remi said with determination. "Slim and sweet and very huggable." He was stroking the inside of Kris's hole, looking for the textured bump of his prostate. He knew as soon as he found it because Kris suddenly jerked, his eyes flying open.

"Oh, baby," Kris cried. "There, right there. Oh fuck, don't stop!"

Remi grinned. He had no intention of stopping after getting such an amazing result. He did add another finger, though. Kris squirmed deliciously against him. "You look so beautiful," Remi said, his voice hoarse. He heard the slight awe in his words, as did Kris he suspected, from the way he opened his eyes and looked at him.

"Fuck me," Kris whispered. He pushed himself against Remi's fingers and kissed him, hard. "Fuck me with your big cock, Remi Washington. I want to feel you inside me."

Remi should have known Kris was a dirty talker, but damn, it was a turn-on.

"Are you ready?" he asked, a little dubious. His hole still felt tight around Remi's fingers. But Kris shook his head.

"I'm fine," he said. "Need you now, goddamn it."

Remi laughed at his petulance. "Wow, you're a bossy one, aren't you?"

Kris preened and rolled his body against Remi's. "You know it, baby," he rasped.

Remi was so turned on he was dizzy. He pulled his fingers out and wiped them on the comforter so he could roll the condom over his straining erection. Kris watched him hungrily. But when Remi went to position himself behind Kris, Kris shook his head.

"More lube," he said, nodding toward Remi's cock.

"Oh," Remi said, thrown. "Sure, sorry."

Kris reached out and took his hand. "Don't be, sugar," he said warmly. "I like that you're learning with me." Then he licked his lips and spanked the side of Remi's thigh. "Now let me see you stroking that big dick. Get it dripping wet for me."

Remi snorted, feeling a bit embarrassed. But he wanted to make Kris happy above anything else. So he grabbed the lube once more, coating his fingers. Then he kneeled, displaying his cock while he rubbed the slippery substance all over it.

Kris's eyes danced as he took in the sight, his breathing shallow. "Oh, fuck, yeah," he hissed. "That looks so good. Come over here and jam that thing inside me."

Remi crawled over him. Kris grabbed one of the pillows from the bed and put it under his hips, angling his ass up toward Remi's cock. Normally, Remi would just use one hand to angle himself inside, but he soon discovered he needed a bit of help pulling apart Kris's ass cheeks. But soon enough, his tip was breaching the hole.

"Holy fuck," Remi hissed. "Oh, man, Kris, you're so tight. This is awesome. Is this okay? Does it feel okay?"

Kris was biting his lip and gripping the bed sheets, but he nodded emphatically. "Yes, yes," he cried. "Just keep going."

Remi didn't want to go too fast. He was worried it might be too much for Kris. So he took his time pushing inside, inch by inch. Kris moaned and wriggled beneath him. Now Remi's hands were free, he used them to run up and down Kris's sides, feeling every desperate breath he took. Then he leaned down and kissed between Kris's shoulder blades. His skin was damp with perspiration and he tasted salty.

This was everything Remi could have dreamed of. He'd often wondered – hoped – that one day he would get to experience this kind of intimacy with a guy. But to be doing it with Kris, who had become so important to him, was incredible. He groaned as he bottomed out. Even with the condom on, it still felt amazing. So tight and hot. Perfect.

"Kris?" he asked, not able to think of any other words. Kris was panting and still gripping the sheets.

"Just…give me a sec," he panted.

But Remi was concerned. Women didn't usually have that kind of reaction. Yeah, he had quite a big cock, but it wasn't a monster. But obviously it took a bit more effort to get inside an ass than it did a vagina, and he'd never done anal with a woman before.

"Are you all right?" Remi asked anxiously. "Have I hurt you?"

Thankfully, Kris laughed and looked over his shoulder at him. "It's fine," he assured him firmly. "It just takes a minute to adjust. Come here and kiss me."

Remi propped himself on his elbows and captured Kris's lips with his own. They kissed sweetly with his cock nestled perfectly inside Kris's ass. Gradually, Kris began to undulate, rolling his cheeks against Remi's crotch. Remi groaned.

"Fuck, that feels good," he rasped into Kris's mouth.

Kris nodded. "Fuck me, baby," he said between kisses. "Fuck me hard with your big, gorgeous cock. Make me scream."

"Oh, baby," Remi uttered, trying out the word for the first time with his new lover. He thought it might have felt weird calling a dude that. But with Kris, much like everything else, it felt just right. "Like that?"

He slid his dick out most of the way, then pushed it back in, angling his hips so his cock curved upward, searching for Kris's sweet spot again. It took him a couple of thrusts, but Kris suddenly scrabbled to grab hold of the bedsheets again and he figured he'd nailed it.

"Oh, yes, baby, *yes,*" Kris wailed. "Harder, baby, just like that. Fuck, *yes!*"

In no time, Remi was really pounding into him. Sweat was running down his back and dripping from his forehead onto Kris's skin. They were slippery and in perfect sync and it was difficult to tell where one ended and the other began.

Jesus, he wasn't going to take long to come at this rate. But he desperately didn't want this to be over.

As preoccupied as he was, a dark thought managed to sneak into his mind. What would happen when they finished? Would it be awkward? What was going to happen to their friendship? Or would Kris be interested in, what, dating? Would Remi have to come out to everyone right away? What would his family think?

He realized he had slowed down when Kris turned and looked

over his shoulder at him. "What's wrong?" he asked. He reached for Remi's hand and gripped it tight.

Remi shook his head. "Sorry," he gasped.

He was being ridiculous. What the hell was he doing thinking about shit like that when he was balls deep in Kris's perfect ass with those beautiful silvery-blue eyes looking up at him so tenderly?

Remi leaned down and kissed Kris. "I just started overthinking, that's all. I'm good."

But Kris shook his head. "Do you want to stop?"

"Definitely not," Remi spluttered. "I'm being stupid. I'm sorry. You're gorgeous and this is so fucking hot and I'm ruining it."

Again, Kris shook his head. "Time-out," he whispered. He kissed Remi then turned, easing Remi's cock out of his ass. Remi bit his lip and cursed himself. He *was* ruining everything. But Kris didn't seem mad. When they were face-to-face, chest to chest, he cupped his free hand to Remi's face and squeezed the one he was already holding. "This is your first time with a man. You're allowed to need a second to catch your breath. If it helps, you are doing *so* well." He rolled his eyes and grinned. "Like, crazy good. I'm having an amazing time."

Remi laughed, feeling some of the tension leave his body. "I'm having a great time, too," he said honestly. "You're so sexy and fun and, god, thank you, Kris."

Kris kissed him slowly. "Pleasure's all mine, honey bun," he said sweetly. "Now, do you want to carry on? I promise, if it's too much, we can just stop right now, I won't mind."

"Well, I'd mind," Remi said gruffly.

Kris laughed and spanked Remi's ass. *Fuck,* he liked that.

"If I remember, I promised to ride you," Kris said with a raised eyebrow. "Would Baby like that?"

Remi nodded, obediently rolling onto his back. "Yes, he would. Sounds hot as fuck."

Kris grinned as he climbed on top of him, lowering himself down on Remi's glistening cock. They both moaned. Yeah, Remi liked this. He could see Kris's face and kiss him when Kris leaned down. He could also see his hard, weeping dick, bobbing around as he moved.

Kris reached for Remi's hands, placing them by his shoulders and lacing their fingers together. Then he started rolling his hips, grinding down on Remi.

"Shit, baby, yes," Remi cried. "That feels perfect. Don't stop."

"Oh, I won't," Kris growled. He was like a small, powerful animal. "I'm going to make you come in my ass. I'm going to make a mess all over you, Remi Washington."

Remi loved the way he said his name like that. It was so possessive. "Kris," he said, trying it out himself. He squeezed his hands and angled his hips up to meet Kris's ass every time he dropped back down. "Kris Novak, my hot little minx."

"Hell yeah, baby," Kris yelled, dropping his head back and exposing his throat. "I want you to come, Remi. Do it, you beast. Come in my ass."

Remi was close. He rutted frantically. Then Kris let go with one hand and wrapped it around Remi's throat. Not enough to hinder his breathing, but enough to make him feel pinned down. God, it was good.

"Jerk me off," Kris commanded. "Make me come on you, Remi. Touch me, oh, fuck."

Remi made a tunnel with his hand, allowing Kris to fuck into it. It was slippery with precum and felt so good. Remi wished he'd played with it more, but there was no time now. They were both yelling and gnashing their teeth.

Remi's orgasm hit him like a train, tearing through his body and snatching his breath away. He buckled as Kris kept riding him, milking every last drop of cum from his cock. Then Kris snapped forward with a bellow as he began shooting white streaks along Remi's chest.

They shivered as their climaxes peaked. Then Remi flopped back into the bed and Kris dropped on top of him. "Shit," Kris whispered with a giggle. "That was…wow."

Remi managed to drop his hands over Kris's back and hug him while he stared at the ceiling fan going around and around, trying to collect his wits. "Is it always that good?" he asked.

Kris lifted his head to give him a kiss. "No," he said with a grin. "It's not."

Remi was aware they should clean up. But he was so sleepy already and Kris felt so good lying on top of him. He hugged him tighter and nuzzled his face into the crook of Kris's neck. "Thank you," he whispered.

It was still light outside, but Remi could feel himself drifting off. The fan was cooling the sweat on their skin and he could feel Kris's heart beating through his chest. He couldn't stop himself from falling into an easy sleep.

21

KRIS

It was dark when Kris woke up, stiff and sticky and slightly sore. For a second, panic gripped him. Where was he? Who was sleeping under him?

But then it all came back to him. Remi. Remi had made a move and taken Kris to bed and it had been *glorious*.

At least, Kris thought so.

Kris hadn't held back. He never did during sex. Life was too short to be coy. He liked his loving wild and free. But this was *Remi*. He said he hadn't done this with a guy before, although he wanted to. Did that mean he was bi? Kris had said all kinds of filthy things to him. How was he going to feel about that when he woke up?

Kris bit his thumbnail. Yuk, there was a lot of dried cum between them. He should have taken care of that before passing out. Remi was going to think dude sex was gross. He looked around the dark bedroom for some tissues, but there weren't any. What he needed, really, was a Wet Wipe, but he doubted Remi would have anything like that.

Carefully, Kris peeled himself off and padded naked to the bathroom. He used his hands to splash a bit of water on himself, giving his chest and cock a wipe-down. Then he found a facecloth that he dampened to bring back for Remi.

He was still sound asleep when Kris returned. Kris perched on the bed and gently wiped down Remi's chest, getting rid of most of the mess. He had dark hair across the top of his pecs and down his sternum, past his belly button where the happy trail lead to a thick thatch where his cock and balls were nestled. It was floppy now, lying up on Remi's belly, all innocent. Like it hadn't given Kris a good hammering only a few hours ago.

Kris bit his lip as he lay down beside Remi. Now he was awake, it was a little too cold with the A/C on and no clothes. There was no way he was shifting Remi without waking him up to move the comforter, so he got up again and took a look in Remi's closet. Sure enough, he found a blanket on the top shelf that he spread over both of them before snuggling down against the pillow.

He watched Remi sleeping, his slow breaths making his chest rise and fall.

Was Kris okay to stay here? Or should he go back to his own bed? He wasn't sure. It would be obvious from the blanket that he had woken up in the night, so he couldn't claim he had slept through until morning. But would Remi mind if he stayed in that case?

Kris rubbed his eyes. Maybe he should have held back a bit when they'd been fucking? He knew he was full on with his dirty talk. But Remi seemed to really enjoy it.

Except for when he'd stopped halfway through. That worried Kris. Although he had double-checked, he was still slightly nervous that Remi had experienced some second thoughts. As a rule, Kris stayed away from 'straight' dudes who wanted to bone a fem guy then immediately insisted they weren't gay. Remi didn't seem like that sort, but Kris couldn't be sure. Until yesterday evening, he would have sworn Remi wasn't queer.

Although, Kris had wondered if he had been flirting several times over the past couple of weeks. Perhaps he had been? He *had* said he'd wanted to try having sex with a man. Kris allowed himself a moment of pride that Remi had chosen him.

But why?

Kris had nothing. No house, no job. He only had clothes because his friends had been kind enough to donate them. Even when he had a job, he was just a bartender. Remi saved people's *lives* for a living. Why would he be interested in silly, twinky Kris?

Maybe it was just an experiment? A bit of fun to check if he liked cock or not? Kris wouldn't be too surprised if that was the case. Fuck, he never, *ever* thought he'd get to experience sex with Remi. After all those hundreds of daydreams he'd had over the years, to know it was now a reality was mind-blowing. So, yeah, perhaps he would have to accept this was a one-time thing and he'd do his best to move on and cherish the memory.

But what if it wasn't just a one-off? What if Remi really liked him, despite all his short-comings? Kris smiled to himself in the dark. For just a second, he imagined what it might be like to actually *date* Remi.

He sighed and chased the thought away. The chances of that were slim. It was better not to get his hopes up. Yeah, Remi said he was cute, but cute could be a novelty. Guys liked to fuck cute. They didn't want to hold hands in public with the fem twink in case it dragged down their masculinity.

Again, Kris didn't really feel that was Remi. But he still didn't know where Remi was coming from. Was he gay or bi, or was this just a bit of fun to try on for size? Now he'd fucked a dude up the ass, was he just going to cross that off some list and move on?

Shit, they were *living* together. If this went bad, Kris would have to move back to his mom's couch. He loved his mom, but not having his own room was kind of stressful and the sofa made his back hurt. He'd rather not leave Remi's. They had been getting on so well. But if the price of getting to bed him was moving out, Kris thought it was maybe worth it.

Christ, if his teenage self could see him now. He'd have a heart attack. Or cry. Or both. *Remi Washington.*

Kris sighed softly. The sex really had been amazing. If that was all he got, he would be happy, he would. But it was tempting to fantasize about what *else* they could maybe do. Kris wanted to give Remi a blow job and feel him come down his throat while he sucked on that gorgeous cock.

He also wanted to cuddle him as he fell asleep again.

He could do that right now if he wanted. He could shift over and snuggle against Remi's large, muscular body. But what if Remi woke up? Would he think Kris was clingy? He huffed and rolled onto his back.

What would be great was if Remi could wake up and they could talk about all this. But in Kris's experience, guys weren't great at discussing their feelings, even gay guys. Would Remi just bottle all this up and brush it under the carpet?

Kris probably wasn't going to get any answers now. He felt like he was radiating heat and taking up too much room in the bed. Like a bomb waiting to go off. This was crazy. If it was a random hookup and he'd accidentally fallen asleep, he would have absolutely made his way out by now. He should leave.

Sighing, he flung back his side of the blanket and swung his legs out. He needed to give Remi his space and just go back to his own bed.

Except at the movement on the mattress, Remi moaned. Kris snapped his head around to look at him. He still appeared to be sleeping, but there was an adorable frown on his face. He mumbled something and fumbled with his arm. Like he was reaching for something.

Reaching for Kris.

His heart in his throat, Kris scooted back beside him. Remi was probably just fidgeting in his sleep, agitated by a dream. But if he *was* searching for Kris, Kris could let him find him and see what happened.

When Remi's hand landed on Kris's leg, he clung tight and pulled, mumbling something incoherent. Kris's heart melted as he allowed himself to be tugged back beside Remi's sleeping form.

Well, it couldn't hurt to stay here in that case, could it? Kris reasoned with himself as he gently pulled the blanket back over his body that it *would* be pretty rude to up and leave Remi just to go in the other room. It might make things more awkward than waking up together in the morning.

Yeah, staying here was probably safest when he thought about it. He didn't want Remi to think he'd used him or anything. If it was only one time, he wanted to make sure Remi understood it was great, even if they were just going to be friends afterward.

But for a moment, as he allowed himself to be snuggled by this big teddy bear of a man, he indulged in a few seconds of fantasy. That he could have this again, regularly. That Remi would want to make him feel safe like this every night.

Kris closed his eyes and let sleep claim him again. He could deal with all these complicated questions in the morning. For now, he could just be happy.

22

KRIS

When Kris awoke to the morning light streaming past the curtains, he was alone.

His heart skipped a beat as he looked around for Remi, but there was no sign of him. Shit. This was what he had been fearing. It was going to be weird and awkward. Goddamn it. Why couldn't he have kept his mouth shut and just had some vanilla sex for once in his life? He'd probably terrified Remi or scarred him for life against sex with men.

Kris knew Remi had cuddled him last night, but he'd been more-or-less asleep. He had most likely come to this morning and been horrified at what he had done with his best friend's younger brother.

Kris squeezed his eyes shut and pinched the bridge of his nose. Regret washed over him, tightening his chest and causing a lump to rise in his throat. He should have pulled back when Remi made a move. But was their friendship already lost by that point?

This wasn't the first time Kris had woken from a night of passion to find himself alone. But he didn't care when it was random

Grindr hookups with guys whose last names he didn't even know. This was Remi and what they had done had changed everything.

Feeling weighed down, he dragged himself out of bed and pulled his shorts and muscle shirt back on. If there was any mercy in the universe, Remi would have gone out to the gym or the store, leaving Kris to shower and change in peace.

Maybe pack.

With a heavy heart, he pulled Remi's bedroom door open to step onto the landing, intending to slip into the spare room and grab his new toiletry bag. But the smell of frying bacon caught his attention as soon as he wafted air through the door. Kris paused. Yes, that was bacon he could smell, as well as fresh coffee.

He bit his lip and looked down the stairs. He couldn't see anything much, but he could hear sounds coming from the kitchen – the clattering of utensils and food sizzling in pans and a voice humming along to the radio.

That didn't sound like someone going through an existential crisis. Nor did it sound like someone regretting an overzealous sexual encounter.

Remi was cooking breakfast and it sounded like he was happy about it.

Kris's heart sped up a little. Not thinking too much about what he was doing, he slowly made his way downstairs. Halfway through his descent, he wished he had checked his reflection in the mirror. But he wasn't going back up now in case he lost his nerve. Instead, he ran his hands through his hair and ruffled it, hoping he looked okay.

He padded softly through the living room, stopping at the threshold to the kitchen, much the same as he had done the previous night after he had come back from the bar. He had obviously interrupted the chicken dinner Remi had been making and spoiled those ingredients when they had gotten…distracted. In their place now were several new pans and mixing bowls.

Sure enough, coffee was brewing in the pot. Bacon and eggs were spitting in a large metal frying pan while Remi stirred some grits. Dear lord, he was only wearing a pair of black briefs as he worked, a dish towel over one shoulder. He must have sensed Kris's presence because he looked up toward the door suddenly. Then his face broke into a beautiful smile that made Kris's heart flip.

"Hi," he said, wiping his hands on the rag and dropping it on the counter. With a glance at the cooking food, he stepped away from the counter, stopping a few feet from where Kris was standing. He leaned over and turned down the radio. "Morning, hi. Did you sleep? How are you feeling?"

Relief raised its head tentatively in Kris's chest. That wasn't the worst reaction in the world. "I'm good," he said. He wanted to appear confident and at ease, but he couldn't stop himself from folding his arms over his chest protectively.

"Yeah?" said Remi. He seemed to notice he was almost naked and also crossed his arms. But he was still smiling and his eyes were wide. Kris thought he looked hopeful. "Sorry, did I wake you?" He gestured to the delicious-smelling mess behind him. "I was going to bring you breakfast in bed."

That lump rose in Kris's throat again, but this time it was from happiness. "You were?" he asked in a small voice. "That's…that's so sweet."

Remi bit his lip and looked bashfully at Kris through his dark eyelashes. "Do you want to take a seat and I can plate up?" he asked. "Or we could go back up to bed?"

As romantic as taking their food back up to bed sounded, there was a lot of it. Also, Kris actually wanted to eat it and then talk about some things. If they went back upstairs now, he was liable to jump Remi again before they did either of those things.

"Here's great," he said enthusiastically. "Wow, I had no idea when I moved in you liked cooking so much. This smells amazing."

Remi grinned as he grabbed a quilted potholder and opened the oven, wafting the slight buildup of smoke away then retrieving a tray of fresh cornbread muffins. "My mom taught me a lot when I was a kid," he said. He glanced over at Kris as a slight frown crossed his face. "My dad doesn't really think guys belong in the kitchen. It's not like he *forbade* it or anything. He just...didn't get it. I guess it was enough to stop me from trying over the years." He smiled at the potholder in his hand. "Mom gave me this when I moved in. I kinda feel like she was encouraging me to try again now."

Kris swallowed around the pesky lump in his throat that refused to go away. "That's awesome," he said out loud. To himself, he thought a couple of things. One, how he could relate to what Remi was saying about his dad, and two, how interesting it was that Remi had started cooking again *now*. When Kris was living here. Not in secret where no one would know. He was doing it *because* of Kris. *For* Kris.

That was pretty incredible.

He watched Remi plate up their large breakfasts and pour the coffee while a warmth settled over his heart. Maybe this wasn't going to be the disaster he had feared. Maybe...just maybe...the crush of his life liked him back.

Stranger things had happened.

Remi placed the plates carefully down on the already-set table and sat himself in a chair. Only once they were both settled did Kris realize this was where they had been last night before the kiss.

Remi obviously appreciated the same thing as his eyes went wide.

"About last night-" they both said in unison.

Thankfully, they both also laughed afterwards. "Um, yeah," Kris said. He could feel his cheeks getting a tiny bit warm, but hopefully he wasn't blushing too much. "How are you, uh, feeling? About everything."

Remi bit his lip and looked at Kris. "Well, you know. Good." He lifted his fork and toyed with the prongs for a second. Then he slammed it back down on the table. "I'm bi," he blurted out, shaking his head rapidly. "I'm bisexual and I've known that for a couple of years and I think I really like you and I know it's fast but last night was amazing."

Kris felt frozen in place. Remi was also now still. He wouldn't quite meet Kris's eyes and his forehead had gone a little shiny with perspiration. But Kris felt like a balloon of happiness had expanded in his chest. "Oh, honey, really?" he squeaked. He bunched his hands up in excitement then sat on them to stop himself from waving them about. "I wasn't too much? I...well, I kind of woke up feeling like I shouldn't have been so extra."

Remi's face broke into a grin even bigger than the one when Kris had entered the room. He reached out and pulled the nearest hand free from under Kris's thigh, squeezing it tightly. "Screw that. That was some of the hottest sex I've ever had. It would have been the hottest if I hadn't freaked out halfway through. But next time, if you want there to be a next time, I won't do that. I promise."

Kris bounced on his seat. "I'd love there to be a next time," he said. "More times. As many times as you like." He wiggled his eyebrows. "I have ideas."

Remi burst out laughing. "I am really sorry you woke up to an empty bed," he said, shaking his head. "I'd hate for you to think last night wasn't monumental for me, in more ways than one."

Kris placed his other hand on top of Remi's. "So, you're bi, huh?"

Remi nodded and blew out a heavy breath. "Yes," he said firmly. "God, that feels good. You – well, you're the first person I've ever told."

Kris was taken aback. "What, *ever* ever?" he spluttered. Not Leon or his mom or one of his buddies at the fire station? Kris sat back in his chair. Wow. "I'm honored. Thank you." On a whim, mirroring the night before, he stood up and walked around to Remi. But this time, he draped his arms around him for a hug. Despite his almost complete lack of clothes, the moment felt tender, not sexy.

"Oh, man," Remi said with a laugh as he hugged Kris back, resting his cheek on Kris's shoulder. "I love how much you hug. It's so cool."

Kris frowned and stood up with his arm resting around Remi's shoulders, looking down at him. "Doesn't anyone hug you, baby?" he asked.

Remi shrugged. "Nah," he said with a rueful smile. "Dudes don't do that, man."

Kris rolled his eyes. Honestly, straight people sometimes. "Well, this dude does," he said, dropping sideways onto his lap and kissing Remi's cheek. They grinned at each other. Remi rested his large hands on the small of Kris's back.

"So, um," Remi said, playing with the hem of Kris's shirt. "Do you wanna, like, do this?" he asked.

Kris raised his eyebrows. "This?" He thought he knew what Remi was asking, but he was too scared to jump to any conclusions.

"Like, uh, us," Remi said. He wasn't blushing, but he did squirm under Kris's legs. "I mean, we're both here, in the house. But if that's too much pressure-"

"Baby," Kris said patiently. "What is 'this'? Sex?"

Remi spluttered, but then he laughed. "Well, yeah, that would be great," he said, squeezing around Kris's waist. "But I suppose I meant a bit more than that."

Kris felt a bit dizzy. "Like…dating?"

After a beat, Remi nodded, but he seemed hesitant. "I'm not out," he said in a rush. "I guess you worked that out for yourself, but, huh, I don't know-"

"Oh, hey, no," said Kris shaking his head. "Babe, you don't have to leap out of the closet like a baby gazelle. You can take it slow."

"I want to," Remi said quickly and earnestly. "Come out, I mean. I do. I just don't know how…or when…"

Kris stopped him with a kiss, cupping his face gently with his hands. "Darling, sweetie," he said sincerely, "take all the time you like. Let's try this thing on for size and see how it goes. You know, give it a spin, like a new car!" He gave Remi some jazz hands. "Then if you feel right, you can start telling people."

But Remi was shaking his head. "No," he said. "I mean, don't get me wrong, that's real nice of you. But I'm not just coming out because I'm seeing a guy now. I'm coming out because…it's me. That's who I am." He rested his forehead against Kris's. "If I happen to have a super hot boyfriend when I do, that just makes me lucky."

Kris tried not to wriggle with ecstatic glee. He couldn't believe

Remi was saying this. "Aww, baby," he whispered. He didn't know what he was more excited about. The fact that Remi wanted to come out regardless, the fact he thought Kris was hot – not cute or adorable, but actually hot – or the fact he had used the word 'boyfriend.' "That's so great," he said, not trusting himself with anything else.

"Thank you," said Remi.

Kris frowned. "For what?"

Remi kissed the tip of his nose. "For helping me work it out. I needed someone incredible like you to push me into admitting what I already knew."

"That you're bi and fly?" Kris asked, swinging his legs and being all cutesy. He was trying to play it cool but deep down, he was over the goddamned moon. He couldn't believe yesterday he had been so distraught and now he was so happy. He felt like he could conquer the world.

Remi laughed at his silly joke. "Damn right," he said. Then he kissed Kris properly, capturing his lips and moving them slowly. "But I swear, I'm not going to sit on this. I just have to talk to my family. Once I've worked out how to do that, I can tackle work and friends."

Kris ran his hand down Remi's sculpted arm. "Do you think they'll have a problem with it?"

Remi tilted his head. "I think my dad is gonna be in a whole world of surprise," he said after a few moment's consideration. "I think I'll start with my mom." Kris nodded. After all, he himself had waited until his dad had skipped town before coming out. He got that, totally.

"Good plan," he told Remi sincerely. "And I'll be here to support you, all the way."

Remi hugged him to his chest, running his fingers through his hair and kissing his neck. "I mean it," he murmured. "I'm so lucky. You're amazing."

"So are you," Kris replied.

Before they could start making out too heavily, Kris insisted on eating at least some of the yummy breakfast Remi had made them. Then he had detailed plans on how he would take them back to bed.

But for a few minutes, he just stared at this wonderful man he had somehow managed to attract. Maybe, just maybe, his luck was turning around?

He could only hope.

23

REMI

*R*emi felt like he was floating in this strange in-between place outside of reality. Like a dream he didn't want to wake up from yet. He and Kris had spent all day together on Friday after their talk. Yes, there had been more fooling around (dear lord Kris gave an incredible blow job) but there had been snuggling and talking and watching dumb game shows together. It had been awesome.

"Come on, who is she?" Channing said. Remi hadn't even noticed him come into the common area. But when he slapped Remi's arm with the magazine in his hand, it got his attention quick enough.

Remi frowned as Channing sat down at the dining table beside him, a grin on his face. "What?" he asked, genuinely confused. All Remi had been doing was a crossword puzzle.

Channing pointed at his face. "That look is the look of a sexually satisfied man," said Channing, loudly enough for the rest of the watch to hear. Remi's gut immediately twisted. "So, come on, spill. Who is she?"

"There's no girl," he said.

It gave him a head rush to even skirt that close to the truth. But he wasn't about to confess to everyone just yet. He still had no idea how he was going to talk to his mom about any of this, let alone his dad or sisters.

Alondra dropped into the chair opposite him and wagged the spoon from the yogurt she was eating at him. "There is something," she agreed with a wry smile. "Have you met someone you *hope* to start sleeping with? You got that glowy look."

Remi rolled his eyes as his phone started vibrating in his pocket. "There is no glow, y'all are crazy."

Except, call it good or bad timing, it was Kris's number ringing him.

"OH!" Channing bellowed, clapping and pointing in triumph. "That's it! That's the face! What's she look like? Let us see."

Remi quickly hugged his phone to his chest to hide the caller ID as he hastily stood up. He was in no way ashamed of Kris. The timing just wasn't right yet. "Y'all are nosy perverts," he grumbled as he stalked off toward the front entrance. "Hey, baby," he said when he was finally able to answer the call in private. "How's it going?"

"Um," said Kris.

Remi immediately stopped walking. Even from that one syllable, he could tell something was off. "What's wrong?" he asked.

"Well," said Kris, drawing out the sound. "I'm standing outside your fire station."

Remi's emotions swung from concern to flattered to concern again. "Is everything okay with the house?" he asked. "Or are you just here for a visit?"

Kris chuckled, lightening the mood a little. "As much as I would love to surprise you at work, baby," he said playfully, "I do respect your boundaries and the fact you're not out yet. And no, everything's fine with the house. Although I had to shoo that cat away again. Do you think she's a stray?"

Remi sighed. It had occurred to him. Although he knew cats sometimes just took themselves on vacation. If they found a house that would feed them, why go home? His mom had always warned him not to leave anything out for a cat he didn't know in case he was keeping the kitty from going back to its rightful owners.

Of course, he hadn't listened this time. But the little black cat was hardly bigger than a kitten and obviously hungry. And now she kept breaking into his house to stare at Kris's fish and bat at the tank. Even with the new top on, Remi was worried she might do what cats naturally do and eat Kris's beloved pet despite their best efforts.

"Yeah," he said, nodding to himself. "Maybe next time she pops up, we can take her to the vet and see if she's microchipped."

"Cool, yeah, good idea," Kris said. His voice was tight with anxiety.

Remi bit his lip and looked around. He was in the front hallway that led out in front of the bays. "So, I'm guessing you didn't come all the way out here to tell me about the cat," he said. "Where are you? I'll come meet you."

"Out by the front where the trucks come out," Kris said with a sigh. "No, you're right. I, uh, well, that guy Epstein called me back. He told me to come here as soon as possible. That it was to do with the fire at the bar. Have you heard anything about it?"

Remi frowned and began making his way out to the front of the station. "No," he said, trying not to let his apprehension bleed through in his voice. "Maybe they just want to talk to you again about what happened at the end of your shift? Or getting your things back from your apartment? Hang on. I'm nearly at you."

They paused the conversation while Remi walked past the engines outside. Kris was waiting there in a slightly more conservative outfit than Remi had become used to. He was in jeans, flip-flops and a T-shirt, with no accessories aside from the sunglasses that Remi had loaned him. Or given him, as he'd already decided.

It made Remi sad to see Kris dressed down to deal with certain kinds of people. It also upset him he couldn't hug or kiss him hello. Well, that was up to him, wasn't it? The quicker he came out to his family, the quicker he would be able to declare to the world that he and Kris were together.

Were boyfriends.

What a crazy thought. He loved it.

Instead he hung up the phone and gave Kris a light tap on the arm. "Hey," he said.

"Hey," Kris said back. He slid his phone into his jeans, then both his hands into the pockets, rolling on the balls of his feet. "So, I'm supposed to go to a Captain Bishop's office?"

"I'll take you," said Remi with a nod. He realized they would need to walk through the common area, but he immediately quashed any hesitations he had. The more his buddies were used to seeing Kris around, the less of a shock it would be to them when they announced they were a couple.

That made Remi realize something, however. "Hang on," he said as they began to wander back inside the station. "There were a couple of other people who came into the station during our last shift. I wondered if they were, well, uh…" He glanced at Kris who raised his eyebrows at him. "Well, I thought they might have looked gay."

Kris burst out laughing. "Oh, honey," he said, lightly slapping Remi's arm. "You can say that. It's not a crime."

"Oh," said Remi in relief, feeling a little foolish. "Well, maybe they also work – or worked – at Bottom's Up? Maybe they're just talking to everyone."

Kris blinked, then grinned at Remi. Remi could see the tension melt away from him. "Yeah, maybe," he said, nodding. He bumped arms with Remi. The touch of skin on skin was enough to give Remi goose bumps. "I'm sure it's nothing. Probably just routine."

Heads turned as they walked past the rest of Remi's coworkers in the common room, but no one said anything. They just smiled and nodded and carried on with whatever they were doing. All except Travis, of course, who followed their progress across the room with a slight frown on his face. Remi did his best not to look at him.

When they reached Bishop's office, Remi glanced up and down the corridor. There was absolutely no one around. So he threw caution to the wind and quickly leaned down to peck a kiss on Kris's cheek.

"Good luck," he said as he straightened up just as hastily. "I'll, um, hover around here for when you come out. Unless we get a call. Then I won't be here. I'll, uh-"

Kris giggled and squeezed Remi's arm for just a second. "Baby, it's fine," he said with a cute smile. "Like you said, it's probably nothing. If you're here when I leave, I'll say hi. If not, I'll see you at home."

Home.

God, Remi loved hearing him say that. It sounded right.

"Okay," he said. "Catch you later."

Kris winked and knocked on the door, leaving Remi behind as he went inside.

24

KRIS

Kris tried to hold onto his optimism as he closed the door behind him and found himself in Remi's boss's office. It wasn't large, but enough to comfortably fit Captain Bishop's desk and the three chairs standing in front of it.

Kris guessed Bishop was the man behind the desk. He had dark skin and was probably in his fifties, judging by the touch of gray in his hair. Kris vaguely recognized him from the night of the fire, although, to be fair, most of that night was a blur. He also featured in a lot of the photos that were hanging on the wall, shaking hands with lots of different people. So he had to be Bishop.

One of the other people Kris recognized immediately. PJ looked tired, but he managed a small smile for Kris. Kris was still hugely pissed about their last conversation, but the guy was clearly at the end of his tether. His eyes behind his glasses were bloodshot and had dark circles underneath, and his goatee had gotten scraggly.

"Mr. Novak, come in," Bishop said, standing and indicating the last vacant seat on the left. "Take a seat."

"Thank you," said Kris politely.

"Hey, man," PJ sighed. "How you doing? You holding up?"

Kris couldn't help but feel a tiny bit of gratitude. PJ wasn't all that bad. He just wasn't very good with people sometimes.

"Oh, I'm fine," said Kris with a little flick of his wrist. "Thank you, sweetie."

"Mr. Novak," said Bishop as they both sat down either side of the desk. "This is Mr. Epstein. I believe you've spoken on the phone."

Kris turned to the slightly haggard-looking guy in the seat to the right beside him. He was probably in his forties but looked like he didn't get much sleep. Everything about him was gray, from his suit to his hair to his tired eyes. But he gave Kris a warm enough smile and offered his hand to shake.

"It's a pleasure to meet you, Mr. Novak," Epstein said. He glanced at Bishop once he let Kris's hand go. "We'll keep this as brief as possible, if you don't mind?"

"Sure," Kris said, splaying his hands out in front of him. "Whatever I can do to help."

He and the two other men watched as Epstein retrieved a small notebook (also gray) from the inside of his jacket pocket. "It's just a quick question, really," he assured Kris. "We've asked most of your colleagues already, but we wanted to give you a bit of time because, well..."

"Because I was almost a little old marshmallow on top of that big old bonfire?" Kris supplied. Epstein gave a small laugh at Kris's attempt at a joke. Bishop laced his fingers together on the desk and PJ chewed on his lip. "Oh, don't worry about me," Kris said. "I'm okay. Fire away. I mean, ask anything you want!" he added hastily. He needed to stop making bad jokes. "What's your question?"

Epstein carefully tore a page from his notebook out and placed it in front of Kris. "We were able to pull up the security log for the door system," Epstein said. He patted his chest down until he eventually located a pen. "Since Mr. Maddox here has explained each employee picked their own code, we're asking y'all to write down that code so we can make a quick comparison to the night of the fire. Then you can ensure we destroy the piece of paper afterwards."

That seemed a little redundant to Kris. What was he going to use his code on now the bar was toast? Maybe on the new system? But he wasn't even sure PJ would rehire him.

Still, he shrugged. "Okay," he said. "Why? Do you think it was an inside job?"

"Someone used a code to access the downstairs of the bar at approximately two thirty am," Epstein said. He threw both Kris and PJ apologetic looks. "That's when we estimate the fire started. We have to rule everything out."

Kris felt a little sick. He tried to remind himself they didn't know anything yet. However, it was difficult not to worry. Surely nobody he knew had set this fire?

He scribbled down his six-digit code and handed it over to Epstein. He then slowly opened up a battered-looking tablet and, from what Kris could see without peering too obviously, fumbled his way through a couple of emails. Presumably he was looking for one from the security company.

"How's the restoration going?" Kris asked PJ convivially to break the awkward silence. "Is the building good to repair or do you need to start from scratch?"

PJ sighed and rubbed his chin. "No, the contractors are confident they can save the bar. But the insurance company are putting a hold on the claim until the investigation is closed."

"Oh, well, hopefully that won't be for much…longer…"

Kris trailed off as Epstein stood, handing both his tablet and the bit of paper Kris had written on over the desk to Bishop. Bishop raised his eyebrows and took both items, looking between the two. Then he raised his eyebrows and turned his eyes on Kris.

"Mr. Novak," he said. "Is there *anything* you would like to amend about your previous statement? Now would be the time."

"Er, no," Kris said. "Why?"

"Because," Bishop said, "according to this log, the number you just wrote down was the last to be punched into the door leading into the bar from the back corridor."

Coldness washed over Kris. "W-what?" he stammered.

"Are you sure?" PJ asked. He stood and held his hand out to Bishop. But Epstein intercepted and took the tablet and piece of notepaper back.

"Sorry, Mr. Maddox, I, uh…" He looked over his glasses, then through them again, like he wanted to be sure of what he was double-checking. "Yes. We have it logged that Mr. Maddox's code was used at just before twelve thirty am on the door from the bar, then into his office and then on the door to exit the building to the parking lot about half an hour later. Then…the code you just gave us was used to leave the bar area at about one thirty, then to access the parking lot…then to come back inside again approximately an hour after that."

Kris's whole body was vibrating. "No," he managed to utter. "No, I just went up to my apartment. I never left the building."

Epstein frowned, making notes in his little book. "Is there anyone who can confirm that?"

"Well, no," Kris said. He could feel the panic rising in his chest. What the hell? They couldn't seriously be suggesting that *Kris* set the fire, could they? "I-I live alone."

"Kris?" PJ said. When Kris turned to look at his former boss, he was horrified to see he was tearful. "Why?"

"Why?" Kris spluttered. "What do you mean, why? I didn't do this. That's insane! Why would I torch my job *and* home! And *why-*" he added emphatically, "the hell would I leave the building and then come back an hour later? If I did this – which I didn't – why wouldn't I just do it when everyone was gone?" He threw his hands out. "And why would I *then* go up to my apartment and wait to be roasted alive?"

"Perhaps you went to get supplies?" Epstein said with a frown, still looking at his tablet. Like he was trying to work out a math problem, not accusing Kris of fucking arson.

"Why isn't there another code entry to show anyone leaving the building?" Bishop asked.

A wave of dizziness rushed over Kris. "Huh?" he asked.

Epstein pointed at his screen. "The captain's right," he said, shaking his head. "There's nothing to show anyone leaving. There's just that single code used at two thirty."

PJ shoved his hands through his hair. "You," he cried, addressing Kris. "All those ideas you came to talk to me about. Were you...did you think if you did a little fire damage, I'd listen to your ideas?"

"PJ!" Kris shrieked in utter disbelief. "No, that's – *no.* I don't know why my code is showing up on the log, but I swear to you, *I didn't do this."*

"Mr. Novak," Epstein interrupted, his voice firm. "Did you give your code to anyone? Or leave it lying around?"

"No," said Kris, certain of that. He'd never even written it down, as far as he knew. But it was just his mom's birthday, so maybe someone had worked it out? He pressed his fingers to his temples. This didn't make *any* sense.

"Are you seeing anyone or did you let anyone into your apartment who might have found a way to acquire your code?"

"I-" Kris tried to blink the tears back from his eyes. "I don't think so. I mean, I wasn't seeing anyone – I mean, I'm not. I'm not seeing anyone." Bishop's eyes narrowed. Kris felt like he was under a microscope. He could practically feel the betrayal radiating off PJ from the other side of Epstein. "I didn't do this," Kris said weakly. "I swear."

There came a knock at the door. "Not now," Bishop said loud and clear. But the door opened anyway.

"I'm sorry, Captain." Kris felt sick with relief at the sound of Remi's voice. "But I heard shouting. Is everything okay?"

Bishop frowned at Kris again. Suddenly, Kris didn't feel so relieved that Remi was there.

"Actually, Washington," Bishop said. "Come in and close the door. We might have a couple of questions for you."

25

REMI

Remi had no idea what was going on, but Kris looked upset and Bishop looked grim. Epstein stood from his chair and offered it to Remi, moving to stand on the other side of the desk with Bishop.

Remi arched an eyebrow, but Bishop extended his hand, indicating Remi should sit in between Kris and his boss. Remi only just noticed PJ was as white as a sheet.

Remi had a bad feeling about this.

"Washington," Bishop said. "You were aware that Mr. Novak lived at the building on Jefferson and Row before we arrived on the scene, is that correct?"

"Uh, yeah?" he said. "I mean, yes, sir. Kris is the younger brother of my best friend, so when I worked out the address was taking us to that bar, I remembered that he lived there."

"So you know each other well?" Epstein asked.

"What does this have to do-" Kris began, but Bishop held up his hand.

"Please, Mr. Novak," he said. "I'd rather not have to ask you to leave the room."

Remi looked between Bishop and Kris. Kris looked distraught. Remi desperately wanted to hold his hand, but of course, he couldn't. Not yet. Bishop knew his dad well enough through mutual friends that there was no way it wouldn't get back to him.

"Uh," Remi said, shaking his head, trying to compose a response to Epstein's question.

In some ways, he knew Kris in the most intimate ways you *could* know someone. He knew what his skin tasted like and the beautiful expression on his face when he came. He had also been around him pretty much his whole life. But *know* him? His most private thoughts? The ins and outs of what made him tick?

"We weren't really friends before," Remi admitted. "But as I think you all know, I offered Kris my spare room after the incident. So, now, yeah, I guess we know each other a lot more."

"Are you romantically involved?" Bishop asked.

Remi was so unprepared for the question he couldn't help but splutter. *"What?"* he cried, feeling like the temperature in the room had shot up ten degrees. "No, of course not, no. We're just friends."

"You seemed particularly distressed when we arrived at the scene?" Bishop asked.

Remi blinked, aware his expression was one of incredulity. Why the hell was his boss acting like this? "Yeah, because it was my best bud's brother inside," he said. "I've known him since he was a kid. That's all. What – what is this about? Why are you asking about how we know each other?"

"Because *my* security code was used to gain access to the bar just before the fire started," Kris spat out. He had his arms and legs crossed over and tears were shining in his eyes.

"Has Mr. Novak ever discussed anything to do with arson or starting fires in general?" Epstein asked.

Remi put his hands on his head. "What the hell? No! He's – he obviously didn't do this. We *rescued* him from that building. Besides, there's really not that much skill in starting a fire. You just strike a match. Why would he need to ask a firefighter about that?" He scowled at Epstein, then Bishop. "Come on, guys, this is my career here. I'd never help someone with arson."

Epstein held his hands up. "We just have to cover all the bases here."

"So I got tips on how to start a fire," Kris said, barely holding himself together. His voice was shaking and one of the tears escaped, falling down his cheek. "Then I left the bar after closing, came back, set fire to the place, then jogged upstairs to call 911. Is that right? Is that what you're saying?"

"Mr. Novak," Bishop said, holding up his hands.

"No, no!" Kris all but shrieked. "I want to make sure I get this straight! So I torch the place, destroying my job and everything I own, so I can – what was it? Take over the bar with all my crazy ideas for the relaunch? That's insane! It's *insane!*"

"Kris," Remi said urgently, placing a hand on his knee. He quickly took it away though, in case it gave the wrong impression. "Calm down. There's got to be a logical explanation for all this."

Kris gave him a heartbroken look. "Yeah, I just gave it to y'all. It makes perfect sense, doesn't it? Don't worry," he added, turning to Bishop. "I made the bit up about asking for help. Any *idiot* can start a fire and I wouldn't want to endanger Remi's career."

"None of this makes sense," Remi insisted. But as he looked around the room, he was met with Bishop and Epstein's skeptical faces and PJ's angry one. "Oh, come on, y'all!" he cried. "You don't actually think Kris did this?"

Bishop sighed and leaned forward on his desk. "You and I both know what some people are capable off, son," he said sadly.

"Not *Kris!*" Remi said. "I know he wouldn't do this."

"Because he's your boyfriend?" PJ asked. "Or at least he's got you wrapped around his finger." He shook his head. "I know what he's like, don't take it personally."

"No," Remi said firmly. "He's not my boyfriend and I wouldn't do that. I wouldn't let myself be...what? Seduced into committing a crime? I'm not that stupid. And to what end?"

"Look," Kris said loudly. He hastily wiped his face and sniffed. "Are you actually going to charge me with something? Are you getting the cops involved?"

Epstein sighed. "No, Mr. Novak. Not at this moment. But I think it's best that you don't leave town."

"Washington will keep an eye on him," Bishop said. He arched an eyebrow at Remi. "Won't you?"

"Uh, I guess," he said. He knew his boss and Epstein were just going by the book, but fuck! This was awful.

"Can I go now?" Kris asked.

"Yes," Epstein said.

He'd barely gotten the word out of his mouth before Kris bolted from his chair, lunging for the door and dashing back out into the corridor.

"Kris," Remi called, chasing after him without even thinking. "Hey, wait up. Hey!"

Kris stopped in the hall, hugging himself tightly with his gaze on the carpet.

Remi stopped in front of him. He made to touch his arm, but then he pulled his hand back. "What the hell?" he asked in disbelief. "How was it your security code used? Why are they accusing you of this?"

"Who cares?" Kris said with a mirthless laugh. "There's no evidence to the contrary."

"No, it's all circumstantial," said Remi. "And-" he leaned closer "-*I* care. You know that."

Kris scoffed. "Oh, don't bother," he said sadly. "This isn't your problem. It's mine."

"What?" Remi asked, genuinely confused. "What are you talking about? Of course it's my problem."

Kris looked up to the door of the common room. Through the glass, Remi could see his colleagues trying not to be too obvious as they watched the two of them talking.

"No, it's fine," Kris said, shaking his head. "You've got your career and your reputation on the line. You don't want anything to do with me."

"Kris," Remi hissed. "That's bullshit. Why are you saying that?"

"Because it's true," Kris said. He finally looked Remi in the eye with half a hollow smile. "Don't worry. I won't do anything stupid in front of your friends. We wouldn't want them to think you're some kind of queer fire starter, would we now?"

Remi took a step back. He felt like he'd been punched in the gut.

"Kris?" he said, a pleading tone to the word. "Where's this coming from? I'm sorry I couldn't tell the whole truth in there, but you know why. I have to sort this out with my folks first. I have absolutely no doubt in my mind that you're innocent."

"How generous of you," Kris said. He rocked on his heels and hugged himself tighter, tears pooling in his eyes. "I'm sorry. I have all this shit to deal with, but I don't really feel like being something you have to 'sort out' right now. I'll see you later."

He pushed his way through the door to the common room before Remi even registered what had happened. "Kris, wait," he called out belatedly. But Kris was already halfway across, ignoring all the stares he was getting from the team. Remi chased after him, hoping he could stop him out front before he ran off. "Kris!"

"Ohh, lover's tiff?" Travis said with a snigger.

Remi stopped and spun on his heels. *Fuck you,* he snarled. He managed to grab the back of a chair to stop himself from lunging for the older guy. Jesus, he needed to get it together.

Travis looked horrified. So did everyone else in the room. "Wow, dude?" Channing said.

"Is everything all right?" Greg asked from the sofa.

Remi balled up his fists and shook his head. "Swell," he managed to grind out. He could deal with his colleagues later. Right now, he needed to stop Kris. He turned around and dashed after him, slamming his way through the doors into the garage.

But Kris was nowhere to be seen.

He wasn't outside either. God fucking damn it. He must have run as soon as he'd hit the sidewalk.

Remi felt all churned up. He'd obviously missed something. It was bad enough that Kris was being accused of arson, but now things had somehow gone sideways between them, too.

Remi had absolutely no doubt there was something weird going on. Someone must have gotten hold of Kris's code or something. He'd seen the nightmares, the way Kris had cried when he found out the attack was arson, how delighted he'd been working on new ideas for when the bar reopened. There was no way he'd done this.

But then they'd gone and asked personal questions and…*shit.* Why hadn't Remi just told the truth? Why was he still so terrified to come out? That would have been horrible, though, coming out like that. He wanted to do it properly, not be bounced into it by people he didn't really know.

Did Kris think he wasn't serious about committing to him? Was *Kris* no longer interested in being together? What had he meant by all those things he'd said about Remi's career and reputation? About Remi not caring or feeling like this was his problem because it was happening to Kris?

Remi spent the rest of his shift in a distracted state. His colleagues appeared to realize something was deeply wrong with him and left him alone. The hours dragged by. They didn't even get any calls to pass the time, and although he went to the break room for some peace and quiet, Remi couldn't sleep.

He thought about calling his mom. He thought about just coming out on Facebook and getting it over with in one fell swoop. But he didn't do either of those things. He had to speak face-to-face with his family about this. It was desperately important to him that they understood. And he didn't want to trivialize his coming out by just dumping it on social media then running away.

What he did do was message Kris. Several times. But Kris wasn't responding. Remi could see the texts were being delivered, but not once did he see the moving dots pop up to indicate Kris was typing a reply, let alone actually sending one.

Worry swirled in his gut, getting stronger as the small hours of the morning ticked by. Kris wasn't something Remi had to 'sort out.' He wasn't an inconvenience or whatever it was he had misinterpreted. He was deeply important to Remi. Remi was *besotted* with the guy. He couldn't stand the thought that he had hurt him in any way, but the fact that he had was painfully obvious by the time the sun came up.

Remi couldn't even get anything more out of Captain Bishop about the investigation. He was obviously pissed at Remi when he had shown PJ and Epstein to the front door after the meeting. Then he had stayed in his office, refusing to come out and alleviate any of Remi's anxieties.

Eight am couldn't come any sooner. Remi had his bag ready to go, staring at the clock until it struck the hour. And then he was out of there. He didn't even bother saying goodbye to his team, who all knew he was in a thunderous mood anyway, heading straight for his car. The sooner he saw Kris again, the sooner he could make everything better.

He realized something was seriously wrong when he opened the bug screen to get to his front door and something toppled out from between the two doors onto the porch.

It was Kris's spare key.

Remi snatched it up. "Oh, no," he murmured, hastily jamming his own key into the lock. "No, no, no. Kris, what have you done?"

The house was unnaturally quiet when he finally made his way inside. Remi dumped his bag on the sofa and dashed upstairs to the spare room without even taking his shoes off. His heart was pounding, knowing what he was likely to find before he even saw it. Still, it was a kick in the gut when he reached Kris's room and the door was open, the bed made, and all of Kris's possessions were gone. Even Tay Tay, the fancy goldfish, was no longer in her tank.

"Fuck!" Remi yelled. His phone was in his hand, dialing Kris's number in a flash. But the damn call rang out, so he tried again. And again. "Kris," he cried, leaving a voicemail on the third attempt. "I don't know what's going on, but please talk to me. Why is all your stuff gone? Please, whatever I did wrong, I want to fix it. Just tell me where you are."

But another hour went by in which Remi heard nothing. Despite his lack of sleep, he wasn't the least bit tired. He had to fix this, now.

He started making more calls.

26

KRIS

Kris poked listlessly at his collard greens. He hadn't had any appetite for over twenty-four hours now. Not that this had deterred Hunter Duke in any way.

"Do you want some more mashed potatoes?" he fretted as he dished up the pot roast he had spent most of that Sunday slaving over. His dining room table was groaning under the weight of all the pans he had laid out with the greens, black-eyed peas, cornbread and macaroni and cheese.

Kris did his best to smile at his gracious host. "No, thank you. Honestly, this looks amazing." He managed to swallow a forkful of food, even though it churned in his stomach.

He also attempted not to acknowledge Chase sitting next to him, his expression full of pity. Or the way he and Hunter squeezed hands under the table, no doubt thinking up the best way to try and cheer Kris up next. He appreciated their efforts, but he wasn't done wallowing in his misery just yet.

They weren't the only ones on a mission, though. Lyla, Chase's five-year-old daughter, hopped down from her chair, her cloud of red curly hair bouncing as she skipped up to Kris's side. With her came Trooper, the seven-month-old three-legged Labrador puppy who served as her constant companion. She was wearing a Spiderman T-shirt and Wonder Woman pants. Apparently, super-heroes were her favorite at the moment.

She tugged on Kris's T-shirt. "Uncle Kris, why are you still sad? Do you want to play with Trooper? His special power is To Make You Not Be Sad. Isn't it, Trooper?"

Trooper thumped his tail on the floor to affirm that, yes, this was indeed his superpower.

Kris sighed and smiled as best he could for her. "I'm sorry, hon. I'm being a stick-in-the-mud. Can I get a cuddle to maybe cheer me up?"

"Sure!" Lyla cried. "I bet I can eat more greens than you."

"I bet you can't," Kris cried.

She scrambled up into his lap, and, once he'd handed her the fork from her own plate, they ate off his plate together. Reluctantly, he could admit that with her encouragement, he was able to tolerate a few more mouthfuls.

"Daddy says greens make you strong like Black Widow," she chatted on. "She has red hair like me. I'm going to be a superspy or a chef when I grow up. Or a soccer player."

"You can be anything you want, sweetie," said Kris. He glanced at Chase, who was beaming at him. Kris was never sure if he talked to Lyla okay. Kids were kind of a mystery to him. But he also trusted Chase would set him right if he got anything wrong.

For a while, they spoke about this and that. Apparently, the hospital was going through some bad times, which obviously affected Hunter's work as a physician assistant at the doctor's office. It was all a big scandal, apparently. From the way things currently stood, it looked like Hidden Creek Memorial was going to be scaled down and lose its urgent care unit.

And here Kris was moping over a broken heart.

"Obviously, you're welcome to stay here as long as you like," Hunter insisted, like they were picking up from an earlier topic.

Kris sighed. He was incredibly grateful that Hunter had been willing to put him up for a couple of nights, but he knew he couldn't linger. This was why he hadn't accepted his offer of a room in the first place. *Chase* hadn't even moved in yet, even though Kris knew they had talked about it. Kris just felt like he was totally intruding on this little family who was just starting their journey together.

But to escape Remi's place quickly, he had taken it. They had even set up a large plastic storage box with water for Tay Tay to swim around in rather than her temporary Tupperware. This wouldn't last more than a few days without supplies, but maybe by then, Kris could work up the courage to ask Leon to rescue the tank from Remi's and install it in their apartment. If they weren't able to let Kris stay, they might at least be able to house his fish for a while.

"What did Remi actually *say?*" Chase asked, again.

Kris could tell he was desperate for them to patch things up. Kris had only admitted there might have been a little something going on now that it was over. Chase had interpreted that as there was something worth saving. But Kris knew better.

He speared a strip of beef and wasted a few moments pushing it around in his potatoes. "It wasn't so much what he said, but the way he acted. Like, I knew it was stupid to think this could actually work between us. But urgh. I just felt so damn small in that office. He was so *offended.*"

"But you also said he's not out of the closet yet?" Hunter asked.

"And it was his boss that accused him of helping start the fire," chimed in Chase. "He was just defending himself and worrying about getting fired."

"And that he stood up for you to them over the alarm code and how ridiculous you setting fire to your job and home would be," Hunter added.

"And," Chase said, waving his fork at Kris, "that he ran after you and didn't seem to know he'd done something wrong."

"But he *did,"* Kris said, trying not to shout with Lyla in his lap. She looked up at him and frowned anyway.

"Who did what?" she asked.

"Honey," said Chase sweetly. "Why don't you go play outside for a bit before your bath?"

She gasped and wriggled down from Kris's lap faster than he could blink. "Come on, Trooper," she cried, already running for the backyard. "Let's go see if the volcano has erupted yet!"

Chase smiled at his daughter's enthusiasm for her imaginary expedition.

"What exactly did he do that was so awful?" Hunter asked. Kris's expression must have been bad because Hunter quickly held up his hands. "I'm not saying it *wasn't* awful. Just, well, do you think you might have taken something a bit personally or out of context?"

Chase reached forward and grabbed Kris's hand. "Because you've been through a really shit time, we know that, we do."

"Thanks for reminding me," Kris grumbled.

Chase squeezed his hand. It only reminded Kris of his and Remi's first kiss. But Chase wouldn't know that.

"All I'm saying is you're allowed to be sensitive and raw," Chase explained. "But maybe if we can work out what button in particular he pushed, we can work on fixing this with you."

Kris huffed and laid down his fork, giving up on his food and gulping down some iced tea instead. "It's my fault," he said. "I expected too much. Not just from Remi, from work as well. I'm just…not made for those things."

Hunter frowned and tilted his head. "What? A job you like and a partner you love?"

"I don't *love* Remi!" Kris spluttered. "My god, it's just a stupid crush from forever ago. That's why it was never going to last. I was in love with the *idea* of him, sure. And now I'm just mourning the reality that it's not how it is."

Hunter rolled his eyes. "Dude, you are *so young,*" he said with affection. "Stop acting like your life is over at twenty-one! You don't have to have everything right now."

"But that's the point," Kris said, trying not to let his fear come through in his voice too much. "I have *nothing.* No job, no home, no boyfriend, no goals in life. All I have is a pet fish! The only reason I even have clothes is because I somehow have awesome friends."

"There you have it," said Chase excitedly, clicking his fingers at Kris. Hunter rubbed his back and smiled at him, but Chase was still looking at Kris. "That's what you have. *Friends.*"

Hunter nodded. "My mom always used to say, 'Show me your friends, and I'll tell you who you are.'"

"And if your friends are awesome, so are you," said Chase proudly.

Kris chuckled and had to accept the compliment just a tiny bit. "Okay," he said reluctantly. "I guess my life isn't a hundred percent bad. But that doesn't mean anything is going to work between me and Remi. You should have *seen* his face when PJ asked if he was my boyfriend. He was horrified."

Kris took a moment as a lump rose in his throat and tears burned the back of his eyes. Fuck, he was an idiot to think Remi would ever want to be seen in public with a silly twink like him. Remi would want some other hunky guy he could go down the gym with, like Hunter. Not someone trivial and slutty without a brain cell in his head.

"He's also been calling and texting nonstop," Chase said gently, rubbing the back of Kris's hand. "It's not like I've been looking at your phone, but it's kind of hard to miss."

"Why don't you just give him a chance to explain?" Hunter suggested kindly. Urgh, Kris hated when he was all reasonable and soothing. It was so hard to ignore.

He felt his lips betray him and twitch with half a hopeful smile. God, he would give anything for them to be right. After only thirty-six hours together, he knew he didn't want to give Remi up now he'd finally, unbelievably gone that step further with him. But even with his friend's hopeful faces looking back at him, he still couldn't truly convince himself that Remi would really endanger his perfect straight life by coming out of the closet for Kris.

Like he said, he was hoping to do it for his own sake. But now Kris was entangled in more trouble, Remi was bound to see there were better, more compatible options out there for him.

Kris kept going over this business with the fire in his head. He *knew* he hadn't given his login code to anyone else. So how had someone gotten in to start the blaze, and why? He kept coming back to the fact that it had to be a hate crime, possibly from one of the people who had been sending through those nasty messages. The idea that Kris could be involved in anything that homophobic made him sick. What if people thought he was one of those gays who secretly hated himself or something? That would devastate him.

Adding that to the crushing disappointment of realizing having Remi as a real boyfriend was probably something that had only ever existed in his dreams made him thoroughly miserable indeed.

He suddenly became aware that his melancholy thoughts had made him go quiet. He shook himself and laughed, rubbing the unshed tears from his eyes and pretending to flick his hair. "Oh, she's gone all dramatic," he cooed. But his friends weren't fooled by the looks of it.

Thankfully, he was spared any further questioning by a knock at the door. Hunter blinked and looked between Chase and Kris. "Don't worry. I'll get that. It's probably Girl Scouts selling cookies or something."

They watched as Hunter left the dining room. Kris bit his lip and fiddled with his fork again, hoping Chase wouldn't push him too hard on Remi. Kris felt like if he really looked hard enough at how he felt, he might have to admit his heart was breaking.

"Uh, Kris?" Hunter's voice floated from down the hall. "Could you come here?"

Kris glanced at Chase with a frown, but he was met with a matching look of confusion. Chase shrugged. "Do you want me to say you're dead?"

Kris snorted, the joke cracking through a thin layer of his self-pity. "No, baby, it's cool," he said, getting to his feet. "I'll go see what's up."

He crossed paths with Hunter in the hall as he was walking back to the dining room. Kris raised an eyebrow at him, but Hunter just shook his head and jutted his chin toward the partially closed door. Fuck. Was it the police, come to take him away? They couldn't *really* charge him with arson, could they? He hadn't *done* anything.

Kris kept walking, refusing to indulge in the hope that was attempting to blossom in his chest. Because there was only really one person he wished might be on the other side of that door, despite the logical side of his brain telling him otherwise.

Therefore, he couldn't really stop himself from gasping when he pulled the door inward, bringing a gust of warm evening air inside as he was faced with the sight of Remi Washington, dressed up in a shirt and dress pants, holding a dozen red roses in his hands and wearing a look of naked hope on his face.

27

R E M I

The first thing Remi had done was call his younger sister, Darcy. He had to admit he'd skirted around the identity of the person involved, the specific nature of the problem and, as much as he'd been able, used gender-neutral pronouns. He was sure Darcy hadn't been fooled one bit and was holding back a million questions, but in the end, they had come up with a kind of plan together.

Then had come the really hard part. Finding Kris. Remi had started by texting Leon, trying to casually ask if he'd seen his brother without setting off any alarm bells. The last thing Remi wanted was for Leon to think Kris was missing. But Leon was stressing about the imminent arrival of his and Ava's baby, so didn't question Remi too much. However, he also didn't know where Kris might be.

Without having anyone else's number, Remi decided to get hands dirty. First, he drove to Rocket to see if Kris might have met any of his friends for brunch there again, seeing as it was a Sunday. Unfortunately, he was nowhere in sight, so Remi had been prepared to try the coffee shop or some of the other eateries in town. But then he'd remembered JJ's.

Feeling only slightly foolish, he'd driven to the grocery store with the hopes of talking to the same checkout clerk, Chase, who had encouraged Remi in the first place. But he wasn't on the shop floor, and a quick word with one of the other clerks confirmed Chase didn't work Sundays. Remi then asked about deliveries from the Miele farm, thinking of the other guy, Gabe. Apparently, they weren't due to make a delivery until tomorrow. That was okay. Remi could still work with that.

Rather than wait around for Gabe to maybe show up, Remi drove to the Miele farm. Everyone knew where that was, even if he hadn't visited before. He felt a bit nervous walking up to the front door and knocking, but his desperate need to set things right with Kris propelled him onward.

The door was opened by a cute guy in his mid-thirties who smiled and nodded at Remi. From what Remi recalled of Orion Miele from school, he'd say there was some family resemblance there.

"Hi, can I help you?" the guy asked pleasantly.

Remi rubbed his palms together and tried not to look too nervous. "Hey, I'm sorry to bother you, but I'm in a bit of a jam. I'm looking for a buddy of mine, Kris Novak. I'm worried he might be in some kind of trouble." That much was true. He was genuinely concerned Kris might do something really dumb while he was in such a bad state. Remi would never forgive himself if that happened. "He's friends with a guy who works for the Miele farm. Gabe…something?"

"Spicer?" the man said. Then he smiled fondly. "Yeah. He's also dating my nephew, Orion."

"Ryan Miele?" Remi asked cheerfully. "Aww yeah, I played ball at school with him. Great guy. I'm Remi Washington, by the way."

"Pete Miele," said Pete, offering his hand out so they could shake. He had a firm grip. Remi appreciated that in a person. "You said you were looking for Kris? You don't mean Kris from Bottom's Up, do you?"

Remi's heart skipped a beat. "Yeah, actually, I do. You know him?"

Pete nodded thoughtfully. "He helped me out when I was *real* low a few months back." He smiled, a fond expression on his face as he glanced off to look across one of the fields surrounding the farm. "If I was fifteen years younger," he said wistfully, shaking his head.

Remi couldn't help the prickle of jealousy that flared through him. But that was totally irrational. Of course Kris had a past with other guys. It was the present that mattered now.

And the future.

Whatever emotion had flitted across Remi's face, Pete caught it. "Ah," he said sympathetically. Then he gave Remi the warmest smile and nodded, and Remi knew they were okay. "I'm afraid he's not here and neither's Gabe. He finished work on my mom's yard about a week ago. He's probably at home with Ryan. If you hang on, I'll give him a call?"

Remi exhaled in relief. "That would be great, man. I really appreciate it." For some reason, Remi felt like he could trust Pete. Besides, he was tired of hiding, and having someone realize Kris was more to Remi than just a friend felt so fucking good. "Kris isn't picking up my messages. I know he's getting them, but, uh, he might be more willing to talk to another friend right now."

Pete narrowed his eyes. "You fuck up?" he asked.

Remi bit his lip and nodded. "Think so, sir," he admitted sheepishly. "I'm trying to make it right."

Pete had pulled out his phone and pressed a number to call. "Roses," he said pointedly to Remi before the call connected. "A dozen of them, red. I think my mom might be able to help you out there." His eyebrows went up as the other person picked up. "Ryan, how's it going?"

Pete turned back and wandered further into the house, leaving the door open. Remi stepped back off the porch to give him some privacy. He had butterflies in his stomach, acutely aware that time was of the essence. Kris had already been upset for almost twenty-four hours. This was a horrible way to start their relationship. Remi needed to do whatever it took to make this right as fast as possible.

He suspected that involved coming out. He needed to pull his thumb out of his ass and just do it. Remi's dad was going to take some time to adjust, no matter what. It was just a case of how bad his reaction would be. Manageable or horrified? Remi really couldn't tell which direction he would go.

Pete came back after a few minutes with a thumbs-up as he pocketed the phone again. "Ryan was with Gabe, and once I explained the situation, Gabe was willing to say where Kris has gone. He also assured me he's okay," he added, much to Remi's relief. Then he held a finger up. "Gabe threatened to beat your ass if you're going to be a douche, though."

Gabe Spicer was less than half Remi's size, but his protectiveness warmed Remi's heart. "I'm going to do everything I can to be a gentleman," Remi assured him. He had to take a second to clear his throat after a lump threatened to rise. "Kris is very important to me, sir."

Pete leaned over and squeezed Remi's shoulder. "Good," he said. "Here's what you do."

And that was how, several hours later, Remi had found himself on the porch of Hunter Duke's house, dressed in black pants and a blue button-down, twelve beautiful red roses wrapped in paper clutched in his hands. Kris didn't look quite like his usual fabulous self. There were dark circles under his eyes, he was wearing full-length jeans and his tank top was a simple one with a cartoon cat on it. But even without any makeup on or wax in his hair, he looked beyond gorgeous to Remi. His heart flipped in his chest at the mere sight of him.

Kris's expression was one of complete surprise as he stepped out onto the porch, allowing the front and screen doors to swing shut behind him. "Remi?" he asked.

Remi had so many eloquent things he wanted to say. He had even rehearsed some words on the drive over. But they all flew out of his head at the sight of his forlorn lover. "I fucked up," he blurted, trying not to let his desperation show. "I should have told PJ we were dating and I should have told Epstein to shove the idea you would ever start that fire up his ass. I should have acted like your goddamned man and not let irrational fears get the better of me."

Kris's mouth dropped open. "What?" he whispered.

Remi shifted on his feet. A drop of sweat from the heat and his own nerves ran down his spine. "That is," he said, "if it's not too late? If you still want to date. If...if you still want to be my boyfriend?"

Kris's arms flew up to hug himself and he blinked rapidly, his silvery-blue eyes suddenly glassy. "But...why?" he asked.

Remi shook his head. "I don't have a good enough excuse," he said. "The official investigation, the accusation, I guess it threw me for a loop. I thought about my dad finding out I'm bi from some arson report, which is stupid because how could he? And I thought if I tried to say I knew you better than it seemed I did – you know – basically how could I know you that well if we weren't dating, right? And I was worrying about my job, especially when the captain implied I could have helped start the fire and, fuck, that was selfish of me, and-"

"No," said Kris softly. But it was enough to stop Remi from rambling.

"No?" he said, his anxiety immediately spiking.

Kris visibly swallowed. "Why would you want to be my boyfriend?"

Remi was so stunned he was momentarily rendered mute. "W-what?" he eventually managed to stammer. "What do you mean? Because you're amazing. Because I'm crazy for you. Unless…fuck, if that's not what you want, I guess-"

"NO!" Kris shouted, making Remi jump.

He wasn't the only one. The sudden movement made him realize that they had an audience at one of the windows. A small red-headed girl was watching them with her chin in her hands, a smallish golden Labrador panting by her side. When she saw Remi glance her way, she waved then gave him an enthusiastic thumbs-up.

Kris glanced behind and waved sheepishly back at the child, then he looked back at Remi. "No," he said again, slightly calmer. "That's *not* not what I want. Uh, I, oh god, Remi." He rubbed his hands over his face, his expression wretched. "Okay, the truth is… the truth is I've had a crush on you forever. And I mean *forever*. I realized I was gay when I was thirteen because I just couldn't get over you and it's so pathetic I didn't want to tell you. But I just couldn't imagine this could be real and it was so easy to believe you didn't really want to date me yesterday, or come out or any of that stuff because I'm not worth all that trouble, and-"

It was Remi's turn to interrupt. He stepped forward, careful of the roses in his hand, and flung his arms around Kris, burying his face against Kris's neck and inhaling his sweet scent deeply. From through the glass, Remi heard a faint girlish squeal of delight.

"You are worth *all* the trouble," he insisted. He would like to have pretended his voice was muffled from his mouth being snuggled against Kris's soft skin, but there was no denying his emotions were getting the better of him. "I'm so sorry I made you doubt that even for a second. I still want to come out to my family, soon. But I don't want to go through something like yesterday again. I – so – uh – yeah. Kris Novak, would you like to be my official boyfriend?"

Kris leaned back to look Remi in the eye. Then he cupped either side of his face and stepped on his tiptoes to kiss him gently. "I would love to be your boyfriend, Remi Washington," he said with such sincerity it made Remi's heart melt.

"So," said Remi devilishly. "Forever, huh?"

Kris swatted his arm and swooned, the back of his hand placed against his forehead. Then he made a show of taking the roses from Remi's hand. "Oh, honey bear. These are for me, I take it?" he asked. Remi nodded, resting both hands on Kris's hips. Kris touched the nearest rose to his nose and inhaled slowly, a smile spreading over his face. "They're gorgeous," he murmured. "And, yes. Forever. You are and always have been, a stone-cold hottie, as well as an extremely sweet man."

"So are you," Remi said, swaying them gently back and forth. "I'm sorry it took me so long to realize that."

For a while, they simply embraced on the porch. Remi briefly worried who might see them, then he chose not to care. This was just the push he needed to be honest with his family – his dad especially – sooner rather than later. For now, he just took all the comfort and pleasure he could from having Kris back in his arms.

"So," said Kris after a while. "How brave are you feeling?"

Remi smiled and turned his head to face him. "Pretty brave," he said confidently.

"Brave enough to meet some of my friends and their very rambunctious kid?" Kris asked. He fluttered his eyelashes and flicked his eyes toward Hunter's front door.

This was it. Remi was officially, publicly, proudly about to announce he was Kris's boyfriend.

"Hell yeah," was all he said.

He was ready.

KRIS

When Kris stepped back into the spare room, the first thing he noticed was the black cat had snuck her way back into the house again. She was curled around the corner of the fishless tank, looking forlorn. But at the sight of Tay Tay in her box, she sat up with interest.

"Hey, Kitty," Kris said warily. "Good Kitty."

But the cat simply regarded them as he gently submerged Tay Tay's box back into her aquarium. Kris watched anxiously as she swam out into the bigger body of water. She came up to the glass where Kitty pressed her nose against the side. Fish and cat looked at each other for a moment. Then Kitty settled down, closing her eyes again by the side of the tank, and Tay Tay swished her golden tail and fins, swimming back in between the plants. It seemed they had reached a truce.

"Why do I get the feeling that cat is here to stay?" Remi came up behind Kris and wrapped his arms around Kris's body, kissing his neck, then resting his cheek on top of Kris's hair.

Kris watched his little fish happily flit about and absently stroked

Kitty's head. "I don't think she's the only one," he said, then bit his lip.

Remi hummed against his neck. "I'm so glad you're home," he said.

Kris's heart fluttered at that word. Because, as terrifying as it was, this *did* feel like home. Remi had outdone himself, spending his afternoon baking a peach cobbler that had made the house smell delicious as soon as Kris had stepped through the door. It was warm and welcoming and everything he wanted in a place to live.

He felt so content. After their reconciliation, he and Remi had rejoined Hunter and Chase to have dinner together. Chase could barely contain his excitement at the turn of events and Lyla had immediately introduced herself to 'Uncle Remi.' They all accepted Remi without question, and Remi had not only been charming, but he'd also held Kris's hand throughout the whole meal.

Then he had insisted on taking Kris home, picking up the bags from Hunter's spare room that Kris had failed to unpack and loading them into the car. The drive had been a quiet one, the sexual tension between them mounting the longer they were alone. Kris was amazed they had made it all the way upstairs to his room with his stuff before one of them had cracked and put their hands on the other.

Remi's lips found their way back down to Kris's neck as his hands slipped under Kris's tank top, caressing his hips and stomach. Kris shivered and moaned, letting his body melt back against Remi's hard chest. He hadn't thought he would feel this again.

Without warning, Remi suddenly swooped down and picked Kris up in a bridal carry. Kris shrieked and giggled, clinging to Remi's neck as he carefully took him out of the spare room, trusting Kitty to be left with Tay Tay as they moved into Remi's room.

"This was how you rescued me," Kris whispered, looking into Remi's beautiful brown eyes. "My hero."

Remi kissed him gently as they crossed over to the bed. "My savior," he whispered back.

Kris allowed himself to be undressed by Remi's steady hands. It was hard to believe this was still only one of the first times Remi had bedded a guy. He was confident in every action, which was hot as hell for Kris. He lay back and watched Remi strip him naked, kissing his way along Kris's thighs, belly and collarbones.

"You tease," Kris whispered as Remi sucked on one of his nipples and ignored his straining cock.

Remi grinned up at him. "Damn right," he told him, his voice husky.

He stood, his gaze not leaving Kris's as he took his time undoing each shirt button, one by one. Kris stroked his leaking cock while he watched. "Yeah, baby," he rasped, drinking his lover's body in with his eyes. "You're so gorgeous, I can't even."

"So are you," Remi said, grinning as he dropped his shirt to the carpet, then made short work of his belt buckle and fly. In one motion, he shoved his pants and underwear to his ankles, then kicked those and his shoes and socks free. Even though there was a playful element as he bounced onto the bed to hover above Kris, the way his hands ran up Kris's body was purely sensual. Unlike their first few times together, this wasn't propelled by lust.

This was making love.

"Come here," Kris said, encouraging Remi down to kiss his lips. With Remi's body gloriously smothering Kris's, Kris found room to slip his hand between their bellies and wrap his fingers around both their cocks, squeezing tight for them to thrust into, side by side. "Is this okay?" he asked.

"Amazing," Remi said with a nod. "Oh, Kris, Kris." He managed to get one hand behind Kris's neck, then spread the other across Kris's lower back while Remi held his weight up with his elbows so he wasn't crushing him. "Baby, you feel so good."

They took their time, sliding together while they kissed, their cocks throbbing as they rubbed against each other and Kris's firm grip. Looking into each other's eyes, they knew when to speed up without talking, increasing the pace and chasing their climaxes together.

"Come with me," Kris whispered, not moving his gaze away from Remi's. "Baby, oh, Remi, you're so gorgeous. Do it, baby. Come all over me."

Remi captured his lips with his own, their kisses desperate as they wailed against each other's mouths, their breaths mingling. Kris came first, gnashing his teeth and digging the fingers of his other hand into Remi's hip. As he spurted white, hot cum over their chests, Remi began doing the same, their seed mixing together.

"Fuck," Remi said with a chuckle. He ran his fingers through Kris's hair and kissed him leisurely. "How are you so great?"

"Practice, baby," Kris said, fluttering his eyes. He had hoped Remi wouldn't be one of those guys who lost his shit at the mention of Kris having previous partners. Sure enough, he just snuggled on top of Kris, squidging their mess together and nibbling at his collarbone.

"Hmm, can't wait to practice more, in that case."

"Practice does make perfect," said Kris sagely.

They kissed until they became too cold and uncomfortable. "Is it usually this messy?" Remi asked. Although he laughed, he did wrinkle his nose.

Kris shrugged and kissed the tip of his nose once it unwrinkled. "With two guys, yeah, it can be. You get used to it."

"Oh, I'm sure I will," said Remi quickly, kissing Kris back.

Kris waggled his eyebrows. "For example, by jumping in the shower together?"

"Ohh, that sounds good," Remi said.

Remi allowed Kris to lead him by the hand into the bathroom where Kris made short work of getting the hot water going. Not that he had spent several hours imagining how they might go about this…

Kris hopped in first, inviting Remi after him where he handed him a round loofah loaded up with shower gel. "Wash my back," he demanded cheekily.

"You are such a brat," Remi huffed, shaking his head. Kris just laughed and turned around.

Remi's hands were heaven as they swept all over him. Soon, Remi ditched the loofah and was just using his hands, skimming his fingers over Kris's spent cock and balls and rubbing the entrance to his hole. Kris moaned wantonly as Remi gently fucked him with his fingers. Kris wasn't going to come again so soon, but it felt gorgeous all the same.

"You're so smooth," Remi said between placing kisses on the side of Kris's neck. He was sure to have a hickey by tomorrow and need to wear a scarf. Or maybe he wouldn't, he thought wickedly.

Remi slipped his fingers out, giving Kris's hole one last caress. Then he hugged Kris from behind, resting his chin on Kris's shoulder. The water ran down both their bodies in soothing little streams.

"What, baby?" Kris asked, hugging him back and looking over his shoulder at him.

Remi bit his lip. "I have a question," he said.

"Shoot," Kris said.

"You're…well, you're extremely well groomed," Remi commented, looking slightly bashful. "And I'm not. Is that something I should think about? The hair, I mean?"

"Aww," Kris couldn't help but coo. He turned in Remi's big arms and cuddled him tightly. "That's so sweet! No, baby, you don't have to if you don't want to. It's just something bottoms are expected to do."

He rolled his eyes. He'd learned that the hard way. It only took one guy complaining of a 'gross' rim job to make you pretty hot on hair removal in all the key areas.

But Remi frowned. "Expected?"

Kris shrugged. "Yeah, the guy getting fucked is generally expected to be a certain way and ready to go at any time. It does make it more pleasant for everyone if there's no hair," he said, nodding with his cheek against Remi's pec. "Then there's the bleaching and douching. I even have to be careful what I eat on days I think I might get lucky." He glanced up at Remi with a rueful smile. But Remi was looking down at him with mild horror. "What?" Kris asked, confused.

"Guys get mad if you don't do all that?" he asked.

Kris blinked the water from his eyelashes and rubbed Remi's back. "Some of them," he agreed. "But…I feel good doing that stuff for me, too, not just for someone else."

Remi grumbled something under his breath and hugged Kris tighter, kissing his wet hair. "As long as you're happy, I like you however you want to be," he said firmly. "You're perfect just as you are, Kris Novak."

Kris wasn't able to speak for a moment. Remi must have sensed something was up because he tilted his head toward him. "Sorry," Kris mumbled and managed a weak smile. "I...okay, I really don't want to think too much about my dad right now. But I've always known one of the reasons he left was because of me. He never really loved my mom, but me he couldn't stand. I was always a dirty..."

"Don't say that word," Remi insisted with a scowl.

Kris nodded and kissed his chest above his heart. "For a while, it killed me. My dad was so repulsed by me he *left the state.* He still talks a bit to Leon, but Leon hates him almost as much as I do. Anyway, I...I put on this act of how I wanted to be. Loud and proud and cute and giving no fucks. But I still never know if I'm actually good enough. Wanted. So..." He cleared his throat, embarrassed. "To hear you think I'm okay however *I* think-"

"No, not 'okay,'" Remi interrupted crossly. He cradled Kris's face gently between his large hands. "Perfect. Gorgeous. Kris, you're one of the brightest colors in the whole rainbow. Like the best crayon in the box. Don't ever feel like you have to do anything to impress me other than be yourself, however you see fit."

Kris bit his lip, but one sob was all it took and the tears were coming. They only lasted a minute or so, but Remi held him the entire time, making soothing noises. "Thank you," Kris hiccuped eventually, rubbing his face in the water starting to run cold over them both.

When they left the shower, the faucet turned off, it was Remi who led Kris this time. He handed Kris a big fluffy towel, too, and they dried themselves off, occasionally stealing kisses from each other with sweet little laughs. Kris was so happy he could almost have floated away.

"In all seriousness though," Remi said as they ruffled their hair. "If it makes a big difference, I'll get a wax or whatever."

Kris blinked at him. "Well, a cream is easier and much less painful," he told him. "But I feel the same. I want you to have your body however you like it." He bit his lip and stroked Remi's chest hair. "You're a sexy beast."

"But what about bottoming? You said it's nicer if there's less hair?" Remi asked.

"For rimming, I guess," Kris said, then cackled at how Remi blushed. "Oh, I will eat you out soon enough, don't you worry," he teased. "But you're not bottoming, so…" He watched Remi's facial expression, then felt like the penny dropped. "Oh…would you want to try bottoming?"

"Unless it's not something you'd want to do?" Remi said evasively.

But Kris shook his head. "Guys who look like you, well, a lot of them would never dream of it. God, that's so hot, Remi." Kris dropped his towel and grabbed his gorgeous boyfriend for a kiss. "I'd love to top you. And we'll just groom the way we want to for each other, yeah?"

Remi dropped his towel and picked Kris up again, much to his delight. "Promise," he said as Kris swung his legs and hugged his hunky man.

"Promise," Kris agreed.

REMI

Remi never usually paid much attention to The Hidden Creek Horn. For a start, who even read local newspapers anymore when you could find everything much quicker online? Still, every Monday the damn thing ended up flung onto his front yard by some teenager earning less than minimum wage on a bike.

Usually, Remi would grab it before the sprinklers turned the rolled paper into mulch or a neighbor's dog chewed it up. But then he would just toss it into the recycling. For some reason, that Monday he decided to unroll it and glance at the front cover, perhaps hoping to hear something about the business going on with Hidden Creek Memorial.

What he got was a photograph of Kris.

'Local bartender, Kris Novak, accused of inside arson job' blared the headline.

"Fuck," Remi hissed. His hand tightened around the paper and crunched it up. He stalked back inside the house. "Kris?" he called upstairs to where he'd left his boyfriend lounging with his phone in Remi's bed. "We have a problem."

"I know," Kris called back miserably.

Remi jogged back up the stairs. He had been intending to bring them up coffee and bagels, but his appetite had vanished.

He found Kris sitting in a pool of blankets around his waist, frowning at his phone and chewing his lip. His white-and-purple hair was sticking up at odd angles, making him look adorable. Remi wished he wasn't so stressed.

"My mom texted," Kris said as Remi sat on the bed beside him. "And Leon. As well as Chase, Gabe, Hale, Koby and Pete Miele. And I think half the damn bar customers have messaged into the Facebook page. At least there's only a few of them that are nasty, the others are really sweet."

"They saw the paper, huh?" Remi asked with a sigh, showing Kris the front page. He winced and Remi put his arm around him. "Fuck this shit."

Kris let out an exasperated noise and flopped against Remi. "What the hell am I going to do? Everyone thinks I'm guilty."

"But you're not," Remi said firmly, believing it one hundred percent. "How about I call Epstein again and see if they've made any more progress?"

Kris sniffed and looked up at him. "Would you?" he asked in a small voice.

"Of course," said Remi, wrapping Kris up in his arms. "I'll help you do everything we can to put this behind us."

It was still before nine o'clock, so Remi wasn't that surprised he got Epstein's voicemail. Remi left him a message telling him to get in touch with him or Kris, then he called Bishop. It was his day off as much as Remi's, but this was important. Unfortunately, the captain didn't have any new information for him, but promised he would keep in touch. Remi was glad things were okay between him and Bishop after the interview had gotten so heated. He would hate to lose his captain's respect.

Remi was feeling somewhat in limbo when a text from his mom happened to pop up. Remi raised his eyebrows as several thoughts flashed through his mind at once. "Baby?" he asked Kris, who had been frantically replying to messages trying to assure everyone he was okay. "Do you have any dinner plans tonight?"

"No," said Kris, immediately smiling. "Why? Are you going to take me out?"

"Actually…" Remi said. Right, this was it, no more fucking around. "My family is getting together. I thought…only if you felt up to it, maybe you would want to come with me and, um…"

"You want to come out?" Kris asked. Remi nodded and Kris put his hand on Remi's knee. "Only if you feel ready," he said sincerely.

"I'm so ready," Remi said, gripping his hand. He sighed, vowing to be as honest as he could with Kris from now on. "I don't know how my dad will react. He's pretty traditional. It's not so much the gay thing, actually. It's…he has very firm ideas about boys and girls, men and women. I just know he's going to say I don't look gay and tell me it's a phase." He winced. "Just to warn you."

Kris shrugged. "Then you tell him you're bi and have known that for years and you'll give him time to come around." He lifted Remi's hand and kissed the back of it. "No matter what, I'll be by your side. Okay?"

"Okay," Remi said back.

For a while, he allowed himself to be distracted by Kris, both of them finding comfort in each other's arms. But then Remi's phone starting ringing. He sighed, but then Kris's phone began ringing too. They looked at one another in confusion.

Remi was being called back by Bishop, so he answered quickly, then left the room so he and Kris wouldn't be competing to be heard. "Hi, Captain," he said, loitering in the hall. "Is everything okay?"

"I think so," Bishop said. "You said to let you know if there was any news. Well, Epstein wants to meet again. Apparently, a witness has come forward."

Remi's heart leaped. "Is that good news or bad news?"

"I honestly couldn't say, son," Bishop told him. "I just thought I'd inform you as a courtesy." There was a pause. Remi was fully aware that Bishop didn't have to tell him any of this. "I assume you'll want to come to the meeting with Mr. Novak?" he asked.

"If that's allowed?" Remi said. "And if it's what Kris wants."

Again, Bishop paused. "I'll make an exception," he said. "We'll see you boys at midday. Don't be late."

"We won't," Remi promised.

He frowned as Bishop closed the call. Remi wanted to be hopeful about the witness, but he didn't trust his and Kris's luck at the moment. Then there was Bishop's attitude toward him. Remi licked his lips. He was pretty sure the captain suspected something was going on between him and Kris, but he couldn't tell if his reaction was good or bad.

He added that to his list of things to worry about later and returned to the bedroom to see Kris looking how he felt. "That was Epstein," he explained, holding up his phone. "He wants to meet at midday."

Remi nodded, indicating his own phone. "That was Bishop. He agreed I could come along."

Kris nibbled his lip. "Should I be worried?" he asked.

"I don't know," Remi replied truthfully.

They spent the next couple of hours in quiet agitation. At least they were able to comfort each other with regular hugs, but they would both be happier once the meeting was over. Remi drove them over to the station with plenty of time to spare, giving Kris a kiss in the car for good luck before they got out.

"Whatever happens," Remi promised him. "I've got your back this time. I'm sorry-"

"Don't you dare apologize again for last time," Kris said sternly. "I should apologize more for jumping to conclusions. There. We're even."

Remi grinned and kissed him again. "Come on, you brat. Let's go see what all this is about."

Remi didn't mind so much when they had to walk through the common room this time as he didn't really know the guys on first watch. He nodded to a couple of them as he and Kris walked past, but on the whole, nobody really paid them much attention.

Bishop had his own office throughout the week. He just usually wasn't in it unless they were on shift. Remi knocked on the door, waiting for a response before opening it. He allowed Kris to step in before him, trying not to let his guilt over the previous meeting cloud this one.

There were five extra chairs set out this time, two of which were already occupied, with Bishop behind his desk as usual. Remi nodded at Epstein, who rose to greet him with a handshake.

"I'm sorry I missed your call," Epstein said. "I was in a meeting at my kid's school." He sounded preoccupied.

Remi clapped the older guy on his arm. "He okay?" he asked quietly. Bishop was discussing something with the other person seated near him who Remi didn't recognize, so he hoped they wouldn't be overheard. Kris was quietly standing in between the two groups, a frown on his face.

Epstein shook his head. "Oh, I don't know," he said sadly to Remi. "Suspended, again. Anyway, I'm sorry. It's not the time nor place."

Luckily, Bishop rose at that moment. He smiled at Remi and Kris. "So glad you could join us. This here is Harrison Brown. He phoned me this morning, offering to speak to us with information relevant to the fire investigation."

Kris blew out a breath that sounded like relief, then crossed over the room to shake hands with the black-haired teen in the other chair. "Harrison, right," said Kris enthusiastically. "Great to see you again, buddy."

Harrison looked to be about seventeen or eighteen. Remi surmised if he wasn't in school, maybe he was eighteen and already graduated, so perhaps he just looked a bit young for his age. He looked cut up about something. He was wringing his hands and his eyes kept flitting between Kris and Epstein. "I'm sorry I didn't say anything earlier," he said anxiously. His voice was higher than Remi expected. "But when I saw the paper this morning, I knew I had to do something."

"Oh, am I late?" PJ asked loudly as he walked into the room. Then he stopped dead as he spotted Remi and Kris before pointing to them. "What are they doing here?" he asked Bishop incredulously.

"This meeting concerns Kris, apparently," Bishop said smoothly, taking his seat once more. Remi had only just noticed that, like himself, Bishop was dressed in a shirt and pants rather than the department uniform. It was kind of disarming. "Remi requested to accompany him and I agreed. I hope we can all be civil, Mr. Maddox."

"Now wait just a minute," PJ said. "I have the right to be uncivil. My whole *business* went up in flames. Okay, Kris, I get if we're still looking into this door code business. But why exactly are you here?" he asked Remi.

"It's fine, sweetie," said Kris with over the top sugar. "I asked him to be here."

"I'm with Kris," said Remi firmly. "Someone has to help him fight his corner with all these ridiculous accusations flying around."

"But he's not your boyfriend," PJ muttered, rolling his eyes.

Heat rushed over Remi's skin, but he only paused for a second. "Actually, I am," he said. He wasn't able to look at Bishop, but he maintained eye contact with PJ. "Thanks for pushing me to out myself, though. That was really classy of you."

There was a beat where nobody reacted. Then Kris reached out and took Remi's hand. Remi smiled at him. He felt dizzy and like he might puke, but also very proud.

"Well," said Epstein, pushing his glasses up his nose before removing his notebook from his pocket. "Congratulations all the same, gentlemen. How about we take our seats now? Young Harrison here has something pressing he wishes to add to the investigation."

PJ scowled as he grabbed the nearest chair to him. Remi sat with Kris, who placed himself as close as he could to Harrison and gave him a hug before he sat himself down. Remi glanced at Bishop. His expression wasn't all that readable, but he did nod at Remi.

Hopefully that meant he was okay with the fact one of his guys was queer.

"Hey," cried PJ abruptly, peering at Harrison from across the room. "You're that girl who didn't pay for her cranberry juices the night of the fire, aren't you?"

Girl? *Ohh,* Remi thought. That was why he looked younger than he'd first assumed.

"I *told* you," Kris replied firmly, "that I would cover that. But then the bar burned down."

"Yeah and you want to get a witness statement from someone who *stole* from us that night?" PJ scoffed. "Sounds reliable to me."

"Okay!" Kris snapped, waving his hands. "Everyone needs to stop yelling right now, okay?"

"Gentlemen," Epstein cried again. "Can we please calm down?"

"Agreed," Bishop rumbled.

PJ bobbed his foot while glaring at Harrison, waiting for Epstein to unlock his tablet. "Okay," PJ said loudly as soon as Epstein was done. "Let's get this over with. At this point, I don't care what else happens in the investigation. Kris is no longer with the company and won't be coming back. I just want to get on with reopening my business, if I even can. The insurance is being a bitch."

"The bar is my *home,*" Kris shot back. "Why should I have to leave?"

"Uh, how about, the fact that you're an *arsonist?*" PJ replied in mocking tones.

"There's no proof of that," Remi interjected.

Harrison raised his hand. "Can I-" he uttered in little more than a whisper.

"We need to hear the witness statement," Epstein said. "If you gentlemen can't calm down, I will have no choice but to get the police involved."

"We don't need the police and we don't need any witness," PJ scoffed. "She's unreliable. I don't care what she has to say."

Bishop and Epstein looked thunderous.

But it was Harrison that spoke.

"You're trying to discredit me," he said in a loud voice. His words wobbled considerably and rose in pitch, but he bunched his fists and looked tearfully at PJ. "You keep saying I'm a thief and misgendering me to undermine what I have to say." He angrily rubbed at his eyes, then turned to Kris. "I…no one knows I was at the bar that night. I shouldn't have been there. My folks wouldn't like it." He scowled at PJ. "But I *knew* as soon as I'd left, I'd forgotten to pay for my drinks. I hung around until closing to attempt to find a way back in, but the front door was locked by the time I tried it. I went around back, looking for a different way in because I hadn't seen Kris leave and I knew he would understand. That was when I saw *you* going back in."

"What?" Kris said.

"It's my business," PJ said, rolling his eyes. "I come and go all the time."

"What time was this?" Epstein asked Harrison, clearly interested.

Harrison bit his lip and looked around the room. Remi was trying not to show how excited he was by this revelation, but he squeezed Kris's hand excitedly.

"About two thirty?" Harrison said, not sounding sure.

"I never saw you," Kris said to PJ.

PJ shook his head and scowled. "I probably just forgot my keys or something."

"Then why isn't it your code on the security log?" Epstein asked, glancing over pages in a notebook he had retrieved from his pocket. "Why is it Mr. Novak's?"

"Look, this is ridiculous," PJ said, raising his voice slightly. "It's not a crime to be at my own bar. It *is* a crime to set fire to the curtains and burn the damn building down." He flung his hand out toward Kris. "Why hasn't he been arrested yet? I take it back. Let's get the police involved already."

Epstein was flicking back and forth between pages in his notebook, a deep frown on his face. "I don't believe the start of the blaze was ever disclosed."

Remi's heart skipped a beat. Kris sat up straighter in his chair, his grip on Remi's hand tightening.

"I beg your pardon?" PJ said, blinking a couple of times.

Epstein shook his head. "I purposefully withheld details about how and where the fire began so as not to cloud the investigation," he said. "How did you know the blaze originated at the back of the dance floor where the curtains hung?"

PJ looked between him and Bishop. Remi felt giddy with glee.

"I – what? I mean, I don't know. One of your guys must have said something?" PJ gibbered. "How else would I know? Someone must have mentioned it."

"Or you used Kris's code to get in the building to throw the blame elsewhere," Remi said, narrowing his eyes at PJ. "And set the fire yourself."

"That's insane!" PJ blurted. "Why would I destroy my own business?"

"I don't know," Epstein murmured, scrolling through his phone. "But I would love to talk to your insurance company and your bank. In fact, I think I had someone pull those records already. There was no reason to look at them before. Give me one second…"

PJ had gone incredibly pale. "No, I, wait," he stuttered. "That's crazy. You're taking the word of a teenager over me? I have nothing to gain from this."

Epstein's gray eyebrows shot up as he read something from his phone. "I'm afraid your finances say otherwise, Mr. Maddox. You appear to have run this business into the ground. Were you hoping the insurance claim would make you solvent again?"

"That's crazy," said PJ again. His voice was weak, though, and he was even paler and sweating now.

"It makes a hell of a lot more sense than Kris burning down his home *and* his job then staying in a burning building," Remi said, looking toward Bishop for support.

"It does," his captain agreed. "I think it *is* time we got the police involved. Mr. Maddox, if you'll stay with Mr. Epstein and myself. The rest of you are free to leave."

PJ continued to splutter and yell about his innocence, but Remi, Kris and Harrison were more than happy to get the hell out of there.

"Thank you," Kris said to Bishop and Epstein as he rose to his feet. "Thank you for not giving up on me."

"It's all right, son," said Epstein kindly as Bishop tried to placate PJ. It was difficult, seeing as he more than likely knew he was now facing jail time. But Epstein ignored him for a moment as he addressed those who were leaving. "I'm sorry you were dragged into this whole mess in the first place. I'll be contacting the Horn as soon as possible so they can retract their article and set the record straight." He then laid a hand on Harrison's shoulder. "What you did today was very brave," he told the young man solemnly. "Thank you for your help. I hope you don't face too much fallout from this."

Harrison managed a small smile, although he did wince as PJ yelled at the back of his head again. "I'll be okay," he said. He looked fondly at Kris as Remi herded them toward the door and away from the yelling match. "I had to help. Kris has been so kind to me."

Epstein nodded. "You boys look after each other, now."

"We will," Kris promised.

It sounded like Bishop was calling the cops, so Remi steered Kris and Harrison out the office door, leaving it up to his boss to make sure PJ didn't make a run for it. Once back out in the hallway, the three of them looked at one another.

"Oh my god, my hero!" Kris wailed, throwing his arms around a startled Harrison. "You didn't have to do that! Oh my god, I can't believe you would put yourself on the line like that for me! Are you crazy?"

Harrison had gone bright red, but as Kris released him, he was smiling. "Of course I had to," he said. "I couldn't let them accuse you like that. I'm just sorry I didn't do it sooner. But we have to look after our community, don't we?"

He looked between Kris and Remi. Remi realized with a start Harrison was including him in their community, too. He was the B in the LGBT. "We do," he said around the lump in his throat. He pulled Kris to him and kissed the top of his hair tenderly. "Thank you," he said to Harrison.

Harrison wrinkled his nose. "Eww," he said, showing his teenage years. "Get a room, guys."

The three of them laughed as Kris lightly punched Harrison on his arm, showing his affection. Remi felt like a weight had been lifted from his shoulders, so he could only imagine what Kris felt like.

This was the start of a new chapter in all their lives. There was just one last thing Remi had to do before they could make it official.

30

KRIS

Kris still couldn't believe it was all over. Remi's captain had called him an hour ago to explain that when the police had arrived, PJ had cracked and confessed everything. Yes, he had run the bar into the ground with his appalling business practices. Kris had often wondered how much it had cost them to update the systems all the time and continuously switch suppliers, never mind how lousy he was at sorting the staff schedules and paychecks.

Apparently, he had started the bar with money from his dad and never really turned a profit. So his solution had been to cash out with the insurance claim and either start again or run off back to Houston. He'd used Kris's door code after watching him enter it several times, wedged the back door open so he could get out again without re-entering the code, then set fire to the building.

With Kris inside.

He shivered in the warm Texas air just thinking what could have happened. Apparently, PJ was adamant he had never intended to endanger Kris's life. He had intended for the blaze to be contained and insisted to the police he was going to call the fire department if no one else did in time. But the sociopath didn't seem to understand how nearly it had all gone terribly wrong.

He was facing charges of attempted manslaughter as well as arson. Kris hoped they threw the book at him. Not only had he almost gotten Kris killed and framed him when that failed, but he had always been a lousy boss who never cared about the community he claimed to support.

"Are you all right?" Remi asked as they walked up the driveway to his parents' house.

Kris blinked himself out of his reverie. "Oh, baby, I'm fine," he said, trying to shake off the 'what ifs' that were swirling in his mind. He hadn't died. He hadn't been convicted of a crime he didn't commit. And, best of all, the experience had brought him to the man of his dreams. In a way, he had PJ to thank for Remi. So maybe Kris could spare a good thought for him here and there.

Remi looked like he wanted to take Kris's hand. But they were standing outside his folks' porch and Remi was understandably nervous. Kris touched his shoulder briefly in place of the hug he wanted to give his boyfriend.

"Never mind about me, silly," he said. "I'm just processing everything. I'll be fine. How are you feeling? If you need to hold back on this for another week or two, I'll support you, one hundred percent."

Remi smiled, that slow, affectionate one that made desire curl in Kris's belly. "No," he said. "Because I desperately want to kiss you right now. So the sooner I come out, the sooner I can sweep you up in my arms and take you back home again to my bed."

"Oh," Kris squeaked. He fanned his T-shirt away from his chest.

"Well, you know, I'm down with that plan. Is it getting hotter out here? I feel kind of hot."

Remi chuckled and bit his lip, looking down at Kris through his eyelashes. Those looks always made Kris feel like he was about to be eaten up. "You *look* hot when you get all flustered like that, baby," he said. "You're going to make it hard to get through this dinner."

"That's not the only thing I'll make hard," Kris whispered, taking a step forward.

Then he jumped backward, his heart jumping in his chest as the front door swung open. Remi's younger sister, Darcy, leaned out, raising her eyebrow at the two of them.

"What are y'all doing hanging around out here?" she asked suspiciously. "Come on, we're all here already."

And by all, she meant all. As Kris and Remi followed her out into the backyard, Kris realized it wasn't just Remi's family that had come together. "Mom?" he said as he stepped out onto the back patio. "Leon?" Ava was there, too, looking tired and enormous but very happy. She waved to Kris while his mom and brother came over to hug him.

"We were just so relieved to hear the good news," his mom said. "Bettina invited us over to celebrate."

"That news article almost gave me a heart attack, bro," Leon admonished, ruffling Kris's hair. "I've never known so many people pay attention to the damn Horn before."

Kris smiled sheepishly. "Sorry," he said. "It's all fine now."

"And we're glad to hear it," Remi's mom said. She pressed a beer into Kris and Remi's hands each. "We knew it couldn't be true. Thank goodness it was all put right so fast."

Kris didn't want to be rude, so he vowed to at least hold the beer for a little while. Bettina obviously meant well and didn't know about his disinterest in alcohol. But Remi took it from him.

"Actually, Mom," he said cheerfully, handing one beer to Darcy and the other to his brother-in-law, Thom. "We don't really drink anymore. Have you got any sodas?"

Bettina looked confused at them both, but then she nodded. "Sure," she said. "Dr Pepper okay?"

Kris smiled gratefully at Remi. "That would be great, thank you." He turned back to his own mom as they found seats. "I was lucky a witness came forward to help. It took a lot of guts from them to do that."

"Why?" Remi's older sister, Jamila, asked from where she was sitting playing with Kendra.

Kris shrugged, not wanting to go into it too much for the sake of Harrison's privacy. "It's complicated," he said. "But they could have some trouble for sticking their neck out for me. I hope they won't."

He and Remi had dropped Harrison off at his home after leaving the fire station. He seemed okay about facing his parents, but Kris got the impression he was hoping it wouldn't get back to them that he'd been at a gay bar. Kris wished him all the luck in dealing with that situation, however it went down.

"We?"

Kris looked over at Remi's dad, who was, as usual, manning the barbecue. Remi's mom handed them their sodas and also looked at him. "What's that, hon?" she asked her husband.

Remi's dad frowned and pointed his tongs at Remi. "You said 'we' don't really drink anymore. Like, is this some new house rule?"

Remi licked his lips and glanced at Kris. Kris wanted to hold Remi's hand so badly, but he had to allow Remi to do this himself, at his own pace. Remi looked around the whole group, sitting in his folks' garden, and took a deep breath.

"It's more of a 'me and Kris' thing," he said directly to his dad. "We do a lot of things together now and, um, well, Kris doesn't like drinking so I don't really need to either."

"You can if you want, though," Kris said clearly.

Remi smiled at him. "I know," he said. "But it's not like I love it."

Kris smiled back. It was feeling more and more like he and Remi were meant to be together. They were so in sync.

"Hang on a minute," Leon said. He frowned and waved the neck of his beer between Remi and Kris. "Am I missing something here?"

"Yeah," said Darcy slowly. "Are you trying to tell us something, Remi?"

Remi looked at his dad, as did Kris. Clive's jaw was clenched. Kris's heart skipped in apprehension for Remi.

But Remi just nodded. "Actually, yeah," he said. "There is something I would like to say." He took a deep breath. "I'm bi. Bisexual. I've known it for a long time, but I was too afraid to come out or try anything with a guy. But, um…"

"Holy fuck, you're boning my brother," Leon cried, jamming his hands into his hair.

"Leon!" Kris's mom cried.

Darcy snorted. "Thank you for *that* mental image," she snickered.

Remi leaned across and took Kris's hand. Kris's heart leaped in his chest as he turned and they shared a look of pride and happiness.

"We're dating," Remi said. "And I hope you're all okay with that."

"Wow," said Ava, rubbing her swollen belly. "Congratulations, y'all, that's awesome."

Leon scowled and jabbed a finger at them both. "So long as neither of you breaks the other's heart," he grumbled, "I guess it's okay."

"I think it's cool," Darcy announced, nodding and looking around her family.

Unfortunately, their reactions weren't quite as enthusiastic. Jamila and her husband looked stunned, to the point where she was staring at Remi in shock, unaware that little Kendra was tugging at her skirt to get her attention. Remi's mom had her hand over her mouth, and his dad…

Well, his dad was just shaking his head. "You're not gay, Remi," he said, just like Remi predicted.

"No," he said firmly. "I'm not. I'm bi. I like men and women. It's not a phase. I've known this about myself for a long time. I'm dating Kris and I'm serious about him. We're serious," he added. He looked at Kris, as if seeking confirmation.

Kris was only too happy to help out. "Remi's right," he said sincerely. He purposefully toned down any excitement he felt so as to endear himself to Remi's dad. "I'm so totally honored to be his boyfriend and I promise to take good care of him."

"Oh," said Remi's mom. She nodded faintly and looked between them. "I…but, Remi, what if you want kids?"

"Mom!" he blurted out. "We've only been together a few days, for crying out loud!"

Kris laughed and thankfully, so did Darcy, Leon and Ava. Even Jamila managed a weak smile.

"That being said," Kris assured Remi's mom. "Same-sex couples do still have kids. It might take a little longer, but-"

"No," said Remi's dad firmly. He finally placed the tongs down and came out from behind the grill. "No, Remi, this is crazy. I get if you want to experiment, but you two have nothing in common. You're not like him."

"And what's that supposed to mean?" Kris's mom asked, hurt clear in her voice. God bless her. She wasn't the fiercest of women, but Kris always knew she had his back. Even if it meant standing up to her best friend's husband. "Are you saying Kris isn't good enough for Remi?"

"No," Remi's mom said loudly. "Clive isn't saying that at all, are you, Clive?"

Remi's dad looked between Remi and Kris, apparently lost for words. "I-" He waved his hand between the two. "I'm just saying, why ruin your life over something that won't last, son?"

Kris had been expecting something like that, but it still stung. Remi's hand tightened around his, though. "You're being rude, Dad," he growled.

Remi's mom sniffed. "He's also being a jerk," she said hotly, crossing her arms over her ample chest and narrowing her eyes at her husband. "Where's your memory?" she demanded. "Folks told us we shouldn't date. Said a white boy and black girl had no business getting married, and if we did, it wouldn't last." She sniffed again and shook her head. "Not natural, they told us. Well, that was thirty years ago, and I'll tell you what I told them back then. Love don't know no color. So why should it give a good god damn about gender?" She stood up and leaned over Remi to give him a hug. "I can't say you haven't shocked your mama," she told him. "But I'm happy for you. And so will your father be, once he gets his head out of his ass."

Remi's dad was wide-eyed and didn't look entirely convinced. But Remi smiled at him and stood up. Kris joined him. "I know this is going to take some time to process," he said calmly. Kris was proud of him for not flipping out. "We'll give you some time. We've had a hell of a day and we need some time to ourselves. I'll be back over soon, and if you have any questions at all, please ask." He pointed at the grill. "And, Dad? Move that propane tank before you blow the whole yard up."

"You don't have to leave, do you?" Kris's mom asked. Kris smiled and let Remi go to hug her.

"It's fine, Mommy," he said, kissing her cheek. "We've got a lot of things to sort out." He turned to face Remi's dad, who was sheepishly moving the propane like Remi had said. "I know this is a lot for you to take on, Mr. Washington," he said. "But you don't have to understand everything at once. You just need to respect your son and love him like you always have." He smiled. "I know you can do that."

Remi's dad didn't seem to know what to make of Kris's words. But everyone else waved them goodbye and appeared to be okay with the turn of events. Remi seemed eager to leave the families to their thoughts and opinions for a while, so if he wanted to head home, Kris was more than willing to do so.

Back in the car, Remi looked a little shell-shocked. Kris rubbed his leg. "Are you okay?" he asked.

Remi blinked and turned toward him. "Yeah," he said after a second's thought. "I am. I think that was the best it could have gone."

Kris leaned over and hugged him, tucking his face into the crook of his neck and inhaling his musk in deeply. "We've had a long, tough day," he said, placing a gentle kiss on his warm skin. "Let's head home."

Remi turned and rested their foreheads together. "You're my home," he said.

Kris thought he did very well not to tear up at that. "I'm so lucky," he told Remi. After all these years, it had been so worth it to be with Remi in the end, just like he'd dreamed.

31

REMI

Remi felt strangely like he was floating outside of his own body as he drove them both home. He had enough wits about him to keep his eyes on the road, but he couldn't really believe what had just happened.

He'd come out and the world hadn't ended. His family hadn't disowned him. Yeah, his dad hadn't been keen on the idea, but that wasn't a shock. Hopefully, he would come around.

Despite everything, he and Kris were here, pulling into his driveway, happy and unified. The fire may have brought them together, but it could also have torn them apart. Remi was relieved more than anything that Kris's name had been cleared and they could start to put this sordid business behind them. They could be a couple and come out to their other friends and colleagues.

"I love that smile," Kris said as Remi killed the ignition. He turned to see Kris with his head tilted, looking wistfully at him. "You look so relaxed and content."

"That's because I am," Remi said, leaning forward and capturing Kris's soft lips with his own. "Are you hungry?"

"For food?" Kris asked, waggling his eyebrows. "Not really."

"Me neither," Remi admitted.

Grinning, they both scrambled out of the car. Kris beat Remi to the front door, so Remi crowded behind Kris and kissed his neck while Kris struggled with his key to let them inside. Remi wondered if any of his neighbors noticed. He'd soon find out if any of them had an issue with him and Kris, but that was a problem for another day. Right now, he only had one thing on his mind.

Finally, they tumbled into the living room together, laughing and giggling as Remi kicked the door closed behind him. Kris turned and jumped into his arms, wrapping his legs around Remi's waist and kissing him fiercely. "Take me to bed, baby," he rasped, then bit Remi's lower lip. "I want you naked and moaning in about thirty seconds."

Remi groaned, his cock already straining in his pants. "Yes, sir," he said, not caring how desperate he sounded. He managed to get them up the stairs without any major incidents, pulling Kris's shirt off before they even reached the bedroom.

There was no slow seduction tonight. As soon as Remi placed Kris on the carpet, they both began yanking their clothes off until they were both naked and hard, and Remi tackled a squealing Kris onto the bed.

"Hmm," Remi hummed, kissing up his neck. "What do you want to do, gorgeous? I'm all yours."

Kris rutted against him and ran his hands through Remi's hair. "I want you to come so hard you scream," he said wickedly. "Do you want me to fuck you?"

Remi pulled away to look him in the eye. "Would you want to?" he asked, nerves taking away some of his fire. "I haven't done any of those things you said."

Kris scoffed and kissed him passionately. "You're perfect, remember?" he said, running his hands down Remi's arms. "We can try it, and if you don't like it, we'll switch." He licked up Remi's neck and bit his earlobe. "There's *lots* of other ways I can make you come, and I love getting fucked by you. So it's win/win."

Remi's mind had turned to jelly. "Uh," he uttered as Kris's hands continued to skim over his skin, then caressed his leaking cock. "Oh, baby, I, where do you…how?" He gulped then took a breath to focus. "Please fuck me, please. I want your cock inside me."

Kris giggled devilishly and smacked Remi's ass. "On all fours, big boy. You just concentrate on staying upright, and your baby will do all the work."

Remi nodded, turning to do as he was told. He felt vulnerable while he waited for Kris to come back, presumably from getting lube and condoms. But as he relaxed into it, he found putting his trust in Kris oddly calming. He knew Kris wouldn't hurt him, even though they were about to do something Remi had never attempted with anyone else before.

He felt Kris's lips softly kissing down his spine, then slippery fingers stroked at his entrance, making him moan. "Good, baby," Kris murmured. "You feel so tight. Are you going to let me in?"

Remi nodded, his head hanging between his arms. "Yes, Kris, fuck."

Kris pushed a finger inside, up to the knuckle and pulsed it back and forth. "That's it, sweetie. I've got you. You feel so good."

Remi bit his lip and concentrated on his breathing as Kris continued to whisper dirty sweet nothings in his ear and fill him with two of his fingers. By the time Remi heard him ripping the foil from the condom, he was trembling on his hands and knees.

Before going straight back around to his ass, Kris crawled up beside Remi and turned his face so they could kiss. "All good, baby?"

"Amazing," Remi assured him. He sounded kind of out of it to his own ears, drunk with lust and desire.

Kris grinned. "It's about to get a whole lot better," he told him.

Then he was gone, back to Remi's ass where he made short work of parting his cheeks and pressing the tip of his cock against his hole. It was obviously different from the fingers that had breached him just before. Kris wasn't huge, but Remi could still tell the difference when he pushed the end of his dick past the ring of muscle, filling Remi up completely.

He moaned, like he knew Kris wanted him to. It kind of burned, but not in a completely unpleasant way. Like menthol on the tongue. Kris was using both hands to rub up and down Remi's back and sides. "Oh, yes, feels so good, baby," Kris cried. "Oh, honey bun, yes! Take it, gorgeous, take it up your sweet ass."

Remi moaned like an animal and clutched fistfuls of the bed covers as Kris pushed all the way inside him. "Fuck, baby," he gasped. He could feel the sweat running down his face and tasted salt on his lips. He was too full, it didn't seem right. But Kris was kissing down his spine and telling him how beautiful he was. Gradually, he began to relax, accepting the intrusion in his body and appreciating how wonderful it really felt.

Slowly, Kris started to rock gently in and out of him. They were both gasping and moaning, filling the room with their sounds of pleasure, until Kris pressed something electric deep inside Remi and he bellowed like there were fireworks exploding through his body.

"Holy fuck," he cried, tears in his eyes. "Oh, yes, baby. There, like that. Don't stop!"

Kris smacked his ass and began pounding into him at that angle, again and again. "I've got you, sweetie. Do you like that? Is that so good?"

"So good, baby," Remi said. He was grunting every time Kris hit his prostate, gasping in ecstasy with every thrust. "Fuck yes, harder, *harder.*"

Kris grabbed his hip with one hand and reached around to jerk him off with the other, his hand already slippery from where he'd prepared Remi's hole. "That's it, baby, come for me. You're so gorgeous. You feel so good."

Remi gritted his teeth, his climax building rapidly as Kris worked him back and front. "I can't…" he uttered. "I'm going to…"

"Do it, baby. Come hard. I want to see it all."

Remi let go. He trusted himself to Kris and allowed the beautiful orgasm to roll over him, sweeping him away like waves crashing on a beach. He wailed as he squirted all over the bed covers, emptying his load while Kris still slammed in and out of him.

Remi shuddered but still managed to keep himself up on his hands and knees. Kris slowed down again, rubbing his back and kissing his shoulders. "Well done, gorgeous," he said, his voice a little breathless but full of affection. "Are you okay? Did you like that?"

Remi nodded, so tired he wanted to fall asleep on the spot. But he dug deep. "So good," he slurred. "Good for you? Did you come?"

Kris kissed his back again and gently slid out from his ass. "Not yet. Come on, let's lie you down." He pushed Remi around, pulling at the comforter until he was able to crawl under the dry covers. Through half-closed eyes, Remi could see Kris was still hard as a rock as he pulled the condom off.

"Baby," Remi said weakly, groping for his cock.

Kris giggled. "I was going to sort myself out," he said, hovering over Remi and kissing him sweetly. "But do you feel up for helping me? You won't have to move. I'll do all the work."

He said that a lot. Remi frowned. "I *want* to do some of the work, though," he insisted in his blurry state.

Kris kissed him once more. "Why are you so perfect?" he mused, brushing some of Remi's hair back. "Okay, would you like to suck me off? It's okay if you don't-"

Remi snorted. "Stop thinking I'm going to freak out," he managed to say. "I'm bi. I like the cock and the pussy. Get that dick in my mouth."

Kris dissolved into peals of laughter and kissed Remi hard on the mouth. "I love you," he said. Then he froze. "I mean, uh, oh-"

Remi held either side of his face with both hands and kissed him to stop him from talking. "I love you, too, sweetheart. It's okay."

Kris smiled, tears making his eyes glisten. "Oh, okay. That's, wow…that's so nice."

"Shut up," Remi said fondly. "You're so adorable. Of course I love you. You're amazing."

Kris nibbled his lip and gave Remi a bashful look. "All right, I believe you," he said with a grin. "Now enough of this mushy stuff. Do you still want to give me a blow job?"

Remi surprised him by smacking *his* ass for once. "Get over here, you beautiful man."

Kris snorted and pushed Remi flat on his back, crawling over him so he could angle his dick into Remi's mouth. He didn't take it as far down as Kris had with his before, but he was surprised how much he enjoyed the sensation right away of having his heavy cock sliding between his lips and over his tongue. The look on Kris's face and the moans he made were even better, though.

Remi had been serious when he said he wasn't going to freak out just because it was something new, but it still took a moment to wrap his head around. Was he doing it right? Was Kris enjoying it or just being noisy to make him feel better? But he decided not to worry too much over those details, because Kris didn't seem the kind to fake sex. If he didn't like something, he had told Remi he would make it known. So when he grabbed the back of Remi's head and fucked his mouth, praising the heavens, Remi trust he was doing okay.

"Remi, I'm going to…" Kris uttered.

Remi squeezed either side of his hips, encouraging him to keep going. He was still shocked when the cum hit the back of his throat, but he drank it down, swallowing everything Kris gave him, massaging his throbbing cock with his tongue. It was bitter and he gagged a little, but he thought he did a pretty good job. Kris was certainly grinning when he flopped beside Remi and pulled the covers over them both, snuggling against his side.

"You've ruined me," Kris said. "That was amazing. Oh my god, I'm never going to sleep again. I'm just going to demand sex twenty-four-seven."

Remi looked at him, lying on his chest, so happy and glistening in his freshly fucked state. "Twenty-four-seven sounds perfect," he said. "So, stay."

Kris frowned and looked up at him. "I'm not going anywhere," he said.

Remi's heart sped up again, despite recovering from the sex. "I mean…I know it's fast, but you don't have a place right now. You could…just stay living here."

"You mean, move in?" Kris asked. His eyes were bright and Remi thought maybe this *wasn't* the worst suggestion he had ever made.

"Or," he said, stroking Kris's blond-and-purple hair back. "Just don't move out. Just stay and see how it goes. I don't want to put any pressure on you, but-"

"But twenty-four-hour sex?" Kris supplied with an impish grin. Then he leaned up and kissed Remi softly. "I would love to," he said. "And it's not too fast. I've waited my whole life for you. I don't want to waste another second."

Remi hugged his perfect boyfriend tightly. "I'm sorry I missed you all those years," he said. "But I think we did it right in the end."

"We did," Kris agreed.

Remi could feel sleep creeping over him, but he wanted to hold onto this moment. Kris loved him. They loved each other. Kris had agreed to stay with him. They had such an exciting journey ahead of them. Even his family seemed to be all right with him coming out. Hopefully his dad would come around soon enough.

"Don't worry about your job for now," Remi said, addressing one of the thoughts that floated into his mind. "We're okay for the time being. We can work stuff out after the dust has settled from the fire."

Kris squirmed against him, kissing his chest and rubbing his tummy. "Actually, I have an idea about that," he said sleepily.

"Oh yeah?"

Kris nodded. "You'll have to wait and see," he said cryptically.

Remi smiled and gave him one last kiss on the head. "Okay," he said.

Kris had waited for him. Remi knew now he would wait for Kris forever. In fact, Remi was pretty sure Kris already held claim over his forever.

And he couldn't have been happier about it.

Many hands make light work.

Kris had never really understood the true meaning of those words until now. He weaved through the parking lot at Phoenix, admiring all the stalls that had been erected for the grand reopening and rebranding of Hidden Creek's LGBT bar.

In the end, the timing had been fortuitous. Construction of the LGBT center had come to a close around the end of August, meaning when Chip Carter had invested in resurrecting Bottom's Up, he had simply used the same company and transferred them over to the different site.

It had been a risk, going back to Chip and asking if he still wanted to partner with the bar to expand the town's queer scene. But Kris reckoned if Chip and his partner, Tyler Florman, were interested in his plans before, he took the gamble that they would be even more eager once Kris took on the business himself.

The last month had been a blur of bank loans and paperwork as

Kris bought the bar off PJ, who was indeed facing jail time. As it transpired, PJ had also been behind most of the increased hate mail the bar had been receiving over the past couple of months. He had apparently thought that would make the fire seem less suspicious, but had also used Kris's code as a failsafe in case the fire department did investigate the blaze as arson. He really was a nutjob.

Kris, Chip and Tyler were now all part-owners in the business, but Kris was the new manager. He had enrolled in a couple of courses at Hidden Creek Community College, but already he was learning so much just being on the job. As terrifying as this venture was, he had never felt more alive.

The reopening would never have happened so fast without the army of volunteers that had come equipped with paint rollers and electric screwdrivers. So many of Kris's friends, the bar patrons and the wider LGBT community had offered up their services for free to bring the bar back to life in a mere four weeks. It had been pretty overwhelming to see so many people come together for the place Kris felt so strongly about.

Now here they were on a gorgeous Saturday afternoon, celebrating the new space in all its glory. It had felt right to rename the bar to mark the start of a new era. Like a phoenix, it had risen from the ashes, and Kris hadn't had any trouble coming up with what to put on the sign out front.

Phoenix was his. He was doing something with his life, something he *loved*. Like his original proposal to PJ, he was determined to make the space so much more than just a place to drink. They had purposefully started the event in the afternoon and used the area outside so people of all ages felt welcome.

Cas was selling his handcrafted carpentry wares, the sounds of his wind chimes filling the air as the wood clicked and clacked gently together. Koby had specifically made a selection of smaller metal sculptures and his sister, Ginger, had set up a stall with her colorful, sparkly handmade soaps. Doris, the slightly grumpy lady who ran the coffee shop, Grind, was making a killing selling iced teas and lemon and poppy seed muffins. One of the elementary school teachers was offering face painting for all ages and the gaggle of bi girls from the local college who used to play their air hockey tournaments at the bar was doing a great job selling raffle tickets.

Kris smiled as he watched Remi taking photos next to the fire truck the department had lent them for the day. Remi wasn't on duty, but he and a few of the people from his watch had agreed to donate their time on their day off for the bar's opening event.

On the whole, Remi's work buddies had taken his coming out in their stride. Kris had met several of them now at one of the other sports bars in town that the firefighters tended to frequent. Kris had made it clear, though, they would be welcome any time they wanted to come to Phoenix. He understood the nature of found family more than most and he wanted to get on well with the firefighters in Remi's work family as much as his biological family.

In both of those families, there was one voice of resistance they had to contend with. But Remi's dad was slowly starting to be less hostile over the idea of his son dating a man. The guy from Remi's work, Travis, wasn't really changing his tune so much as keeping quiet about it. But Remi seemed to count that as a win, so if he was happy, Kris was happy.

And he was *so* happy. Kris couldn't stop smiling as he made his way inside the bustling bar. As part of the reconstruction, they had added a few windows along the wall, so the place didn't feel so oppressive during the day now. Most of the current staff were manning the bar, busy filling orders and flirting with patrons of all genders. A phoenix mural had been painted behind them with the words 'Love is Love' emblazoned on the wall below.

One of their new customers, a fun guy called Peter, had offered them free advice on a new security system. Apparently, he worked for the government or something. Kris was more than happy to update the system after the trouble he'd had with PJ. As well as overhauling security, Kris had put his foot down and insisted on installing gender-neutral bathrooms. This was a safe space and he didn't want anyone getting distressed about taking a damn leak. So far, all these changes were going down well with staff and patrons alike.

One of the most significant additions to the new bar was the kitchen Kris had organized to be installed out back. They only served standard bar food and snacks like burgers and fries, but it gave the place a wider appeal. A nice bonus was that the staff only had to be over eighteen to work there, not twenty-one.

"Hey, Harrison," Kris called over the serving hatch. "How's it going?"

"Busy," the teenager called back with a big grin on his face as he plated up some onion rings and slaw.

It was amazing the difference a month could make. Of course, it hadn't been all smooth sailing for his new young friend. Kris hadn't been surprised to find out that news of Harrison's witness statement had gotten back to his parents, forcing him to come out as both gay and trans. They had been pretty shitty about the whole thing, but luckily, Kris not only had a job to offer Harrison, but one that came with a newly refurbished little apartment above it.

Kris knew Harrison had a tough time ahead of him. But he also had a community by his side that had his back one hundred percent. Kris felt extremely hopeful for him.

It was a diverse crowd both inside and outside the bar. Kris had invited numerous groups and entertainment acts from Houston and any of the neighboring towns that had LGBT organizations. Currently, Miss Honey Bee, a golden, sparkly drag queen with two-inch nails and four-inch heels, was sitting reading a picture book to a gaggle of enthralled elementary school kids, putting on all the funny voices for the rabbits and puppies and bugs. A dance company was going to perform a number of routines later and several other queens were going to wow them with a lip-sync battle.

While surveying the scene, Kris caught eyes with Mr. Epstein. They gave each other a wave. Instead of his customary gray, Epstein was dressed in the most hideous Hawai'ian shirt Kris had ever seen. Kris loved it.

Epstein was doing his best to stick to the edge of the room, giving his son the room he needed to meet other queer kids his age. Remi had explained to Kris the trouble Tommy Epstein had been getting into at summer camp. But apparently, after helping Hidden Creek out with their gay bar, Epstein Sr. had encouraged his son to open up over several conversations, eventually giving him the support he needed to come out.

Since then, young Tommy hadn't gotten himself in trouble again at summer camp or school once.

Kris smiled, turning his gaze around the rest of the bar. To his surprise, Kris also saw Mandy, Trixie and Lola, his excitable former classmates, handing out information leaflets explaining the differences between various gender, sexual and biological expressions. It warmed his heart to see them growing and educating themselves as well as others.

"Quite the little empire you've built here," a warm voice murmured in Kris's ear as strong hands wrapped around his waist. Kris beamed as he looked over his shoulder and found Remi's lips to kiss.

"Oh, baby," Kris said, his heart full of joy, "I'm only just getting started."

"I know," Remi said.

He had taken off his heavy gear and was just in his department sweats and polo. Kris rubbed his arms, firm and secure around him, and looked over at everything going on. He bit his lip as tears prickled at the back of his eyes.

As much as he wanted to sound confident to Remi, like he'd taken all this in his stride, Kris still couldn't really believe all he had achieved. He had come from lowly bartender with a miserable boss who didn't care about their patrons, to running his own business in the community that he loved so much. Later, his mom and brother were going to swing by with Ava and his brand-new nephew, Julian. Kris couldn't wait to show them all he had created with the help of his friends and the man he loved.

Things with Remi were still almost too good to be true. It was incredible how well they had slotted into each other's lives. Kris got immeasurable joy from watching Remi continue to blossom in the home they were building together. Having been so soulless when Kris had first arrived, it was now filled from top to bottom with their love and passions.

Remi had made sure not to put pressure on Kris, but Kris was confident he wasn't going to move out again. He had abandoned the sofa bed and Remi's room had become their room, with Remi insisting Kris add some personal touches of his own to the décor.

Remi still referred to the house as a butterfly after the transformation Kris had put it through. It was funny, but Kris had discovered the other day that butterflies needed build up their strength by tearing their way out from their cocoons, otherwise they would be too weak to survive out in the real world.

He thought he might know a thing or two about that himself.

Tay Tay's aquarium had been moved downstairs into the living room where she continued to thrive. It turned out, after a quick trip to the vet, that the skinny black kitty that had been breaking into the house more and more often was *not* microchipped and nobody seemed to be looking for her. So Kris and Remi had adopted her, and Remi had renamed her Sasha Fierce.

Most days, Sasha could be found sleeping next to Tay Tay's tank, keeping her unlikely friend company. There had been no further attempts to eat the goldfish for dinner.

Compared to the shell that Remi had been living in two months ago, his house was now a home. Their home. When Kris had moved his belongings from the spare room to Remi's, Remi had made an off-hand comment about how the space would be good for a nursery one day. Kris wasn't sure Remi even knew he'd said it out loud, but Kris had heard him.

It was too early to be thinking about such things, really. But Kris couldn't help it. Who knew what position they would be in five or ten years from now? Perhaps there would be the pitter-patter of tiny feet?

"What are you thinking about?" Remi asked.

Kris smiled over his shoulder at him. "Us," he said honestly. "Our future."

"I hope you have *long-term* plans for that future," Remi said, kissing Kris's temple. "Because I do."

"I do, too," said Kris said, thinking what those words might mean for them in a few years' time.

For now, they hugged each other tightly, watching friends and family and people they hadn't met yet, all coming together to celebrate love, acceptance and happiness.

Kris couldn't think of anywhere he would rather be.

ABOUT THE AUTHOR

HJ Welch is a contemporary MM romance author living in London with her husband and two balls of fluff that occasionally pretend to be cats. She began writing at an early age, later honing her craft online in the world of fanfiction on sites like Wattpad. Fifteen years and over a million words later, she sought out original MM novels to read. She never thought she would be any good at romance, but once she turned her hand to it she discovered she in fact adored it. By the end of 2016 she had written her first book of her own, and in 2017 she fulfilled her lifelong dream of becoming a fulltime author.

She also writes contemporary British MM romance as Helen Juliet.

Newsletter: https://www.subscribepage.com/helenjuliet

facebook.com/HJWelchAuthor

twitter.com/helenjwrites

instagram.com/helenjwrites

ALSO BY HJ WELCH

SCORCH (HOMECOMING HEARTS #1)

Blake has never had a boyfriend before. Because he isn't gay. Until recently, he was part of one of America's most successful boy bands. After their record label ruthlessly dropped Below Zero, Blake has no choice but to head back to his hometown with his overbearing family.

Elion never thought he'd get another chance with his high school crush, the pop star hunk Blake Jackson. Not when his life is the opposite of exciting, stuck as a barista in the town he grew up in. When Blake walks back into his world though, Elion feels like there might be something between them after all.

All Blake wants is to pursue his first love of dance again. But in order to do that, he finds himself the star of a reality TV show, and the producers are determined to spice things up. They don't care that Blake isn't gay, not when Elion makes such a cute boyfriend. The pair send the ratings through the roof and find themselves forced to continue the charade. At least for the time being.

As reality and fiction begin to blur, falling in love becomes a tantalizingly possibility. Dangerously so, as a real-life superfan decides that Blake belongs to him and will do anything to claim him.

Elion will have to fight if he's to keep the man who has fallen into his arms. But Blake will also have to fight to keep Elion safe from harm.